# The Heart of a Gangsta

**Ca$h Presents
The Heart of a Gangsta
A Novel by *Jerry Jackson***

# Lock Down Publications/Ca$h Presents
P.O. Box 1482
Pine Lake, Ga 30072-1482


Visit our website at **www.lockdownpublications.com**

**Lock Down Publications**
**Like our page on Facebook: Lock Down Publications @www.facebook.com/lockdownpublications.ldp**
**Cover design and layout by:** Dynasty's Cover Me
**Book interior design by:** Shawn Walker
**Edited by:** Lauren Burton

Jerry Jackson

# Chapter 1

## *The Big Come Up*

### *Savarous Jones*

"That's the truck right there, my nigga." Pimp looked in the direction his li'l big homie, Donte, pointed to and saw the white and gray F-150 parked across from them. Two dudes were inside, looking somewhat at a loss out in this area.

Pimp dialed a number in his burner cellphone and watched as the driver picked up.

"Yo, where you at?" the driver spoke.

"I'm in the black Ford with the tinted window right in front of you, let's do business, get it out of the way so I can get back to Atlanta," Pimp said in a smooth, demanding voice, not taking his focus off the two dudes.

"Check," the dude said, and the phone went dead in his ear. Pimp grabbed the Nike bag off the back seat and got out as the dude approached him with a friend in tow. Donte then stepped out of the car. Everybody nodded their attention.

"You got that?" was the dude's only question. Pimp opened the door to the Ford and pointed to the bag sitting on the driver's seat.

"Check 'em out, baby. Make it quick, though."

The driver looked at pimp, then to his friend, and then got into the Ford. He opened the Nike bag and the strong smell of cocaine hit his nose before he even touched the work. He finally looked at two kilos of cocaine and got out. He nodded his head to his partner, who held a brown paper bag. He passed it to Pimp.

"If this shit good like it smell, then I'ma hit you up in a week or two. Maybe I'll come down to the A so we can link up on some shit," the driver said while grabbing the work off the seat. He gave Pimp dap.

"Bet dat. Just hit da cell, my nigga"

Donte jumped back into the Ford, and Pimp did, too. They followed the dude to the stop sign, and when the dude went left, Pimp made a right turn and burst out laughing. Donte did, also, as they gave each other dap.

"Bruh, I'm still try'na figure how you make that shit smell like real dope," Donte admitted and pulled out a blunt of Kush. He lit it up. Pimp was one of them dudes who knew how to do almost everything.

"I'ma put you on game one day, li'l bro," Pimp said and turned a sharp left on a dead-end street a few blocks away from where they just fooled the dudes with fake dope. He pulled up behind his girl's Honda Accord LX. He and Donte jumped in and drove off.

He just made himself a quick 56 grand with flex cocaine, which was really white dirt and bread flower. He knew the dude was gon' be blowed, but hell, he didn't care. The dude thought Pimp was from Atlanta, when really he was from right there in North Carolina. A smile came to his face at the thought of the sweet lick he just hit. That was too easy.

After another 30-minute ride, they ended up in front of a CVS. Pimp reached into the bag and gave his li'l homeboy five grand. Donte's eyes got big.

"Thanks, my nigga!"

"Look, li'l nigga, when you roll with me, you gon' always get money. That's all I want, my dude, real talk. I don't drink, I don't smoke, all I want is some money. Stay around and I will show you magic," Pimp replied.

Pimp was 24 years old. He was well known in his neck of the woods and respected by many for his street smarts and gangsta heart. He was raised by his father through pen and paper, visits, and phone calls from the federal prison in Atlanta. He rested his head at his Aunt Jen's house from time to time until he couldn't take coming in when the street lights came on and the street punishments. He had run away at the age of 14 and followed his dad's instructions to make it in the streets very well. Being a kid, he still made many mistakes, yet learned and got the hang of the ghetto.

He opened the door and got out, leaving Donte inside the crunk Honda once they made it to their destination. Walking inside the CVS, the cool air hit his baby face and sent chills through his body. He waved to the clerk and made his way to the back, where his main girl Yalonda Green worked. She was grabbing her pocketbook when she saw him.

"Oh, I thought me an' you," she paused to kiss him before finishing, "finna fight for being late."

Pimp laughed and grabbed her bag as he followed her out of the store, caught in a lustful stare, captivated by the sway of her walk. When they made it to the car, Yalonda saw Donte bouncing around to the music.

She turned around to face Pimp.

"Pimp, what I tell you about driving around in my car with these stupid-ass niggas? I swear, this is my last time repeating myself." She snatched the driver's door open, and Pimp gestured for Donte to get in the back. He smiled at his girl's cute mug.

"Baby, drop Donte off," Pimp said while taking the Ja Rule CD out of the CD player. Yalonda looked at him and rolled her eyes.

Donte sat in the back seat, looking out the window. He knew Pimp's girlfriend didn't like him. As a matter of fact, she didn't like anybody, it seemed like. Hell, he didn't like her either, though. She was too stuck up and thought she was better than everybody. The only reason he hadn't said nothing about how he felt was because Pimp was his big homie.

Even though Pimp was 5'7" and Donte was 6'1", Pimp was still big homie to a lot of niggas in the hood. Donte had major respect toward Pimp and vowed to stay loyal, no matter what.

After dropping Donte off, Yalonda hit I-95 and headed to her town house in Fayetteville, NC. She was tired from working all day and staying up all last night talking to her twin sister about her no-good husband. Pimp didn't make it any better when she realized he had company today to be dropped off. That's something he always did, and it got to her.

She looked over at him and back to the road. His eyes were closed and his seat was let all the way back, asleep with a calm look upon his face like he didn't have a care in the world. A smile came to her face because sometimes she hated him, but all the time she was in love with him. He always did the little things for her, always paid attention to her and gave good advice. Even though she was five years older than him, she still followed his lead.

He was the man of her house. Even though he had his own place in Baby Atlanta, it was like he stayed with her; he had keys, and what he said always went, no matter what. Though at times she'd force her two-cents in just to try to put her foot down.

Forty-five minutes later she finally made it home. By then Pimp was on his cell phone, wide awake, talking to his father. It was always good seeing how the two's relationship worked. It was like none other, and Yalonda was on the outside looking in. Pimp was very secretive about his and his father's dealings, and she supported that fully.

When the car stopped, Pimp climbed out, still talking, and took her bag from her, which made her smile like always. Yalonda locked the car up and grabbed the pocket of his jeans as he led the way toward her door.

She was madly in love and couldn't help it. Pimp had plenty of game, yet it wasn't that. His sex was the bomb, and that wasn't the cause, either. It was just pure love with pure intent.

When they met three years ago was the day she fell in love with him. She remembered it like yesterday.

*"Come on, Yavonda, Rico ain't thanking 'bout you." Yalonda pulled her twin's arm as she tried to fight with her baby daddy, both her heels in her hand, pocket book hanging from the other hand as Yolanda pulled her away from looking stupid.*

*They were at the club in Baby Atlanta. The whole Silentmoney crew was there, and Yalonda just loved herself some Velt, one of the group's rappers. She was out to have a good time, flirt, exchange numbers, and leave after getting her white t-shirt signed. She had to get back to her normal, single life, though the club was long overdue. Being stuck under her boyfriend Steve for four years in a hectic relationship, she needed the club vibe, but now it was time to go.*

*It was like fate when Pimp made a mistake that night and bumped into her. He held her captivated without knowing he did so, but what really did it was when he grabbed her arm in a soft manner, making sure she was ok. When he was sure she was, he nodded his head and kept it moving.*

*Throughout the whole night she watched him from a distance, surrounded by so many people, all at his beck-and-call. She knew for a fact he shook at least 30 to 40 guys' hands that night, and gave just as many hugs to the females who approached him.*

*Yalonda knew at that point she had to meet this guy. She just didn't know how to approach. Fearful of rejection, she just looked and walked around the club. It was closing time, in the ladies' room she overheard two girls talking about him. She learned his name was Pimp, or Baby Face.*

*Quickly she made her exit and found her sister by the bar. Pimp was leaving when she caught his arm. His whole crew turned.*

*"You forgot to ask was I okay when you damn near knocked me over. And most importantly, you forgot to ask my name."*

*The eight or nine guys with Pimp all started laughing, yet he didn't. She didn't care how she sounded; she wanted to get to know this man.*

*He turned to his boys. "I don't see shit funny."*

*They all hushed, then he turned his attention to Yalonda.*

*"I'm sorry, Ms. Lady, for being rude, yet I took it as you being ok. And my reason for not asking your name was because I would've asked for a number, hug, and maybe a kiss. Yet I know someone as beautiful as you have to have a man, and I wouldn't wanna step on anybody's toes, 'cause if you was mine, ah, nigga bet not step on these." He pointed to his shoes.*

*He was so small, short, and skinny, but his demeanor spoke boss. He was this pretty boy, but a leader. He looked like an underage kid in the club full of grown people, but at the same time he carried himself like an old school cat.*

*"Well, my name is Yalonda. I don't have a man, and I won't be okay until you give me a hug," she smiled.*

*He smiled also and embraced her. They exchanged numbers, and that was where their love life began.*

Once inside the townhouse, Pimp put her bag down and went straight to the sofa. Yalonda rushed to the bathroom, bouncing like a little girl, happy she had an off day and a chance to spend it with her man. She was ecstatic to have her some him.

When she returned to the living room, she noticed the money on her table. She sat next to her man and kissed his cheek.

"Hey, Daddy!" she spoke loud enough for his father to hear, 'cause Pimp was still on the phone with him. She adored the relationship they shared, even though she was on the outside looking in. Pimp was very secretive about his business with his father, and Yalonda supported that fully.

"He said 'what's up.' Go iron that white t-shirt for me right quick," Pimp told her.

Yalonda looked at Pimp funny. She just knew he wasn't about to leave. It'd been three days since they'd been together. She had plans to be with her man, but this nigga had plans himself.

She rolled her eyes and got up, lips sticking out, but still in the process to do as told.

Minutes later he hung up the phone with his father, then looked at the money on the table. Pimp sat up in a slow, lazy movement. He grabbed a folded-up stack, which was ten G's, and put it to the side. Everything else he stuck inside the brown bag. He then got up and pushed the ten stacks inside the jeans he wore. He pulled off the white t-shirt, tossed it on the sofa, and picked up his phone. He pressed one, then listened as it rang. Somebody pick up on the other end, and he made his way into the bedroom with Yalonda.

"Hello?" It was a female.

"Honey, what's up?" Pimp said and took the white t-shirt Yalonda handed him. Honey was one of the four girls who worked for him. She was his veteran, his number one go-to, so that's who he mostly calls to check in on shit. Pimp sat on the bed with the phone clenched in his fist and listened.

"Nothing much on this end. It's been real hot 'round here, so me and the girls is just chilling at the room, waiting on you."

Pimp put his hand in his curly hair and closed his eyes before saying, "Y'all go to da movies, then meet me at Applebee's at ten on Pacer-Ferry, okay?"

"Okay, boo. Bye," Honey replied.

Pimp hung up the phone and laid back on the bed with his eyes still closed, tired for many reasons. Yalonda was placing the iron back into the closet while talking over her shoulder.

"So, you leaving again? When will I see you this time? In two or three weeks, huh?" She was not getting the proper time that was due in this relationship. She kicked off her shoes, then started to strip for a shower.

His eyes opened slowly. He sat up and began to put his shirt on while saying, "So you don't want to go out and eat later?"

"Yeah," she stopped mid-way through peeling her pants off and looked at her man with disgust, "When it's me-n-you, not yo' hos and homeboys."

"Man, miss me with that sucka shit. You know Honey. Dem on my payroll; you know that's how I eat. I was doing this shit before we met, and you ain't trip it then. It ain't like you don't know 'em. Hell, and they know you my wife," Pimp replied while standing up.

"Girlfriend, nigga. I ain't got no ring on my finger, and just 'cause I met them stupid-ass hos don't mean you ain't fuckin' them. I damn near got to beg for the dick whenever I can catch it. And yeah, you was doing this when we met, but you still paid attention to me and my wants."

Yalonda kicked off her pants, standing before him in cotton white panties and a bra to match, creating lust in his eyes.

"And I still don't pay attention?" he asked.

"Nope, 'cause if you did, you'd notice yo' ass been missing for the last three days," Yalonda shot back, now with her hands on her hips, rolling her eyes and neck to stress the point.

Pimp smiled and looked at the clock, then back to her. "Girl, getcho butt in the shower. I'ma be back to get you at 8:00 p.m.," he said.

She just turned around and walked toward the bathroom. Pimp smiled.

# Chapter 2

## *On a Money mission*

Outside, he pulled some keys out of his pocket and pressed the remote to disable his alarm on the 2007 Acura RDX SUV truck he was still paying out the ass for. He climbed inside the soft, gray leather interior with red wood trim and cranked it up. The Playa to Playa CD was in the Kenwood no-face CD player. He pressed three to put it on his favorite song, *Miss Lady*.

The smooth surround sound embraced his ears as he cracked the brain open and pulled off. A slight smile came to his face when thoughts of Yalonda surfaced in his mind. She had every right to be mad at him, because yes, he had been running the streets non-stop for the last two weeks on a money mission.

She just was so cute when mad, it was funny to him even though he felt her. He couldn't neglect his woman though, no matter what. Yalonda was his heart. She was everything he wanted mentally with a woman and beyond what he wanted physically, or so he thought. The turn-on to him about her was she never flaunted her beauty like most women. She was just a good, down-to-Earth person with goals in her life. She showed him how to love, to open up and console and vent. She'd given him more light to the rainbow he already had.

Pimp was a mature twenty-four-year-old, smooth as a baby's skin and as rough as the hardest human being in the ghetto, slum, or dirt. Growing up alone in the streets had its advantages, yet it had its disadvantages as well. He learned the four-pocket hustle from an old-school player named Silky. Plus, he embraced the gift to gab from his father and other pimps. He knew conversation ruled the nation. His disadvantage came along the way. Growing up in the hardest of the projects, a lot of times he had to prove himself. Before he was known, people thought he was weak because of his curly hair and light skin. The pretty-boy baby face got a lot of people beat up, or even worse, shot. The name 'Pimp' came from Bobby Gray, a mac, player, and con. For years straight Bobby Gray was his role model and friend.

*"Say, Pimp, lemme show you something," Bobby Gray said when they met at the corner strip 301. Pimp walked over holding a soda and chips, which he called trap dinner.*

*"You see that girl over there at the bus stop?" He pointed to a woman sitting with a little girl. "Go tell her you from South Beach, FL. Tell her you and your mom stuck all the way up here."*

*Pimp took off to do as told. The woman just looked at him and asked, "What's the problem?" He couldn't give no answer because Bobby Gray ain't tell him everything. He just walked off, feeling stupid.*

*"What happened?" Bobby asked with a smile.*

*"She asked 'what's the problem?'"*

*"And what you say, young blood?" By now Bobby was laughing hard, which made tears appear in his eyes.*

*"Nothing, I – I."*

*"Listen, Pimp, always remember everything is on the bitch. Never approach a ho, girl, or woman without knowledge of what to say. Always make her believe in you. Don't allow her to talk, and you got 'em."*

Pimp smiled while turning down Park Drive. He sure did miss ol' Bobby Gray. He pulled the SUV up next to a black cutlass and cut it off.

He steps from the ice-blowing A/C to the spring break heat. He looked to his left, then right before making his way to the door, which opened without him knocking.

"What's up, my nigga?" Pimp said and gave pound to Shaw. Shaw was one of Pimp loyal friends. Once inside the crib, he pulled the 10 stacks out and passed it to Shaw.

"That nigga been crying like a bitch," Shaw said and pointed to a closed door.

"You go in, right?"

"Naw, I just cut the T.V. up on that stupid mothafucker, that's all."

Pimp nodded his head and opened the door,

When he walked into the room, there was a white guy tied down to a chair, looking scared shitless and overdue for a shower. He had obviously been roughed up prior to Pimp showing up. It was a funny scene, but Pimp was there to conduct business, not to laugh and play games. Pimp walked through the door, closing it behind him. He made eye contact with the white guy as he approached him. Duct tape covered his mouth so he could not speak. Pimp snatched the tape off of his naked lips.

"Whoa! Listen, dude, I must be th—"

Just as soon as his words ran out of his mouth, Pimp punched them back into his mouth.

"Shut up cracker!"

The blow created blood and a fresh, open wound Pimp cared nothing about.

The white boy dropped his head. "Sorry, sir, but—"

"But yo' mother's name is Amanda, your dad's Jeffery, and they own Zale's, that jewelry store down on Mabelton Road," Pimp said, knowing he would hit the dude where it hurt.

The white dude looked up fast, his face turning steamy red as tears formed in his eyes. "What have you done to my mother?" the white dude screamed, then broke down crying, but it didn't faze Pimp at all.

"They will be dead if you don't comply and give me the info I need."

"What info? What are you talking 'bout? I don't know of no information."

"The code to the safe in that store," Pimp said. It was the only thing holding him and his crew back from busting the shop wide open. He had everything mapped out but the code to the safe where the diamonds were locked up, and Pimp would have to kill either the mom or dad to get that code out of them.

"I swear, I—"

Pimp slapped him hard.

"I swea—"

Pimp slapped him again.

"Bitch, I asked for the code." Even though he was small, Pimp could land a hard blow and even harder slap when he wanted to. He had worked too long and hard on this store with this white dude being the main source. It was either do or die.

"Ok, ok, but my parents. Where are my mom and dad?" asked the guy, he begin to panic

"Oh, don't worry about them. Let them worry 'bout you," Pimp spoke. "What's the code?" He pulled out his gun and cocked it back, placing one in its chamber. He aimed at the dude's face.

"I'll give you the code. I just want to make sure my mother and father are safe."

*Boom! Boom!* Pimp aimed and shot the dude twice in the thigh. "Bitch, the code!" He aimed at the face this time as the dude screamed with all his might. Pimp didn't care how bad it hurt him. He wanted the info.

"Ok! 17-87-5-7-89."

"Repeat the motherfucker," Pimp demanded, and seconds later got the same info repeated. The white dude started moaning and mumbling loudly as Pimp walked out of the room, back to where Shaw sat on a lazy-boy chair, smoking a blunt. Pimp pulled his iPhone out and hit a number.

"Yo," the other end answered.

"It's a go," Pimp said, looking at his G-shock watch

"Say less," and the call ended.

Pimp looked at Shaw before saying, "Feed that cracker something to eat. I'll let him go later tonight after the move go down as planned.

"Oh, and put some fresh tape over that bitch's legs where I bust 'em at, and his mouth too." Pimp leaned in to give Shaw some pound.

"Ok, I can handle that," replied Shaw, meeting Pimp's balled-up fist in the air for a pound, then Pimp left just as he came in. He was only the mastermind behind this lick, and everything had to be near perfect if he wanted it to be a successful robbery. Pimp jumped into his SUV with one more stop on his mind.

It took 20 minutes for him to make it to the college campus he attended, majoring in business management. He parked the Acura in a quick spot and jumped out, making sure to sound the alarm as he walked toward the building. One thing about Pimp was he was smarter than the average hood nigga. Even though he was from the hardest of the hoods, he still made his own decision to make it through high school and college. Nobody got him up in the morning or dressed him fresh every day. It was hard, but it was worth every obstacle he went through. He was almost at the end of the road with school, and he could finish his life mission.

When Pimp entered the school lobby, the first person he ran into was a white kid named Johnny. He was a genius, and also one of Pimp's loyal meth customers. See, Pimp was one of those guys who was into all types of things. He was one of the guys who could do almost everything, one of the guys who had tried the unthinkable, but his look was different. He looked like he was raised in a nice environment by well-mannered parents. Pimp could pass for a model with his looks. Most females mistook him for a singer because of his swagger. But little did people know, and those who did know him stood clear of his wrath.

"What's going?" Pimp asked, looking around the lobby until he spotted who he was looking for, but at the same time stopping to holla at Johnny.

"Man, dude, I been calling you for two days. Two whole fucking days." They pounded each other as Johnny stressed.

"I been out of town, brother," replied Pimp with a quick lie.

"Well, I need to cop."

"I'll call you," said Pimp, then he walked off without a reply from Johnny.

He walked over to the head director of the school, Mrs. Johnson, who smiled brightly when she saw him approaching. She held a stack of folders that Pimp took from her with a smile of his own.

"How you doing, Mrs. J?"

"Glad you made it before I left. You need these papers, and your transfer is approved. So congratulations, son! Okay?"

"Thank you, Mrs. J."

"I'm serious, Savarous, you are a wonderful young man. You never missed a day, never failed a class. You have a brilliant future ahead of you. I'm proud of you, I really am," Mrs. Johnson said as they both walked to her class to get his transfer papers. He was done with school up here, so now he was headed to Clark Atlanta to get another degree and maybe more.

Mrs. Johnson led the way until they reached her class. It was a place Pimp spent many days grinding to his degree, knowing he was working for a reason, not just a show.

"Thank you, Mrs. J. I appreciate everything, ok? You hear me?" Pimp said once he received the transfer papers.

They embraced lightly, then she smiled again at the man she saw. He looked so young and was so mature with it. Little did she know Pimp was everything the streets offered, except anything falling under sucker shit. Savarous Jones was a naturally-born hustler in all aspects and had the will to kill instantly. Most of all,

Pimp was a man of finesse and had a genuine gift of gab. He had the voice females loved and the looks they lusted. He wasn't all cut up with big, bulky arms. No, he was a slim, light-skinned dude with major league swagger. He had a natural six-pack and curly hair he kept cut low.

All in all, Pimp had everyone around him fooled. Nobody knew him — nobody but his father — but everyone else was lost. And lost was where he left them, because he was in the game to win, and what a person didn't know, a person couldn't tell.

Jerry Jackson

# Chapter 3

## *So Many Situations*

Yalonda walked out in a cream Prada bodysuit and boots to match. Pimp sat behind the wheel, looking at his woman as she strolled his way: standing 5'8" (5'11" in heels), 151 pounds, thick in just the right places with a Buffie ass to go along with her deep brown skin tone. Yalonda knew she was fine, and considered Pimp lucky to have her. She jumped into the truck, leaning over the console to kiss his jaw.

"I see today you on point with the time, huh?" she said while smiling, then passed him a fresh-pressed t-shirt.

"I'm only tryna be better for you, that's all," he replied while taking the other t-shirt off. After the fresh shirt was on, he pulled away from the curve, then caught Yalonda's arm when she was about to take Playa to Playa out of the CD player.

"Girl, watch out."

"Baby, I know you'll kill about the CD, but this Wayne's CD. This the new one. It came out yesterday."

"Oh, the CD out already?" Pimp asked while taking the new Wayne album out of her hands, looking at the cover.

"Yup. If yo' ass ever be around, you would've been knowin'."

"I said I'm tryin' to get better, right?" he asked and turned out of her townhouse unit.

"Yeah, you right, baby," she said and smiled. Each moment she got to spend around him was a plus, 'cause Pimp stayed on the go doing something. Ever since she'd met him, Yalonda had watched him hustle many different ways. It was sometimes unbelievable, the things she saw him pull off.

When they first met and she was learning him, Yalonda was ready to give up and just leave Pimp to his own world. She could never forget the day she found out he had girls working for him.

She was ready to go Rambo on him and them hos until Pimp explained their positions.

Shortly after she saw in action just what the girls did. He had one who would steal clothes and jewelry. One danced and sold pills in the clubs, on top of setting different niggas up. Pimp had a girl who ran fake checks and credit card scams, and his top girl, who really didn't do shit if anyone asked Yalonda, but for some reason Pimp liked the bitch.

Yalonda saw firsthand that her boyfriend, small as he was, was one hellava dude who was about his issue, and that was a trait that made her fall in love like never before. She was proud to be a part of Pimp's life and vowed loyalty to him. She wanted kids with him, a future, a lovely life together with him and only him.

She knew she'd have to bear with him and his hos. She would need to trust harder and have faith. Pimp had a plan. That's what he would always tell her, but he would never say what the plan was. All Yalonda wanted was to be a part of it.

Twenty minutes into the ride, Pimp pulled up to Applebee's.

"Love you," he spoke while placing the car in park.

"Love you too, baby," she smiled. She was just being honest with equal intent.

\*\*\*

*Ring! Ring! Ring! Ring!*

"Hello?"

"Yeah, lemme holla at Honey real quick?" a male voice asked.

"Dis she, what's up?" Honey asked. She wondered whom this stranger was, his voice sounding sexy over the phone.

"Damn, li'l lady, when we gon' hook up? You been putting me off ever since we met. And why ya ain't dancing no mo'?"

"I been on a family vacation. What are you doing tomorrow, though?"

She now knew who the dude was. They met while she was dancing at Heavens about two months ago. Word on the street was the dude had bread. Everybody knew Big Pop from dope slangin' and gun wars.

"Shid, try'na get with you, if possible," he shot back.

"Okay, that's a bet. I'ma call you after 12 o'clock. We'll do something tomorrow, 'cause right now I'm with my sister, whom I ain't seen in a while," Honey lied

"Okay, just hit, li'l lady. I'm on standby," Big Pop said.

Once the phone was hung up, she locked the number in, this was more money for her future husband. If she could get Big Pop snatched up, Pimp would be really happy with her and the big moves she made throughout their relation.

She just hoped some kind of way Yalonda would slip up and do something stupid or disloyal so she herself could snatch him up, because she'd put in too much work for him. She was like his bottom ho in the stable of four girls. All she did was follow Pimp's orders. If it was sex he wanted, then cool, sex is what it was. But most of the time he had her dance at the strip club to spot victims.

Anything Pimp wanted, he got with no problem. She'd been with him almost two years, and yes, it had paid off. Sometimes she felt neglected, but most of the time she got the love she longed to have.

It was 10:33 p.m. when she pulled the rental up at Applebee's. Diamond, Ke-Ke, and Keyantay all got out and waited on Honey. Everybody was dressed to impress and happy to be off that night.

When the waiter showed them to the table, Honey's heart was crushed when she saw Yalonda. She couldn't stand that bitch and her stuck-up ways. She didn't let Pimp see the disappointment on her face, so she just smiled. Standing at the head of the line, she kissed his hand and took her seat. Next was Ke-Ke, then Keyantay, and last was Diamond, who was the youngest girl who worked for him.

Honey noticed some roses on the table and two plates of already eaten food. *So they already ate,* she thought while picking up the menu.

"Boo, Big Pop called me," Honey decided to say, knowing at the same time Yalonda hated the fact she had to share. Anything possible to get under her skin, though, was joy to Honey.

Pimp only shook his head and gave her a deadly look, because he knew what she was doing. He then took out an envelope and tossed it toward her on the table while getting up.

"That's 20 grand. Y'all get five apiece," Pimp spoke.

Diamond eyed the money with lust. Ke-Ke had told her this was how it was gonna be, and she hadn't even done nothing yet. She hadn't been with them even two weeks yet and was loving it with every day that passed.

In high school Diamond was madly in love with Pimp and always dreamed about him. Every girl in her high school lusted Pimp growing up, because he was always the talk of her town. Things like being his only girl were dreams she wanted badly to come true. Diamond knew it would be hard being number one because Honey was the next girl in line, and he already had Yalonda. Diamond knew she had to play her position until her time came to prove she should be the main. Hell, five grand was a lot of money. That would do until her time came around to be his everything.

Pimp and his girlfriend stood up to leave. She grabbed the flowers and her pocketbook. Diamond didn't like her for some strange reason. What reason, she didn't know, but she wasn't feeling Yalonda's stuck-up ways.

"Y'all order so we can go!" Honey said, breaking Diamond from her train of thoughts. She finally looked at the menu after watching Pimp disappear through the doors.

She looked across to Honey and started to say something, but didn't because she knew Pimp had once again pissed her off, and she wasn't try'na lip fight with Honey. She began to look over the menu, lost in thought.

Meanwhile, Honey was in her feelings, because it felt like Pimp was rubbing his being with Yalonda in her face when he knew she was a bitch. She was stuck up, over arrogant, and high and mighty. She was a prissy, black bitch who Honey wanted to go a couple rounds with.

Pimp had to see her loyalty was number one when it came to him. She had proven numerous times she was with him and for him. She had his back like no other. Honey had watched Pimp kill niggas, and never had she spoken a word about it. She saw him cut his friend's throats, and she held that secret.

Honey was his go-to girl, had been since the day they met, so she felt like she most definitely deserved some respect when it came to her feelings. Pimp was a good nigga overall, and Honey appreciated him for taking care of her and for giving her good game, but she wanted more than appreciation. She wanted love like the love she gave.

Pimp didn't share her vision. He had other plans in life, and he wouldn't let anything stop him. Pimp was very smart at the things he did. He was one of those guys who did things today that didn't show effects until months later. He was slick. He was smooth with his journey through life, and most of all he paid her good for her help.

Keyantay really didn't care for Pimp like the other girls. She just liked the money she made being with him. Plus when a person deals with Pimp, they learn something important. Keyantay first met Pimp through her sister, Tiffany, who at the time was a stripper.

Keyantay was younger then, but admired the relationship her sister shared with Pimp, and the many nights of long stories of him and what they had going on all intrigued her. Tiffany tried to keep Keyantay out of the life she lived, but it was impossible.

Tiffany was in a bad car accident and was killed, which brought Keyantay and Pimp together. He arrived at her mother's house to offer his condolences, and that was when he laid eyes on the exotic look she possessed. Soon after that day, she and Pimp started talking over the phone and agreed to get money together.

Keyantay was only 22 years old and already had a boyfriend when Pimp popped up out of nowhere. Even though Pimp knew of her nigga, she didn't let her boyfriend know the deal with Pimp. All he thought was it was plenty of money to get, and Keyantay and Pimp were cousins. She never had sex with him, but desperately wanted to because she'd heard through many stories how good he was in bed. Having sex with him wasn't important, though; it was the money she made being on his team.

Ke-Ke was a girl who just wanted to fit in the picture. She first met Pimp through boosting clothes and check cashing. Pimp saw she had the heart the will to get money, so he put her on the team. Ke-Ke was an ex-cokehead, but Pimp didn't allow drugs, so it was something she had to let go.

Overall, Pimp treated all his girls the same, but used them for different things. He paid them good, and the only girl he'd sexed was Honey, because she'd been around the longest.

All four girls ate their food and left the restaurant, everyone content with their earnings except Honey.

\*\*\*

Inside his SUV, Pimp sat on the passenger side, seat let back, rubbing his stomach as Yalonda drove, heading home to the townhouse. She was grooving to the music while Pimp watched through lazy eyes.

She smiled and bit her bottom lip when she caught him looking. Only one thing was on her mind, and she not taking no for an answer.

Pimp, on the other hand, was tired and only wanted a nice shower and soft bed. He had a lot of things to do tomorrow and needed all the rest he could muster in a day.

"Yo' butt might as well wake up, nigga," Yalonda said while turning the radio down. "I'm gettin' some dick tonight, Savarous. I'm not playin'." She held a mug on her face when she noticed him smile.

"Boo, we got forever."

"No, fuck, we don't. Yo' ass be in the street too much. Stop fuckin' them nasty-ass hos and come home to some good pussy. You wouldn't be so fuckin' tired and wore out."

"You trippin'," was his only reply.

He leaned up to cut the radio back up, but not before hearing her say, "Naw, you da one who's trippin'."

She pulled up twenty minutes after the sex conversation into the townhouse unit. They both jumped out and strolled toward the door. Pimp held her roses as she hit the alarm.

Once inside the crib, he put the roses on the table, pulled out his cellphone, and dialed a number. Yalonda went straight to the bedroom to run her man a bubble bath, still pissed off.

Deep in her heart, she knew Pimp loved her and would do anything to make her happy, yet she knew he was cheating on her. Or at least she thought he was.

Throughout their relationship she had always been faithful to Pimp, and still he sometimes treated her like one of his hookers or something, and she was tired of it.

"Pimp!" she yelled from the bathroom when the tub was filled with water and bubble. He entered the room while hanging up the phone. Tossing the cell, money, and gun on the bed, he stripped down to his white, silk boxers.

"Can I join you, or is you too tired for that, too?" she asked in a sarcastic way.

"Miss me with that li'l girl shit, Yalonda. You know you can join me. Yo ass need to grow up, damn." Pimp shook his head while walking into the bathroom. She started to respond, but didn't because she knew he was mad now. She just stripped down to nothing, then followed him.

Pimp was amazed at his girl's body. To be a couple months shy of 30, she looked good. She stepped into the tub between his legs. While she was sitting down, he leaned back, soaping up a wash towel, and gave it to her. She started at his feet, then turned around and washed the rest of his body while his eyes were closed. She just looked at him and realized it was a bliss love she held inside her, every heartbeat for this man.

Pimp opened his eyes when he felt her kiss his lips. He returned the favor with a warm tongue and a back rub. *I got thirty minutes in me,* he thought and moved his hand down some more and gripped her phat ass.

"Stand up," Yalonda demanded, and Pimp complied. Emerging from the warm water, his semi-hard dick hung in her face. Her beautiful face. Yalonda kissed his dickhead, then with the tip of her tongue made circles around his head, making Pimp's dick grow out to his full length.

Standing 5'7" and 160 pounds, Pimp surprised most females with his dick size. It was the thickness that got the females. Eight inches, but full thickness is what drove females crazy, on top of him knowing how to fuck.

Yalonda took half his dick down her throat and gagged. She pulled away from the dick, look at it, and spit on it before she stroked him with her hand. She then started stroking and sucking at the same time. This made Pimp grab her head and start to fuck her face.

"Shit," he let out on a slight moan, because her mouth felt like some pussy. Pimp looked down at her pretty, chocolate skin tone, beautiful face, and super sexy lips. He took his dick at the base and pulled it away from her mouth.

Pimp stood her up and forcefully turned her around. Yalonda was taller then him by two inches, so when she bent over he slid right into her tightness, which granted a deep moan from her.

"Ah, yes, babe."

Pimp took both her hips and pushed into her deeper. Yalonda ran from the pain, bracing herself against the wall as he started to go in and out of her wetness. Just being with this man was amazing to her. Yalonda turned around to get a good look of his baby face, tatted-up small chest, and natural six pack.

Pimp bit his bottom lip, bent his knees slightly, and went a little deeper than before, making her rise up more into a standing position. He hit it twice deep, then pulled his dick out.

Yalonda patted her pussy, which was dripping cum, then squatted down in front of him. She started sucking her sweetness off him, jacking him at the same time. Pimp gyrated his hips until he felt the pressure of an orgasm building up. He pulled his dick from her mouth and her hands and started stroking it himself. Yalonda opened her mouth and stuck out her tongue as a thick load spilled from his dickhead onto her tongue.

"Fuck!" Pimp kept stroking until he drained every drop in her mouth. Yalonda wasn't a swallower, so she let the cum pour out of her mouth and down her chin and neck.

"Nasty self," she said, looking up to the man she loved.

Jerry Jackson

# Chapter 4

## *A Girl at Work*

She stood 5'5", 138 pounds, with a pecan-light skin tone and thick, long hair past her shoulders. At 23 years old and a mother of one, she was beautiful and blessed. The heels she had on hurt her feet a little, so she decided she would pull them off as soon as she got in Big Pop's car.

Pimp was in Atlanta for the weekend. He took Diamond and Keyantay with him to handle business. A trip to the A would have been nice, but right then she had bigger fish to fry, money and moves to be made. Seeing as she was the number one, Honey always looked to out-do any of the other girls.

Honey was standing in front of the mirror when a horn blew. Her clock read 8:45 p.m., and she knew it was Big Pop. Quickly she grabbed her keys, pocketbook, and money, then went toward the door. She pulled her cell out and pressed one. It rang twice, then Pimp picked up.

"Yeah, Honey, what's good?"

"Hey, boo. I'm on my way out the door, leaving with Big Pop. I'm finna see what he talking like. Wish me luck, okay?"

"Bet dat. Get back at me later," Pimp replied, and they hung up.

Big Pop was driving an S500 2007 Benz. She strolled toward the whip in a J-Lo skirt with the top to match. She noticed her sway had him hypnotized as she maneuvered around the Benz, running a soft palm over its wet-looking paint.

She was absolutely righteous to him. He knew when they first met at the club she was his future wife. Every time he embraced with her physically, his adrenaline got to pumping. His composure was uncontrollable when with this woman, yet at the same time it was obvious she was hiding something about her life. He didn't know what it was and didn't wanna run her off trying to figure it out, so he decided to wait in hopes she would share herself whole, like he was willing to do.

Big Pop was far from a sucka, but when it came to something he wanted, no matter if it was money, a nigga's life, or a woman, he got it. And yes, when seeing a perfect woman with the mentality right, he couldn't help but be highly captivated. He knew he was gonna get Honey, no matter what it took. He considered her, only in his thoughts she was already his girl, and one day reality would surface. Or so he thought.

As soon as she got in the Benz and closed the door, she pulled the heels off.

"What's up with cha, sexy?" Big Pop asked while pulling from the apartment. Lust was in his eyes.

"Nothing much. Where we going, if you don't mind me asking?" Honey said and let her feet rest on the soft, white car rug, plus the cool air relaxed her. Just looking at Big Pop, she knew his money was long, and she knew he liked her, which would work good for the plan.

"I was thinking we'll smoke a couple blunts, then hit the blue light. Why, what's up? Is there anywhere particular you'll like to go?"

"Naw, that's cool. I'm with you today," she replied with a smile. Honey pulled her phone out and sent her best friend Kimberly a text, asking about her three-year-old daughter, Simya.

Simya stayed with Kimberly while Honey ran the streets — not really ran the streets, but made money, paved a way for her and her daughter. Simya's dad was killed before she was born. He was Honey's first love, and it shattered her to watch him die in her arms.

Honey spoiled her daughter for both her mom and dad. She spent as much time as possible with her daughter, making sure to get her every weekend, no matter what. Simya was her life, her world, and everything she did or was doing was to better her and Simya's life.

Big Pop drove to one of his gambling spots in Summer Hill. He rode slowly down the streets, stopping to holla at certain dudes, even collecting money from some, but really showing Honey how plug he was. Honey, being the one with boss game, peeped his efforts.

Instead of thinking otherwise, she thought it was cute. She kinda liked Big Pop, but she was in love with Pimp, and business was business with her.

He pulled the whip up in the yard of a brick home surrounded by nice, expensive whips.

"Come join me, baby girl. It'll only take a second," Big Pop said and made his exit, and she did the same. Inside the nicely-decorated home was a group of men sitting around having drinks. Big Pop smiled coming in, shaking each man's hand.

"Nice to have you make it," one of the men spoke. At the same time, every man eyed Honey with the sexy outfit she wore.

"No problem. This is my lady friend, Honey. I hope y'all don't mind her sittin' in," Big Pop took her hand.

"Not at all," came a reply, and they took seats as business began. Honey quickly learned Big Pop was a major figure, and the guys around him were all legit businessmen willing to help clean up Big Pop's money. She was amazed at what she was learning. Word in the streets was Big Pop was the man around town, and that was her main reason or giving him her number.

Honey knew Big Pop was head over heels with her looks, and from other strippers at Magic City she knew he was sweet on the money and spoiled them overly. Honey made up her mind that she would swindle Big Pop right into Pimp's arms. She would rock him to sleep, rub his ego until he started floating.

The meeting lasted another 20 minutes, then they were back in the whip. Big Pop said he wanted to take her to one of his favorite restaurants, and Honey was willing to go. Hell, anything to get him comfortable.

\*\*\*

He grabbed his ID from the officer at the front desk of the federal prison after seeing his father. It was something he hated to do, but at the same time he loved to kick it with such a strong-minded person.

Pimp's father was a powerful man with an extremely driven mind. Most would call him a mastermind for all the acts he pulled off. It was like he was untouchable in most cases, though the federal government saw differently and planted a case against him. It was a case no lawyer could get him out of, and the feds knew it. That's why they gave him a natural life sentence on killing an federal agent.

He hated coming to a prison because he was already throwing rocks at the front door, but for his father's comfort he would just about do anything. One thing his dad told him when he was coming up in the game was that nothing wrong lasted forever, and half of what's right might last a lifetime. So Pimp watched all his moves, making sure every step was counted.

Pimp already had plans to get out of the game once he was set for life. It was a hard struggle to make it this far, but since his first fifty grand, everything started to fill out just right.

At twenty-four years old, he had $250,000 street money. He was ready to leave NC and move on to his next mission. After a quick flip of dope, he planned to pack up and just go; go until he couldn't move no more.

He slid the ID card in his pocket and began to walk off, but bumped someone and made her coffee spill to the ground. When Pimp turned around, he noticed an FBI tag hanging around her neck.

"My bad, Ms. Lady," was his only remark. Never once did he think to stop and help. All he wanted to do was get as far away as possible.

He jumped in the rental 2005 Impala. Diamond pulled off once the door closed.

"My flop rung while I been gone?" he asked.

"No," she replied. She was very, very cute, Pimp noticed.

Pimp dialed a number with a mug on his face as Diamond turned out of the prison yard. She was beyond happy to be anywhere around him. They'd been together all day. Pimp did not talk much, but it was okay. Without speaking a word, he'd given her hope in the dream she held about them.

"Keyantay, what the fuck I tell you?" Pimp snapped into the phone, then listen before going on. "Bitch – yeah I know. Bitch, I don't give a fuck." He listened again. "Okay, what he say?" After a couple seconds of Keyantay talking, he just hung up in her face.

"Listen, Diamond, lemme tell you something I want you to always remember, okay?" He didn't wait for an answer. "I run a tight ship. Slips count in everything I do, feel me? So I got no room for mistakes and fuck-ups. If I ever tell you to do something, no matter what it is, I want it done like yo' punk-ass friend. I tell her to tell this nigga we'll meet in Buckhead. She turns around and lets him tell her someplace else. See, that's what I'm talking about. I run this shit, not him. Diamond, you the reflection of me. Ain't shit about Pimp weak, feel me? You got to rep me, understand?"

Diamond nodded her head in agreement, because she did understand. She always understood. Even though she was the youngest, she truly felt like she was the best girl on his team. All she needed was her chance to prove she was loyal and highly capable of handling business like he wanted it to be handled.

Diamond knew Pimp was upset, so she really didn't say much, 'cause she didn't want to fuck up her moments spent with him solo.

At this point in her life she knew she was ready to be his number one. She had made up her mind she would do whatever it took to get that wifey position, even if it was crossing every bitch out in his path.

The remainder of their ride was spent silently in thought. Pimp texted back and fourth on his phone, and also directed her through the Atlanta streets, headed to their hotel rooms so they could dress up and meet his people

\*\*\*

When Diamond and Pimp walked into the hotel room, Keyantay was on the phone laughing. Diamond already knew whom it was Keyantay was on the phone with, and boy if only Pimp knew. Or at least that's what Diamond thought.

Keyantay ended her call, then stood her 5'9" frame up. She was naked except for her panties. She walked up on Pimp, putting her arms around his neck like always.

"Baby, I called Montay back. He gon' meet you in the Buckhead Hotel as planned. I'm sorry, boo, for the fuck up." Pimp balled his fist up; she kissed it. "I'm still yo' gangsta bitch, right?" she asked.

"As long as you do exactly what I say, then yeah, you my G.B. for life. Order y'all something to eat," he replied and sat back on the bed. His thoughts couldn't help but go back to the FBI female he made spill her coffee. Maybe it was the look she gave him, or the pure beauty she radiated. Pimp didn't know which one it was, but he felt at that moment something blissful. Yet she was the police, so he left it at that.

He looked at Diamond and Keyantay on the other bed through lazy eyes. Keyantay really thought she had Pimp wrapped around her finger with her watered-down game. Pimp was far from slow.

He already knew she was fucking with E-Bo on the side, which he didn't give a fuck about.

She was only good to him for two reasons, and once he left the North, he would leave them all except Yalonda. Diamond, on the other hand, was his up-and-coming star. She was the total package, plus young. He knew eventually he would make Keyantay set E-Bo up to be robbed blind. She could keep that nigga for right now; it was just her thinking she was slick was a sign of disloyalty.

Pimp was three or four steps ahead of them all because he played the game for perfection. He played the game for keeps at all times, and he trusted no one around him. He just dealt with them accordingly.

Pimp looked at the clock, then to his phone, and just as expected the call came. He let it ring twice before he answered.

"Yeah."

"What's the code?" the caller said.

"17-87-5-7-89" Pimp replied, and as quickly hung up the call, then took the SIM card and battery out of the phone. *Everything is moving as planned,* he thought, and walked into the bathroom to flush the SIM, then the phone.

Pimp was very careful how he did things. He always watched his steps and covered his tracks. He had never been to jail. He was one of those guys who could out-slick the police. Everything the next person got locked up for, Pimp did as well; he just was too smart to let the police catch him.

He left the girls in their room and found his own so he could relax and put his plan together. He had his North Carolina squad down in Mableton, GA robbing a fancy jewelry store. In exchange for some money and jewelry, he would be making a deal with an Atlanta cat named Montay. It was like killing two birds with one stone.

So far, so good. Everything was lovely.

Pimp entered his suite, which was plush since it was the master. He closed the door behind him and found the bed. Pulling out his phone, he dialed Yalonda.

# Chapter 5

*Rules are Broken Loyalty*

She knew one of Pimp's rules was to never drink or do drugs, but she still did, and boy was she beyond high. Whatever Big Pop had in them two blunts they smoked five hours ago, she don't want no more. She was lying on her back on white silk sheets, tired from sucking and fucking all day. Big Pop was also laid out.

They never had a chance to get dinner. It was two blunts and *wham!* His crib was plushed out and beautiful.

Honey must admit, she was feeling this dude in more ways than one, but she had a job to do, 'cause her love for Pimp was great. Being stuck between a rock and a hard place left her confused while laying in the bed with Big Pop's arms around her small waist.

Honey knew what had to be done, yet being around Pop the whole day she had seen something different than what others saw in him. She saw his struggle through years of gold-digging ghetto females, wars and battles with hoods about anything from drugs to respect for reputation. She also saw that li'l boy. Pop never got to play on playgrounds and bike rides. The playgrounds in his projects were dope spots and tuck-away areas for guns.

Big Pop started young for a cat called Ace, an older legend in the hood. He would traffic 10 bombs a day to five corners for months and months, getting the max of two G's a week. Plus Ace took a liking to the fourteen-year-old who was quick on his feet and had the heart to pull the strap when somebody in the streets took him for granted. Somebody —Ace didn't know who — gave the young kid game. Big Pop would never say, though. Being loyal landed him a spot as an over looker of a crack house. A year into that he became the pick-up guy, then on to Ace's right hand man.

Older, rich, and tired. Honey felt his pain, but what really captivated her was when he asked her to be his girl, to share the wealth and live through bliss with him.

*Ring, Ring!*

The phone broke her train of thought. She slowly rose from her lying position to grab the phone out of her pocketbook. Big Pop couldn't help but eye her full, firm breasts as Honey answered her phone.

"Hello?" Honey said.

"Girl, what's up?" Keyantay asked in a low voice.

"I'm busy. Is it a need that you called me? Because if not, I'ma call you later."

"Oh, okay, do that then. And don't forget," Keyantay replied and quickly hung up the phone. She knew Honey was out on a date.

Honey looked at the clock, which read 6:30 p.m. She jumped when Big Pop placed a hand on the small of her back.

"Don't get scared, Ms. Lady. I won't hurt you in no kind of way," he said.

She turned to look him in the face, and his eyes spoke the truth. It felt good, being next to him, with him, and around him. She leaned down and gave him a quick peck on his lips before saying, "I ain't scared, but I do gotta go home."

"You can take the Benz if you coming back later," Big Pop said while grabbing one of her small hands. He placed it on his rock hard manhood. Honey's fingers gripped him tight as thoughts of pushin' the Benz ran through her mind. She bit down on her bottom lip, then allowed her head to fall on his lap. A moan escaped Big Pop's lips when her warm, juicy mouth took him in.

\*\*\*

Pimp, along with Diamond and Keyantay, walked through the door of Romantic. Montay, along with another dude, sat and waited for them to arrive.

When Montay got a good look at the females, he was mesmerized beyond words. Diamond wore an Allure skirt set the showed off her well-shaped legs, and the heels allowed her booty to sit higher than its original height. She had to have on a thong or no panties at all, because when her 5'2" walked, her booty cheeks clapped. As for Keyantay, she wore a jean body suit by J-Lo with boots. She was tall and slim, yet thick and righteous. Montay was captivated.

"What's good, baby boy?" Pimp proceeded to give Montay some pound before taking his seat.

"Shid, you! I'm glad you could make it," Montay replied, still looking at the girls, who also took their seats. Pimp knew the girls' beauty would work on Montay. He was only hoping the price would drop on the drugs.

They sat and made small talk awhile over dinner, then they all rode to a hotel where Pimp had Diamond in the room with him while Keyantay was outside with the other dude.

"So, what do you got for me?" Montay asked, rubbing his iced-out hands together. He and Pimp linked up because Pimp's father and Montay's father were in the same prison.

Pimp smiled, also. "The real deal." He pulled a tote bag from under the bed and emptied the contents onto the mattress. All the ice and gold nearly blinded Montay. "Just give me some work for all this shit," Pimp said. He let Montay play with the four watches and six chains and charms.

"We gotta 'praise this shit, bro. And how much work you talking like?" Montay asked, holding up a diamond necklace with a Jesus head pendant iced out.

"Tell you what, all them watches 80. Just give me half dat. And as you see, the tag on the chains 150. Just give me the 50 on each.

You and I both know the ticket gonna 'praise out to more than that, so you winning by giving me some of that step-on ass work you got," Pimp said.

"Nigga, my shit official," Montay defended his product, laughing.

"Still ain't a hunnid," shot back Pimp.

"So you telling me you want me to give you $460,000 dollars worth of drugs?"

"For over a million dollar worth of diamonds. Fuck yeah, that's what I'm telling you, bruh."

Pimp had a point, and Montay knew this. "It's 35 a brick."

"Give me 13," Pimp shot back, instant with his math, which made Montay started laughing.

He spent 460 grand for 13 kilos and got to keep the cash he was willing to spend. After the deal went down, Montay pulled him to the side. He couldn't keep his eyes off the girl. He wanted to know who this woman was.

"Say, shawty, peep dis. What's up witcha li'l friend, my nigga?" Montay nodded his head toward Diamond, who held the bag at the door, awaiting Pimp for their departure.

Pimp smiled while looking at his young star, then turned back to Montay before saying, "Me-n-you'll talk. Lemme handle this business."

Diamond opened the door and strolled out after Pimp. Keyantay was in conversation with the other dude when they made it to the lobby. She excused herself and joined Diamond on the way out of the big door.

It took 30 minutes to get back to the Ritz Hotel. Pimp had a top floor suite, and Diamond and Keyantay shared a room just below his suite. Pimp sat in the corner chair, looking at the 13 kilos laid across the bed and talking to Yalonda.

His plan was to flip the drugs into more money, then leave the North for a while, just like his father told him.

"Lasting in the game is all about stick-n-move," his father always told him, and those words stuck like glue inside his every bone.

"Baby! Did you hear me?" Yalonda broke his train of thought. He had totally forgotten she was on the phone.

"Naw, boo. What's up?" he asked.

"Oh, so now you don't even listen to me, huh?" Yalonda snapped.

"Girl, I was just mothafuckin' thinking 'bout something. You can miss me wit' that sucka shit. Now, what did you say?"

"Nothing if you ain't heard me the first time."

"Man, what's up?" Pimp asked, getting irritated with her at the moment.

Yalonda already knew he was mad. She liked him upset because that was the only time he showed her real attention. She also knew what buttons to push and how far to take the verbal fighting, because Pimp would snap.

He only hit her once in their relationship, and it put the fear of God in her every moment. She wasn't try'na see those days no more.

"I love you, Pimp. Drive safe." She decided to end the little dispute before it went anywhere else.

Without a reply, Pimp slammed the phone down.

He put the phone on the nightstand and pulled out his cell. He dialed Diamond, which rang twice before her sexy girl voice picked up.

"Hey, Pimp." Pride, joy, and lust could be heard in her words. Pimp smiled to himself.

"Yo, what y'all doing?"

"Nothing. Talking, watching TV," she replied. She really wanted to tell him she was thinking about him and how wet she was at the thought of them making love, but she didn't. Instead she just waited on a respond.

"Come up here at 6:15," Pimp demanded.

"Pimp, it's 6:30 now," she replied while looking at the clock.

"Then you late. You know I hate those who's late, don't cha?" Pimp said in a joking matter.

Diamond laughed in that little girl tone and said, "I'm on the way."

Keyantay looked at Diamond. Joy lit her face as she hung up the phone. She tried to hide the blush, but couldn't.

"Pimp musta told you to come up, 'cause you smiling from ear to ear."

Diamond's smile disappeared. She totally forgot a rule: never let on when Pimp calls for a creep session. *Or does he really wanna talk?* she thought. She didn't wanna rub nothing in Keyantay's face.

"Girl, my bag. But he said I was late, it was funny, I laughed, and—"

"So you're not going to his room?"

"Yeah."

"And then y'all finna fuck-n-suck." Keyantay got up, mumbling under her breath, "I'm surprised one y'all hos ain't hated on me."

"Excuse me?" said Diamond, also getting up.

"Nothing. I'll see you when you get back." Keyantay walked into the bathroom and slammed the door. Tears began to fall out of her eyes, but she willed herself to stay strong.

*Why don't Pimp spend one-on-one time with me?*

She'd been with him a year now and still ain't got the chance to feel him. Nobody did the things she did for him. Nobody risked their necks like she did, yet she was treated like a dog. "Fuck this," she said out loud and snatched the door open!

The door was already cracked open when Diamond made it to the room. When she walked in, he was lying on his back with the phone to his ear, looking like Heaven in the flesh, which made her moist.

She slowly closed the door while making her way toward the bed. Pimp gestured for her to take a seat. She did, her adrenaline pumping at the sight of him and the fact she was alone with the man of her dreams.

The opportunity was there. *Should I approach cautiously, or go buck wild?* she kept asking herself over and over again until she heard Pimp end his phone call. All her courage, all her anticipation, and whatever else she held all folded up into a tiny knot, especially since no TV or radio was on, only heavy exhales of breath.

Pimp put the phone down, and she could only imagine what he was about to do to this little girl, who was pure, soft, and absolutely beautiful.

"Say, Diamond," he called. She turned around to face him. "Do you know how to dance?"

"Depends," was the remark she gave, but at the same time she was confused by the question.

"Strip, shake, make it clap, that kind of dance. Do you know how to do that?"

"Yup," she blushed.

"C'mere." Pimp sat up at the head of the bed, one leg on, one leg off, and pulled her by the waist between his legs. He looked up into her eyes and read them. He then slid one of his hands up her skirt, moving up the soft, warm thighs, then stopped.

"If I touch your pussy, will she be wet or dry?"

Diamond bit her bottom lip. This was the moment she'd waited years for, and now it was there in her face. She was soaking wet, ready, and willing.

"Touch it and see," she replied and stood in a wide-leg stance. Pimp pulled her panties to the side and touched her there to realize it was wet as hell. He moved his hand.

"Strip," he said

On command, she obliged him. Within seconds she was butt naked. He pulled her back between his legs and kissed her stomach, then grabbed both her breasts, which were handfuls. A moan found its way out of her lips.

Pimp slowly let his hands roam her flawless, soft body until he reached her curly pubic hair and pretty pussy.

"Dance," he demanded.

Just when she was about to start, a knock came at the door. Pimp grabbed the seventeen-shot Beretta from under the pillow. He put a finger to his lips, telling Diamond to keep it at a hush while he crept to the door. The first person who came to mind was Montay and his boys, but Pimp was far from a sucka. How did they get past Security?

Keyantay was standing there with a look of hate on her face. He pulled the gun back inside the door behind her. Diamond was sitting on the bed naked with a sheet covering her. Keyantay rolled her eyes, making sure Diamond noticed.

"I need to talk to you, one-on-one," she finally spoke, at the same time glancing at Diamond. Pimp took her small hand and led her to the bathroom.

"What's up?"

"Why you doin' me like this, Pimp? What have I done?"

He smiled while dropping his head, shaking it from side to side because when he first opened the door, he knew what this was all about.

"Is we in a relationship?" He didn't wait on an answer. "Okay then. I pay you good money for being on this team, and you still unloyal. I been peepin' the move with you 'n E-Bo, Keyantay. So you can get that look off yo' face, 'cause a nigga ain't mad. You still my gangsta bitch," Pimp replied, busting her out.

She dropped her head because she knew he was right. She just wondered how the fuck he found out about E-Bo. All she and every girl wanted was a chance to feel him inside them, and it was killing her that Diamond's chance was already there.

"Pimp, I'm—"

"It's cool, ma. We still straight," he cut her off and began to walk out the door, but she grabbed his hand. He saw hurt in her eyes when he turned around.

"Can I join y'all?"

Pimp couldn't help but laugh at the look she gave. He knew she was for real, yet so was he when he stated she'd never get his dick.

"I gotcha on a one-on-one, ma, before we dip."

Keyantay's eyes lit and she showed her dimpled smile as her body fell into his arm.

Diamond saw Keyantay walk straight outta the room, beaming with pride and joy. Seconds later Pimp walked out of the bathroom. He locked the hotel room door, then placed the gun on the nightstand.

"Where did we leave off at?" he asked while sitting beside her. Diamond looked, leaned over, and kissed him. To her surprise, he kissed her back. This was something she knew for a fact he never did, and it aroused her more and more as their tongues danced.

She stood up, allowing the sheet to fall from her naked, flawless body and pushed him back on the bed. First came his shoes, his pants, and then shirt. She wasn't a vet at giving head, but was ready to try to please him in any kind of way possible. She got between his legs, then freed his rock-hard dick, which was pretty big for him to be so small. First she stuck her tongue in its hole to taste his pre-cum, then she took him all into her mouth until she choked. Pimp couldn't help but laugh.

"That ain't funny." Diamond looked up to his face, dick still gripped in her palm.

"C'mere," he said while pulling her to a standing position, he made her stand in a wide-leg stance.

He slid between her legs and proceeded to enter her. She moved back quickly, a shocked look on her face.

"Rubber. We need protection."

Pimp look dumbfounded at her comment. "You dead right," he said, then got up to grab one out of his overnight bag. Once he had it on, he walked back toward the bed.

"Lemme ride you," Diamond said when he approached.

It was a turn-on to Pimp that someone so young wanted to take control. He really wanted to see what she was working with anyway, because someone so beautiful had to have flaws.

To his surprise, she was a pro riding dick, placing her soft, small hands on his chest, rolling and bouncing with every thrust he gave. She then rode him on the floor sideways and let him hit her from the back, which she tried to run from because of the pain. The rubber busted, but he held on for dear life while exploding inside her.

Pimp and Diamond went at it all that night and the next morning before they all pulled out, heading back to NC.

He had to admit Diamond was one of the best fucks he'd ever had. Her small body felt so right next to his own. He knew a rule in his book was about to be broken, and that was thinking with the dick.

# Chapter 6

## *The Big Lick*

Honey was knocked out when Ke-Ke passed her the phone, at the same time hearing a car pull up. Ke-Ke looked out of the blinds and saw it was Pimp.

"Daddy home," she said while unlocking the door.

"Bitch, my daddy dead. I told you 'bout that shit," Honey snapped, then barked into the phone, "Hello?"

"What's good, ma? Can I see you today?" It was Big Pop.

"I don't know yet. Lemme get back at you when I'm fully woke, kay?"

"Bet. Jus—"

She hung up the phone. Keyantay and Diamond walked into the crib. She was hopin' to see Pimp, but didn't. *He musta kept going to that bitch,* Honey thought while going to the bathroom. They all shared a six-bedroom crib Pimp paid for each month, plus the five grand he gave them.

Diamond was glad to be home. She went straight to her room, ready to shower and still drained from last night. She now knew the love she held for Pimp was real. She was happy beyond words, but feared how Honey would feel about the situation. For whatever it was worth, she didn't care how nobody felt.

On the other hand, Keyantay was already giving Honey a rundown on what took place in Atlanta over the weekend. Honey couldn't believe her ears, and it was easy to see the hate and attitude on her face.

"So that bitch got the dick, huh? That's why she ain't speak," Honey said through anger, then picked up the phone to call Pop back. "Fuck Pimp," she mumbled while the phone rang.

Meanwhile, Pimp pulled the rental up to Hertz next to Yalonda's Honda. He let her keep the Acura while he was away so she could stunt a little bit on the hos who hated and the niggas who wanted to sex her.

Once the car was cut off, he reached in the back, grabbing the Adidas bag with the dope in it, more than happy they all made a safe trip to and from Atlanta.

For some reason his mind wouldn't rest on the thought of Diamond and the great sex they shared last night. It was just right. *She* was just right. Pure and still young, beautiful, and willing to do whatever to please him; that was something he liked in her.

He got out and slung the bag over his shoulder with his left hand while using his right to dig the car keys outta the pants he wore. Her smell was still on him even though they showered before leaving the hotel. "Damn," he remarked while sliding into the Honda after pushing the bag inside the trunk.

A fresh 13 kilos, a stash spot, and a team of six workers. He was ready to get money, keep money, and dip. Nothing would stop or slow this mission down. He had to have it like a human being had to have a breath of air.

While turning out of Hertz, he dialed a number into his cell phone.

"Hello?"

"Where your brother at? What's going on witcha?" It was Nevea. When he heard her voice, he realized he had totally forgotten the promise to take her along on the trip to Atlanta.

"Nothing. Hold on," she replied with little emotion and dropped the phone on something hard as he waited for Donte to pick up. He was wondering what Yalonda was doing. He sure did miss his boo and couldn't wait to see her, yet at the same time….

"Yo, big homie, what's up? How was ATL?" Donte's overjoyed voice boomed through the phone, breaking up Pimp's train of thought.

"Good, li'l bro, good. What's up on yo' end, though?"

"Shid, chilling. You know how I do it. When you gon' come fuck with me?"

"Soon. I told you I had something major in the works. I'ma swing through around 11 o'clock, so be on standby, check?"

"Bet, bro."

"Put Nevea on the phone right quick," Pimp cut him off. Donte yelled for his sister to pick the phone up. When she did, Pimp could hear females in the background laughing.

"Hel-lo," she picked up laughing.

"What's up? You miss me or what, ma?"

"Oh hey, Pimp." She paused. "You ain't gave a bitch the chance to get to know you. I can't miss somebody I don't know."

"What you doing tonight? Can I come swing through?"

"I don't care what you do," Nevea replied and said something to one of her friends. She made a promise to not chase Pimp, and she was gonna stick by it. If he came, he came. If he didn't, it was all good.

"I'ma be over around 11 o'clock. Don't have no niggas there, 'cause it me-n-you tonight."

"Whatever."

"I see—"

The phone went dead, which pissed him off. He saw it as a form of disrespect when someone hung up the phone in his face. He was gonna make her pay for that move. She just pulled, and she knew it.

***

Yalonda was standing over the sink with the phone to her ear, still in her work clothes, talking to her twin sister about a guy she just met. Yalonda hated to listen to the, "oh, girl, he so fine, he got money," etc. Yavonda always stressed, but hey, that was her Ace, blood, and best friend, plus there was nothing else to do while washing dishes.

Pimp has been gone for the last two days, and she was missing him like crazy. They only talked once last night and he sounded tired, so she let him go to sleep. Now she was waiting for him to come home. For two days straight she'd been horny, and doing it herself just wouldn't cut it. Her sister wasn't making it better by talking about this new guy.

"Girl, I'm telling you, wait until you meet his friend Nick's fine, bald-headed ass. I don't see what you see in Pimp. You got to know he's—"

"Yavonda, stop!" She refuses to let anyone talk about her man. "Don't do that, 'cause I don't give a damn about nobody else, and you know this."

"Girl, I was…. You dead right. My fault. Anyways, Pimp is my dawg," Yavonda replied and thought of the night she spent with him, how he blew her mind with his skills. And to be so short with a big dick was a major turn on.

"It's cool, girl. I know you only be try'na look out for a bitch," Yalonda replied, then heard a car radio outside. She quickly took a look out the window to find no Pimp. All hope inside her vanished, and all of a sudden she didn't feel able to speak with her sister any longer.

"So, is you gonna double date with me or what?" Yavonda broke Yalonda train of thought.

"Um, only if Savarous can be my date. You know I'm faithful, girl."

"Honey, it's just a simple date. No strings."

"Yavonda, no! Okay? My answer is no. Anyway, lemme call you back. He's on the way home. I need to be ready. Love ya." And without a second thought, Yalonda hung up.

She looked around her empty kitchen, down to the sink, and back out the window again. Still no Pimp in sight. *I should call,* was her thought as she walked to the bedroom, coming out of her work clothes.

\*\*\*

Pimp pulled the Honda up at his condo in baby Atlanta around 4:00 p.m. Tired from so much driving, he still had so much to do in just a little time.

The area he stayed at was nice and low key. Not a human being was in sight as he sat in the car, debating his next move. He knew it was almost over in the North. *Maybe I'll give Texas a try.*

He opened the door and noticed a teenage kid running toward him with a bat. Pimp quickly pulled the Glock from the console and almost shot until he saw the rolling baseball. He stopped it with his foot as the kid approached.

"Thanks, sir," the young boy said. He was no more than 13 years old. He bent down to get his ball and sprinted away quickly. Pimp tucked the Glock and stepped out of the car into the hot air.

The bag thrown over his shoulder, he made his way to the apartment, looking around before even walking through the lobby. When he was sure he was safe and out of harm's way, he pushed through the glass door. Not even paying the attendant any mind, he went straight to the elevator and pressed up.

The girl behind the desk was a young, white, blue-eyed blonde who thought she was a goddess. Pimp never gave her the time or day, never spoke one word to her, and he knew she hated that because she loved attention.

The door to the elevator opened and he stepped in as two white dudes stepped off. Both smelled like police and gave him the eye, then nodded their heads at him. Pimp pressed nine on the panel and watch the doors close behind them.

\*\*\*

"Honey, yo' ride is here," Keyantay yelled from the porch with Ke-Ke and Diamond. They both turned their attention to the yellow Viper Big Pop was pushing. He didn't bother to step out, but they all knew how he looked, and he stayed fresh.

Honey walked out in some Gucci capri pants with the top to match and heels. Her hair, nails, and feet were done perfectly. She turned to the girls before going down the steps and winked.

"I know I look fly!"

Everybody agreed with a nod of their heads because it was a known fact she was.

Big Pop jumped out of the whip as he saw Honey approaching and opened the door for her after he got a quick hug and a peck of cherry lip gloss.

It was easy to tell Honey had him faded in more ways than one.

She settled inside on the black and yellow guts. The air was on cool, plus the music played low. One of her favorite songs by Deniro was on: *White Bitch.*

Big Pop slid his wide frame behind the wheel and leaned over for another kiss before saying, "I gotta make a run. You don't mind, do you? But it'll be quick."

Honey smiled with those flirty eyes, hooking him in for the kill. She leaned over the console, inches away from his lips, and said low, "As long as I'm with you, it don't matter"

Big Pop smiled and pulled off.

\*\*\*

It was 7:30 p.m. when Pimp finally walked through the door of Yalonda's townhouse. She was on the sofa with a bowl of popcorn and a DVD playing. When she saw him, her eyes rolled.

He closed the door. "What's up, pretty? What's with the mug?"

"Nothing," Yalonda replied and sat the bowl down on her glass table, her eyes focused on his neck. She got up, walking toward him to cut the light on, because the glow from her TV could've been playing tricks on her eyes.

Once the lights were on, she followed Pimp, who was headed to her bedroom as if nothing was wrong. When he turned to enter the room, she knew for sure what she saw: a big-ass hickey on his neck.

Blood boiled up to her head, rushing to her brain. A million thoughts ran through her mind, nothing positive though. Tears forced themselves up to her eyes. All her doubts she now knew were facts; yes, he'd been cheating while she'd been faithful for three straight years. And it hurt.

"Iron me a sh—"

"Savarous, what the fuck is that on yo' neck?" she pointed.

Pimp looked at her, then reached to touch his neck. Then he went to the mirror and was shocked to see what Diamond did in the midst of their lovemaking.

He slowly turned around to find Yalonda's arms folded across her chest, barefoot, waiting on an answer. The hurt in her eyes was clear, and it made him feel really bad, because he was busted, no doubt about that.

He made an effort to reach out to her. When she didn't move, he came closer. She took a step back and dropped her arms, which now were fists at her sides.

"Don't touch me, Savarous."

"Baby, lis—"

"Listen, my ass! Nigga, I can't believe you. Instead of going to handle business, yo' ass out fuckin' around." The tears forced their way out of her eyes.

She tried to strike him, but he moved out of reach. When she tried again, he caught her arm, and with one motion he spun her around, holding her, and said, "Okay. I don't wanna fight, boo. I fuck—"

"Let me go! Let go of me, mothafucka!" she screamed.

"Listen, Yalonda! Listen, boo, I fucked up. Okay? Damn, I admit the shit. What more you want?"

He let her go. She turned around quickly. She had a look in her eyes he'd never seen.

"Get out of my shit, that's what. Bye!"

"So—"

"Bye!" she yelled so loud it shut him up fast. He had to respect her crib, but Diamond was about to get it for this sucka shit, plus Keyantay because she must have noticed it on their drive from Atlanta.

In the living room he dropped Yalonda's car keys and got the keys to his SUV, then headed out the door. He decided to grant her a little space because, true indeed, he fucked up and let Diamond suck on his neck. Her pussy was so good he couldn't help himself.

The living room light was on when he pulled up to the six-bedroom brick house he rented for his four girls. It wasn't nothing major: a small front yard, a back yard and pool, plus a couple pits made it home.

Pimp jumped out and walked up the steps. He used his own key to enter the plushed-out crib. Ke-Ke was laid out on the sofa with the phone to her ear.

"Hey, daddy!" she spoke, loud enough to alert the others in the house. He waived, but headed straight upstairs. Before he reached the top, he saw Diamond coming out of the bedroom wrapped in a towel, hair wet and looking more beautiful than ever.

"Hey, Pimp," she spoke with a smile once she noticed him, but her smile was quickly gone when she saw the mug he wore. "What's wrong?"

Pimp didn't speak. He just walked toward her, grabbing her hand.

"What da fuck you see that's wrong with me?" He leaned his neck to the side.

Diamond turned around and touched the spot on his neck softly, then looked him in the eyes before saying, "I told you it was hurting, but I didn't mean to mark up yo' neck like this. I just bit down because—"

Without a second thought, he pushed her out of his face. He tried to walk out of the door, but she grabbed his arm.

"Pimp, wait!"

He turned around and slapped blood out of her mouth. She fell back and he stood over her body.

"Bitch, you know what you was doing. Don't play with me." As he walked off, he decided to not even bother Keyantay, but he did go to Honey's room. She was missing, so he pulled out his cellphone to call her ass.

*\*\*\**

Big Pop went to the waffle house across the street to get them a bite to eat. Her stomach was hurting because her emotions were saying one thing and her head was stressing the next. Big Pop had been great to her. He wasn't ugly, and his bread was long, real long.

The cellphone ringing on the nightstand of the hotel room made her jump. When she looked at the caller ID, it showed Pimp's number.

"Hey, boo. What's up?"

"Where you at, Honey? I need to see you." He sounded mad.

"Baby, I'm at the hotel with Pop. Is everything okay?" She sat up in the bed. She knew everything wasn't okay, and just like any other time, she was willing to be the one to make it ok.

"Fuck naw. Dis stupid-ass bitch Diamond done put dis hickey on me, and Yalonda saw it. I need you to whoop dis bitch ass when you get home. Just call—"

"She did what?" she asked him, surprised. Pimp didn't let nobody get that close to him, but somehow, some way he allowed this bitch Diamond to get closer than she'd ever been, and that alone had her in her feelings.

"Li'l bitch need to get her ass beat. So what's up with this nigga, though? 'Cause you sho' been spending a lot of time with him," Pimp said, and she could hear a bit of jealousy in his voice, which was cute.

"He ready, daddy," she burst out and said. The time was perfect to move into the number one spot, and what better way to do it than giving him one of the biggest niggas in the North?

"Who, Big Pop?" Pimp asked.

"Holiday Inn, 301. Daddy, he ready. Get here. Bye!" She quickly cut the phone off as she heard Big Pop come into the room. He damn near took over the whole doorframe as he smiled at her with a handful of food.

"Let's eat," he said and ducked down to enter the room.

Honey smiled back and slid out of the bed. "I gotta go to the li'l girls' room first." She ran up toward him, stood on the tips of her toes, and still had to pull his shirt down for a kiss. He slapped her ass when she ran off toward the bathroom.

Big Pop could see forever with this girl. Everything about her was for him. He set out the food on the table and took a seat to hear the water running. Then she stepped out, still smiling that smile, and skipped over to the table to join him.

"Thanks, boo. I'm starved."

"What you want to drink, 'cause I forgot. I'ma run outside right quick." Big Pop stood up.

"Anything would be fine," Honey replied while going at her food.

When Big Pop left the room, she made a mad dash for her bag and pulled out some eye drops. She then rushed to get two cups of ice. She squeezed four drops from the bottle into the cup for Big

Pop. She knew only two were needed, but he was a big guy and she didn't need any slip-ups. Quickly she put everything back into place and sat down at the table and food. She began to eat, and happy thoughts of Pimp loving her for this came to mind.

Big Pop soon returned with two cans of soda out of the machine. He placed them on the table and took his seat also. He was a large man and full of love. He was falling fast for Honey, and she didn't even know it.

All he needed was true, honest love from the girl he wanted to be with. If he could get loyalty and love from Honey, she could get the world in return. Right then and there at the table, Big Pop made up his mind that he wanted her and nobody else, and he was willing to do whatever it took to keep her happy.

***

Pimp pulled up at the hotel and saw Big Pop's Viper parked out front. He pulled three cars down and reached under his seat to grab his .357 DE, mask, and black gloves. It was a known fact Big Pop was one if the biggest niggas up North, so Pimp was grateful Honey pulled this lick off.

After he put the gloves on, he put the mask on top of his head and opened the door. With one foot out, one foot in, his cell phone rang. The caller ID showed Diamond's number. He had no time for her right then.

He left the phone in the passenger seat and closed the door. His heart rate started to speed in his chest. His stomach felt light and lazy. He touched the top of his head and made sure the mask was in place, then he touched the gun in his waistband; it was there and ready. He walked toward the entrance door.

The hotel parking lot was clear, not a person in sight. That was a good thing, Pimp thought, because the police in that area were hell. He didn't feel like getting caught up with them today. Pimp made his way inside and took the elevator to the third floor.

The lights were on in the room, he saw under the door. He wondered what was up. *Has Big Pop caught Honey in the act?* was Pimp's thought, but he was too far in the plan to start the doubt now, so he pulled the mask down and gun out. He slowly grabbed the door knob and turned it. The door began to open. Pimp pointed the gun first, not trying to take a chance.

"Daddy!"

He heard Honey's voice, then saw her snatch the door open, looking scared. He saw Big Pop laid out across the bed. A smile came to Pimp's face as Honey fell into his arms.

"'Sup, ma?" He kissed the top of her head as her face was planted in his chest. Pimp made the phone call and was glad he didn't put up much of a fight with the big nigga.

"Yo, y'all niggas pull up. I got 'im," Pimp told Dontae and one of his partners. The plan was to tie Big Pop down and watch him while Pimp and Honey went to his house. Honey noticed the hickey on his neck as he talked on the phone. It was big, too, and Pimp being red didn't help the situation.

He told Honey to get dressed. He decided to go ahead and duct tape Big Pop's feet and hands in case he wanted to wake up. After Honey got dressed, they waited in his SUV for his people to do the dirty work. They took another 30 minutes to get there.

When Donte and two of his friends made it, Pimp left them with strict instructions

"Whatever y'all do, don't let him roll over on his back. Keep him on his stomach, and keep ya bangers out."

The boys agreed to do as told. Nobody really wanted to go against Pimp, no way, especially since seeing he had a major nigga tied up in a hotel room. Right then they all knew Pimp was serious.

The Heart of a Gangsta

# Chapter 7

*Sticking to the Mission*

*days later*

Pimp walked out of the bathroom of his condo and looked at all the money on his bed: all 20 kilos he took from Big Pop's townhouse, a spot only Honey knew about. When she and Pimp had gotten there, they only found the dope, no safe, no nothing important. Pimp knew that wasn't the spot, so he made a call and had Shaw scoop Big Pop's ass up for a few days, 'cause Pimp knew he had some paper.

Two days ago he went out to fix things between him and Yalonda, but she was gone. He tried calling, but her phone was off. "Fuck it," he said to himself and grabbed the bag with the 380 grand inside that he hid in her storage room at her townhouse.

He still had plans to go fuck with Donte for the li'l job he did and for what he was willing to do. Pimp had 33 bricks and almost a million in cash scattered all over his room. It was time to make a move and change up. He was about to leave everything and everyone behind to go on to his next mission, 'cause a million wasn't enough.

Pimp put all the bricks in two suitcases and the money in two duffel bags. He reloaded all the guns he had and left the condo and everything else in it. He was headed to Big Pop and Shaw to get shit over with.

Shaw came to the door. Pimp passed him ten grand. The crib was filled with weed smoke.

"'Sup, Pimp?" Shaw pocketed the cash and moved to the side. Pimp nodded his head.

"Shid, you. How dis big nigga been act'n?"

"Cool'n," Shaw informed.

61

Pimp only smiled 'cause he knew there was more money in his pockets before he left.

Shaw also smiled. See, this was his type of shit. He was well known to kidnap and murder niggas.

Him and Pimp met when they were teenage boys, running around North Carolina, learning life. Shaw was older, but Pimp – like in most cases – was faster than his peers. When they met, they quickly made a bond through action. Back then Pimp had a lick for some mid-grade weed. He needed another guy, and Shaw was down. The lick didn't go as planned, and the boys were forced to kill, and did so without hesitation. After that day, both of them understood their relationship.

Pimp walked into the room where Big Pop was tied down and cuffed, too. He closed the door with money on his mind, murder in his intentions. A wicked smile painted his face 'cause once this was over, he would be a millionaire plus some.

"Big boy, you know what it is."

\*\*\*

"Girl, you miss that nigga, don't you?" Yavonda asked her twin sister, who was looking lonely sitting on the sofa. She'd been in front of the TV for the last three days over at her sister's house to get away from Pimp.

"Yup."

"Well, go get ya man, Yalonda." Yavonda sat down next to her sister. She was tired of her looking so down and out. She put an arm around her shoulder and held her.

"You think I should?"

"I know," Yavonda replied. "Listen, girl, Pimp loves you to death. Okay, he cheated. He's a man. You knew da type of nigga he was when y'all met in the club that night. But overall, Yalonda, that boy treats you like a queen. Men gonna be men, whether we like it or not, boo." Yavonda stood up.

Yalonda knew she was right, yet she also knew it wasn't impossible for one to be faithful, because she had been ever since the day she and Savarous met. She knew she deserved better than this, but she was crazy in love with the man. He loved her, too; she'd known it as fact. She just wanted him to do good by her — not just spoil her with attention, fly words, and great sex, but be faithful.

Since the day she found that hickey on his neck, he'd been blowing her voicemail up, but she refused to answer or call back. It'd been four long days now, and she missed her man, so she decided to get him. Or better yet, let him get her.

"You right. Maybe he's realized what he had and lost, and now he won't get caught up like this no more, huh?" Yalonda also stood up.

"Right."

The sisters hugged each other. Yalonda looked at her watch, then grabbed the picture of her and Pimp. She kissed it, then picked up her keys.

"I'ma call you once I've settled this, okay?"

"Do that, girl," Yavonda said. She walked her sister to the door.

Boy was she glad that girl made up her mind to go back to Pimp, 'cause she wanted to run around her own house butt-naked with her man.

Yalonda climbed into her Honda and was about to call her baby, but decided not to. She'd surprise him, maybe even put the pussy on her boo, because it'd been a while. She cranked up and pulled off, blowing the horn to her twin sister, who waved and blew kisses in the air.

The first place she went to was her condo, where she got under a warm bubble bath. Lying back in the tub, she let her mind wander here and there. She held her leg and turned her foot from side to side. She knew that at her age she was blessed with a beautiful body.

*How could someone cheat on me?* Yalonda thought while dropping her leg back into the water. All she wanted was to live a happy, normal life. Why did it have to be so hard?

She went ahead and bathed really quickly, then climbed out of the water. She walked naked to her room, wishing like hell Pimp was on the bed looking lovely, but he wasn't. So, instead of falling in his arms, she grabbed her sexy, white silk thong set. First she put baby oil all over her body, then slid her frame into her thong. Already she was feeling extra sexy.

The dress she wore was by Gucci. It stopped at her shins with splits up to the middle of her thighs. Pimp love when she dressed like that. She put on some heels with the strings and grabbed her Gucci bag, then car keys. It was time to get her baby back.

An hour later she pulled up to his condo in Baby Atlanta, NC. His truck wasn't there. Pimp gave her a key a month ago, so she decided to go inside, clean up really quickly, set candles up, and call him home. A smile came to her face at the thought of being with him that night. She got out of the car and made it to the lobby door before turning to the Honda, hitting the alarm.

The girl at the desk looked up from reading a book and smiled. Yalonda waved, but kept going. On and off the elevator, she pulled her key out. Goose bumps were all over her body as she stuck the key inside the lock, then turned.

Her heart dropped when the door came open. The living room was empty! Quickly she ran to his room to find everything gone. Her heart was beating wildly inside her chest as she dug around in the bag for her phone. She dialed Pimp's number to find his cell has been disconnected. She tried again and again only to get the same thing. Yalonda looked up from the phone, then around the room. She was confused. *Did he get locked up? Was he calling me days ago to tell me his new address? Will he call me again?* All the thoughts made tears rush out of her eyes.

"Why me?" she screamed and broke down.

After crying almost 10 minutes straight, she willed herself together, then made her way down the stairs. The girl was still at the desk with the book. Yalonda walked up.

"Excuse me, ma'am. Um, Savarous Jones, he's moved. Do you know when?"

The girl looked up from her book into Yalonda's face,

"Yesterday some people came and took all of his things, but it's been two days since I've seen him."

"Did he leave an address?" she asked with hope in her voice.

"Sorry, but he didn't."

"Thanks."

Yalonda felt defeated as she made her way to her car. What was Pimp doing to her? What kind of game was this? Because she didn't like it. She had two more places to go before going home. She just crossed her fingers.

***

Donte was washing his rims when he saw Pimp's girlfriend's car pull up. He wondered what that was about as he stood straight up. The look in her eyes let him know something was wrong. He could tell she'd been crying not too long ago. He dropped the sponge in the bucket as she approached.

"What's goin' on witcha?" he asked.

"Have you seen Pimp?"

"Naw." Now he was confused because everybody knew she was his main girl. So if she ain't seen him, then something was wrong with the picture, 'cause Pimp was gone.

"When was the last time you saw him, den?" Yalonda asked. Donte didn't wanna get in the midst of no bullshit, but he did remember when Pimp gave him ten grand and they rode around talking. He gave Donte the game on the flex, the kidnap, and the perfect get out.

Donte asked him, "You must finna dip?"

Pimp looked at him and smiled, then said, "I just gave you the game to get rich. Two niggas with that knowledge can't be in the same state; it ain't big enough. Stick and move, baby boy. Stick-n-move."

"Well, is you gon' leave yo' number ?" Donte asked.

"Naw, but you gon' hear about it, and two real niggas gon' meet up again." That was two days ago. Donte just put two and two together and figured Pimp left Yalonda alone also.

"He gone. He left da state," Donte replied.

"How you know?" She put her hand on her hip.

"'Cause he told me."

"What you mean, he told you?" Something didn't add up to her.

"Bruh said he was 'bout to leave. If you didn't know he was gone, then that says a lot about you."

"For yo' information, we had a fall out. Anyway, where did he say he was going, Donte?" Yalonda asked. Her heart was broken.

"He didn't say."

"Did he leave a number?" she hoped.

"Wouldn't give it to me," Donte replied, nonchalant.

"You lying," Yalonda pressed.

"That's on my li'l girl. Pimp is gone, and I don' know where."

Donte bent back down to grab the sponge. Yalonda had a hurt look on her face, but there was nothing she could do about it, so he went back to his rims.

Yalonda made a stop at Pimp's hos' house. Only Diamond and Honey were there, and both said they hadn't seen or heard from him. Honey said she even tried calling, but the phone was off. Yalonda read both the girls' faces and saw they were telling the truth. Now she was really confused. Now she had doubts. She believed Donte when he said Pimp was gone.

Tears wouldn't stop falling from her eyes.

She pulled back up to her condo and didn't see his truck or him standing on her steps with some roses. She knew it was over.

She just wondered why.

Jerry Jackson

# Chapter 8

### *Da move*

Pimp was sitting up in the bed at the hotel, looking down at the two bags that held his whole life inside. Everything he worked so hard for. Years of sweat and tears had finally paid off: 980 grand strong and 33 bricks. Now he was ready to do it again, but this time in Texas, where he'd start from the bottom up. Yet first things first, he had to get a place to rest and a place to kick it. He had too much cash money just laying around to leave to go sight-seeing.

Pimp picked up a letter he wrote to his father. He re-read it before sealing it up:

*Ol' Head:*
*My new number is 817-702-9945. I've moved. I've stuck. I'll see you soon.*

He decided the letter would do for the moment. There wasn't much he could say anyway until they were face-to-face, yet he knew his father would be proud. He did well in NC and planned on doing better in Texas.

It'd been two days. He'd rested, and the time read 9:30 a.m. He got out of bed and hit the shower for a minute, then got dressed. He stuck 20 grand in his pocket, his cell phone, and Glock 19. It was 10:15 a.m. by the time he left the room, both bags thrown over his shoulder. He tossed them into the SUV and slid behind the wheel.

The Texas air was different. Well, he was in the South now. He'd get to see how the dirty-dirty do their thang. When he cranked up, K-Kutta came through the speakers.

He pulled off into the new world to see what he could find, how easy it would or wouldn't be for him to get another million or two and leave. *Would it take years or months,* his father always said!

"Once you've seen big numbers, that's all you gon' want. Fuck anything less."

And he was right, because Pimp didn't want nothing but 100 G's or more from then on.

For the next two hours he rode around looking for a nice spot. He found some townhouses that looked alright. The area was mostly white with coded gates. He pulled up to the office to see two white boys on skates fly past.

*Yeah, this will do,* he thought and made his way inside the cool office, which had two black leather loveseats, a table with a lamp on top of it, and a desk with a middle-aged white woman behind it. The place was neat and very clean-looking. Pimp approached the desk.

"How you doing, miss?"

The woman looked up and a bright smile spread across her face. "I'm fine, young man. And what may I help you with?"

"A place to sleep for the next six months."

"I see. Well, there's paperwork that must be filled out before we can do anything. First you must be approved, an—"

"Listen, I know about the deposit and all. I'm willing to pay that plus my whole six months' worth of rent today. Call whoever you need to call to make it happen. I gotta have a place to rest tonight," Pimp cut to the chase.

"I see. And," she paused, looking for the correct words to say. She wasn't used to people like Pimp, and he saw it on her face. "Sir, we will still need to do paperwork."

Pimp pulled out his ID and bank statement. He slid both to her with a smile on his face.

"I'm A1."

They did the paperwork and he went to take a seat to wait. It wasn't long before she called him back, which he knew she would. See, Pimp had A1 credit and a soul food restaurant in his name, run by his aunt.

"The rent is $1,600 a month, $1,000 deposit, and the total for the whole six months will be $10,600, sir. Whenever you can have the money—"

Her words were cut off when he pulled out a bankroll. He counted out 11 grand in her face and told her to keep the extra $400. He just wanted his keys.

The next of couple days Pimp spent getting his crib plushed out. He was standing outside talking to a car dealer on his cell phone about a new Escalade he saw.

He watched the movers grab an 80-inch TV he paid an arm and a leg for, then out of nowhere he heard, "Yummie, this is the one I was talk'n about!"

Pimp turned his attention to the voice. He saw a white girl walking toward the TV, looking bright-eyed. She then looked at Pimp.

"How much it cost you, if you don't mind?"

He pulled the phone away from his ear and spoke. "It's eight grand. I got it for six, though."

"Yummie, c'mere," the woman said. That's when Pimp noticed her friend, a white girl in some jeans so fine it made no sense at all. She wore dark shades he noticed were Prada. Her hair was a honey-blonde mane that reached her lower back. She stood 5'5", around 150 pounds solid. He never in his 24 years of life saw someone so well put-together. The white girl was so beautiful.

"Excuse me, could you tell my friend where you got this TV from?" the other girl spoke. By now he had ended his phone call about the truck.

"Radio Shack."

"You're not from Texas, are you?" the beautiful one spoke. Her voice was even sexy.

"Yes. You can tell, huh?"

"Quite so. Um, nice area—"

"My name is Ivory. This is my best friend, Yummie. I stay in C-11, over there by the flowers," the white girl cut Ms. Beautiful off and stuck her hand out. "What's your name?"

"Pimp." He shook her hand.

"Who?"

"Pimp." He smiled and stuck his hand out to Ms. Beautiful. "And that's only a name, trust me."

"Nice to meet you," Yummie replied. Pimp wanted to get at her, but decided not to since her friend was throwing herself at him.

Both the ladies walked off. When Yummie turned, he saw her ass was fat like a black girl. "Damn!" He shook his head and watched until he couldn't see her no more.

The living room was plushed out with cream leather, glass end and coffee tables, his 80-inch TV along with the DVD player, sound system, radio, and PlayStation 2. His bedroom was plush with a king size bed, black headboard, and dresser. He had a 50-inch safe in his walk-in closet without clothes. He planned on going shopping soon, but first he was about to jump in the shower, mind still on the white girl he saw today. He stripped down out of his clothes to his boxers only to hear his cell phone ringing. He reached in his shorts pocket to pull it out.

"Yo!"

"Yo, what's good, dude?" It was his father.

"Chillin', son. What's word?"

"I just got this kite. I'm lovin' the move you pulled, yo. So, what's poppin'?"

"Shid, son. Really I ain't had the time to move around yet, but I'll do so soon."

"What about the hos?"

"Oh, Pop, I met this white, cornbread-fed honey today. Ma ass fat to death!" Pimp found himself saying. His father always brought it out of him.

"Word."

"Hell yeah."

He was in the mall not even two hours and had spent a grand on clothes and shoes. He also went to Zale's, where he spent 15 grand on Rolex, 20 grand on a necklace and charm, plus two pinky rings, which ran $3,500 a pop. He knew in order to get plunged he had to look and smell like money. Tonight he was gonna hit the clubs to meet and mingle. The sooner he started, the better and quicker he could move on to his next mission.

Pimp saw so many thick hos it was crazy up in the mall. When he opened his mouth, they went wild. He met this hood rat named Peaches who had colorful hair and big breasts. They exchanged numbers because she agreed to show him around the town and turn him on to the major spots. She was nothing he'd even consider on the kicking level, but she would have to do. But just as soon as he found his way around, he was gonna drop her like a bad fly.

After leaving the mall he went to the dealership to look at the Escalade. He liked what he saw and spent 45 grand cash on a 2007, fully-loaded. He then went home and got fresh.

Jerry Jackson

# Chapter 9

## *Link Up, Take Off*

The club was packed as he sat at the bar holding a cup of water with Peaches, who had already downed two cups of Hen. He didn't like how she got so much stupid attention, like a lot of young niggas running up in her face. They'd look him up and down and stroll on. He just shook his head. His eyes searched the crowd for major niggas, and he let it be known to her what his mission was that night. "I'm looking for a connect, ma, not no homeboys." Peaches decided to call her sister's baby daddy, Rod, who said he'd be through. That wasn't until an hour later, so he waited and looked over the crowd.

"Here he come!" Peaches shouted over the music when she saw Rod, dead fresh, walking their way. Rod was a good 6' feet tall, 200 pounds with a lot of golds. Pimp knew he wasn't the man, but he might be somebody.

"'Sup, son?" Pimp spoke once Rod bent down to give Peaches a hug. He looked at Pimp's 5'7" frame a minute too long.

"What's going on, bruh?"

"Rod, this Pimp. Pimp, this my big brother, Rod. I'm finna go mingle. Bye, Pimp!"

Without replying, he stood up. "Shid, we can push if you wanna, 'cause this ain't my vibe."

"Yeah, mine neither," Rod shot back, and they both headed for the exit door. Once outside, Rod climbed in a black Tahoe truck with tinted windows. Pimp followed his lead. He tried to pass a blunt.

"I just want some money," Pimp said.

"Yeah, I feel you, bruh. So, what? First, where you from?"

"New Jersey," Pimp lied.

"So you just?"

Jerry Jackson

"I just move down here. Yo, kid, I'm not the knocks. I just want to get my piece of the pie, that's it."

"So, what you lookin' for?" Rod decided to get down to business.

"Shid, at least 20 kilos."

"20 kilos! Man, damn, I ain't... look, I can turn you on to my people. Lemme get yo' number. I'ma have him call you ASAP," Rod said and took another look at Pimp. Pimp knew he wasn't the man for the dope he wanted to buy. It was no time to play; he needed to get his face known. They exchanged numbers and Pimp left to go get into something else.

Not even an hour later, he got a phone call from Dino. They talked a minute, then made a plan to meet the next day at Simple, a five-star food joint.

Pimp felt like he was getting somewhere. All he did that night was ride around project after project, looking and taking notes. He ran into a young kid named Slim who was on a bike and had a walkie talkie by an ice cream truck, which was crowded with kids and one female – ghetto looking, but with class. Pimp paid her no mind, though; his focus was on the kid. He rolled his SUV window down.

"Yo, shorty!"

Neither the boy, kids, nor girl turned around. Pimp called again, "Yo, shorty!"

This time the girl turned around. Pimp pointed to the boy, who then turned. He rode his bike over when Pimp waived him to the truck.

"Nigga, do I look like a bitch or som'?" The little dude lifted his shirt up and showed a handle of a gun. He had to be about 15 or 16 years older. Pimp smiled because he knew he had the right hood, but the boy had the wrong man. He just didn't have a clue.

"You a young playa," Pimp said.

"Yo, ease up, den. It's hot 'round here. What, you want some work?"

"Naw. Look, get in. Let's rap."

"Rap? Rap 'bout what, man? I'm try'na get cake. I'm on the clock, fool."

The boy was about to ride off, but Pimp stopped him. "Yo, check this out. My name is Pimp. I just moved here a couple days ago. I got that good shit and I'm trying to plug in. When you wanna make some real money, give me a call."

Pimp began to write his number down when the boy said, "What you mean?"

Pimp passed the number out the window, looked around and down at the kid. "I mean you can't be making no money riding bikes. What's ya name?"

"Slim."

"Call me tomorrow, homie, around this time."

Pimp already saw the heart in the kid. He needed someone on his team like Slim to show him good spots to set up.

He made it to his condo just in time to catch the white girl, Yummie, leaving her friend's crib. Pimp made his move.

"How you doin', Ms. Lady?" She wore no glasses this time. A different pair were stuck on her shirt between her breasts. She stopped and smiled. "Oh, hey, um, Pimp."

"Yeah, dis Pimp."

"How you doing? How you like your stay?"

Pimp saw she had gray eyes that were beautiful. She had an exotic look about herself. "It's good. Could be better. Really wish I had a friend to show me around. Really wish it could be Yummie, but I know her husband won't like that." Pimp leaned on his SUV. He had to take in the perfect figure this white girl had.

"You don't see no ring on my finger, but I wouldn't want yo' wife to get the wrong thought about someone showing you around."

Pimp held up both hands to show no rings. She did the same. They smiled, then he said, "Can I take you out?"

"You mean I take you out, but you pay?" she asked, then turned her head sideways.

"Yeah."

Without a reply, she found one of her cards inside her purse. Pimp also wrote his number down on a sheet of paper. Yummie told him to call her whenever he felt like going out.

"Oh, so I can't call to just talk, huh?"

That remark made her laugh. "Yeah, call anytime."

They said their goodbyes and Pimp watched her walk away, thinking to himself that she had to been fucking a black man. She was too fine. As soon as he made it inside, he called.

"Hello?" he heard her answer the phone.

Taking a seat on his cream leather sofa, Pimp picked the remote up and said, "How you doing?"

"Who is this?" Yummie demanded to know.

"Pimp. Is you busy?" She burst out laughing, which was a turn on to him. He could just picture her face turning red, though.

"I just left yo' crazy self. No, I'm not busy. I'm headed home."

"To him?"

"No, to my cat and water bed. I told you I'm single, didn't I?"

"Nope, but I plan to fix that."

"Really?"

"Really," Pimp replied. They carried on talking for two hours straight, non-stop. He found out Yummie was 28 and owned a funeral home. She was born and raised in Texas, had never been married, and didn't have any kids.

He shared his age and name with her. She asked could she call him by his first name, because she liked the way it sounded coming off her tongue. He didn't mind at all. He also told her he was trying to get his hustle on, just to see how she took the news. It sounded as if she had no problem with it. He also told her he had no kids and no wife. Pimp liked the white girl, and what surprised him was she said she never dated a black man, that he'd be the first.

"And only," Pimp said.

"And only," she replied and laughed before hanging up the phone. That night she promised to take him out the next day after she closed up at work. Pimp wondered how she could work at a place like that, being around dead folks all day. He didn't ask her, though, but he had a plan to do so on their date. He wanted to see where her mind state was, what type of shit she was on, if any.

Right there on the sofa he laid back and dozed off. The day had been an alright day for him. He couldn't wait until tomorrow!

\*\*\*

Two weeks later

*Yummie*

All eyes were on her as she strolled toward the pool in a pink two-piece. The men stopped all their movement, and the females rolled their eyes. This was the kind of attention she didn't want, and she told Pimp this, but still he wanted her to join him. Now he was standing by the pool in some blue trunks, smiling.

"Damn, I'm blessed," he said and opened his arms for a hug as she approached, towel in hand. She embraced him with a quick peck on his lips.

"You lucky I don't punch you. I feel fat."

"Girl, you fine. Don't you see them dudes?"

"And that's what I don't like. This is for your eyes only."

Pimp kissed her forehead and pulled the towel from her hand. When he had a grip, he pushed her in the water. She screamed and fell over in the eight feet. He tossed the towel next to his own and then jumped in, also.

Yummie pushed water in his face, then she swam off. He followed. Everything about Pimp she liked. He was good company, and she ain't felt like this in years. He caught her when she stopped swimming. He put his arms around her. Through the water, she felt him press up on her booty. *Damn, he packin'*, she thought and let her head rest on his shoulders. It felt good to be held by a man again. She turned around in his arms and they shared a deep kiss. Yummie reached down into the water and inside his trunks. She took ahold of him as they still kissed. She didn't know what had gotten into her, but all of a sudden she was hot and horny. She'd never been with a black man, and just to feel him up on her did something wonderful. Since the day she met Pimp weeks ago up until now had been wonderful to her. Pimp was the perfect guy in her eyes.

That was the first time they kissed, and the first day they got as close as they were. Something had come over her. It felt so right, so perfect that she didn't care they were in public.

Yummie kissed him deep and griped his dick underwater.

"Let's go!" she moaned once they broke the kiss. Pimp didn't say a word, just followed her out of the pool.

It hurt because he was bigger than she expected, but pain was love and lust. In two weeks' time she was in love. Pimp held her hips from behind as he slid in and out of her. Her face was sideways in the pillow, ass up in the air. This was their second round, and boy was his sex great. Yummie gripped the sheets on her bed as Pimp went deep insider her with long strokes.

"Baby, I'm cumin'!" she yelled into her pillow.

He picked the pace up, which made a their skin slap together loudly. She started shaking and cussin', telling him to stop because it hurt, but he wouldn't. She couldn't take no more, so she laid down flat on her stomach. Pimp's dick came out, but he slid right back in her.

"Better?" he asked in her ear.

"Yes, boo. Yes, don't stop." She moaned and started rolling her hips. Pimp put one hand at her lower back and pressed down as he long-dicked her sideways, making his dick rub her wall, giving her another sensation.

"This pussy good," Pimp said in her ear.

"This pussy is yours. Yes, Lord, it's yours!"

Yummie moaned louder as Pimp kept stroking her deeper. He started to pick up his pace, grinding hard into her now, working for his nut. Yummie buried her face in the pillow and screamed with all her might. Pimp got up on his knees and shot cum all over her back and booty.

"Shit, babe. What the fuck!" Sweat appeared on Pimp. He was breathing hard, dick still in hand, leaking cum.

"Your dick is entirely too big. You nearly murdered me," Yummie said, looking back at him with a lazy look, but pretty smile. He could tell she was drained.

Later that night Pimp was with Peaches and Ron at the club. He got a call from Rod saying they needed to talk, so he met them. Rod wanted to get on his team, seeing that Pimp had took flight with the condo trap, said he knew a lot of people and could jump the work fast. Pimp sat back with his cup of water and listened to Rod speak. Something told Pimp there was game behind this, but something also said there was money to be made, hell he had slim pumping, so he gave Rod a kilo to see what the move was.

Also that night he met Money, the stripper, who was young. She reminded him of Diamond, just a little thicker. She danced for him for a couple songs, then they talked a while. Really his mind was still on Yummie, who he left asleep in the bed. She had some good pussy on her, and a nice head. He planned on getting all he could get before he dipped. Money realized he was no longer paying her attention, so she asked for his number. He gave it to her and got up and left.

"I'll call you tomorrow," she said.

"Bet," Pimp replied.

Inside his escalade, he called Slim. It was 1:30 a.m., but Slim answered.

"Hello!"

"What's up? What y'all niggas doing?"

"Shit, chillin'. What's up?"

"How many ounces you got left?" Pimp wanted to know so he could keep count.

"Couple left," Slim said.

"Ok, I'll swing through later," Pimp said. He would front Slim only eight ounces at a time and gave him a place to stay. So far, so good; Slim did as told.

Before even giving Slim the keys to the condo he told him shit needed to be kept down, 'cause it was the white folks' area and he was young. Plus he had pulled some major strings to get the three-bedroom spot.

"Ok, I'm waiting on you," Slim shot back. Since he ran into Pimp, he had elevated his status. He wasn't riding bikes no more, he was pushing whips. He was no longer sharing clothes, he had his own now. He came a long way from slinging nicks from corner to corner in just two weeks.

In the two weeks he'd been working for Pimp, Slim had to stand up against his old plug, a dude named Cheddar, who had his part of Texas on smash. He wanted Slim to introduce him to Pimp, but Pimp always told Slim to keep him as a secret and never step to him with new or old friends.

Slim just never told Pimp about the pressure he was getting from his hood about fucking with him. Slim figured he had it under control, but little did he know his hood was slowly turning against him for not so-called "keeping it real." Niggas weren't feeling him rocking with an out-of-state nigga at all.

"Check. Just be on standby," and the phone hung up.

\*\*\*

Pimp picked up Money, the stripper girl he met, when she called saying she had a play for a few ounces. She jumped in the Escalade when Pimp pulled up to her crib.

"What's up, sexy," she spoke, getting comfortable.

"What's hap? You good?" Pimp pulled off. He had the eight ounces on him for Slim and four for this play with her, everything tucked up under his seat, his gun laying across his lap, ready for whatever.

"Ok, so this dude from the north always come into the club. He always spending big. Well, last night I was dancing for him and somebody called his phone asking for some work," Money explained.

"And you told him me?" Pimp wanted to know.

"Of course not."

"So how did you make it happen?"

"He just gave me the money, say he was doing his friend a favor. Said he don't deal with drugs, though, but he gave me three bands." Money pulled the money out of her bag and showed Pimp.

"Cool. Well, I gotta take a ride real quick, so sit tight." Pimp mashed the gas into traffic, headed to Slim to make the big play. As they rode the city lights, Money did most of the talking, telling Pimp everything she thought he should know. Pimp could tell she liked him, but Pimp was on a mission, so his time was limited. He could only use her for the right now, while her intentions may be different.

It took them 15 minutes to make it to Slim. Pimp left the stripper girl in the car while he ran inside to drop Slim the package.

When Pimp got to the door, a strong smell of weed was in the hallway, which was a bad look.

It was Pimp's first time at the condo since he moved Slim in, so he was caught off guard. Plus Slim knew it was a no-no to smoke at the condo. Pimp knocked hard on the door since he had left his key in the car. He waited patiently for the door to come open. This was strike two for Slim.

When the door opened, Pimp was face-to-face with some nigga he didn't know, had never seen a day in his life, and he had the nerve to size Pimp up, which had always been niggas' mistake.

"What's up, homie?" The dude was at least 6'4", though Pimp couldn't care less. He returned the ugly look and strolled right past him into the smoke-filled condo. Slim was coming out of the back when his and Pimp's eyes met. Pimp had told him he'd be there in a few hours, so he didn't know he would show up sooner.

"What the fuck going on, Slim?" was all Pimp was able to say. It was obvious he had the wrong shit going on. First the money was coming up a few grand short, then this shit here.

"We was just kicking it, few females, few family members, that's it, bro. I thought you was coming later. They would've been gone, bro, I swear." Slim knew he had done fucked up. He could look at Pimp and tell.

"This shit ain't never 'posed to happen. Fuck, you thinking you can't get no money like this? Get these folks out my shit, my nigga. I'm not rocking for fun and games, nigga, I'm on a mission." Pimp was beyond mad. He folded his arms, waiting for Slim to start putting people out.

The condo was rented for one person, and one person only to be posted, not for a fucking get-together or a pussy-ass party. Reluctantly Slim turned around to his two friends and told them it was over with, that they had to go. The big nigga who had first opened the door stepped to Slim with a scowl on his face.

"Bruh, what's up? What you wanna do?" he asked and looked at Pimp, then back to Slim. Being street and smart, Pimp peeped what the big nigga was trying to say. Pimp reached behind his back and pulled out a plastic Glock.

"Getting the fuck out my shit is what's up, nigga. Fuck you mean? Now what's up, bitch?" Pimp aimed the gun directly at the big nigga's face, who was just as surprised as the others by Pimp's actions. Nobody expected him to just snap like he did.

The big dude just put his hands up and shook his head as the two girls grabbed all their things and headed for the door. Slim was also getting his stuff together, scared for his life. The day he met Pimp he was fronting when he showed Pimp his gun, but right now was real life. It wasn't a game.

"We gone, homie," the big dude said and took a step back. Pimp took a step up.

"Get the fuck out now, nigga, and wait in the parking lot to get murdered if you wan'," Pimp said and meant it. His temper was quick, and he hated to be sized up. Pimp was one of them li'l niggas who had a complex with big niggas trying them on any level.

Without another word spoken, the big nigga and Slim left the condo with a long face. Pimp followed behind both of them, wishing either would try something. He would leave them in the parking lot and leave Texas with no hesitation.

Money noticed Pimp following two guys with his gun out, held down by his side with a mean look upon his face. She quickly sat up, not knowing what was going on. She just watched as Pimp stopped and allowed both guys into their rides, and moments later they pulled off.

Pimp walked over to the car and got in, placing the gun across his lap. He pulled off quickly, not saying one word, and Money didn't either.

Jerry Jackson

# Chapter 10

### *Don't Bite the Hand that Feeds You*

Pimp woke up late the next day to find four missed calls: one from Rod, one from Yummie, and two from Slim. He was still tired, so he lay in his king size bed looking at the wall. His mind went to Honey and Diamond and Yalonda. He was missing his li'l team, hated to leave them, but had to go. Pimp refused to reach out to them because it didn't go with his plan. Going backward was never good.

He decided he'd call everybody back later on, 'cause right then his mind needed to rest, but it couldn't. He knew dope wouldn't sell itself, and Slim not handling business only slowed down the plan Pimp had. Now, instead of an easy run in Texas, Pimp had to watch his back.

*Ring, ring!*

"Yo!"

"Open the door. I'm mad."

"Speaking of the Devil," Pimp laughed while climbing out of bed. He opened the door to see her standing there. She punched his chest.

"Why you leave me last night? And what do you mean, speaking of the who?"

Pimp took her into his arms. They shared a kiss before he said, "I was just thinking about you, ma."

"Why you leave?" She kissed him again.

"Business. Got a call in the middle of the night. Lemme go get dressed so we can go get some'n to eat." With one last kiss, he left her standing in the living room. Pimp quickly got dressed in jeans and a white shirt. He grabbed his gun, his money, and phone to find Yummie waiting on him at the door.

"I didn't like how you just left. Could've woke me first," Yummie said, following him out the door.

"Baby, stop it. Told you it was business."

Pimp locked the door. He pulled her into his arms and kissed her deep. It was one of his good game moves he used on females.

"Or you could have gave me one of those," Yummie spoke through a smile.

\*\*\*

## Slim

He and Poncho sat in a Jay car watching Pimp leave his condo with some white girl. A fine-ass girl. They both jumped into a blue four-door Benz on some nice-size rims.

"Pussy-ass nigga," Poncho said and cocked the 9mm handgun. Slim cranked up and pulled off when the Benz did. He had a little fear in him because it was really about to go down, but Pimp came at him wrong. Plus he ain't even from Texas.

Poncho talked him into robbing Pimp anyway, but Slim knew they'd have to kill him, so he disagreed. Yet Poncho had a way with words, so he talked Slim into it.

He stayed four cars behind the Benz at all times while *White Bitch* by Deniro boomed through the speakers. Poncho passed the blunt.

Poncho was older by seven years and was considered big homie to Slim. Slim worked for a big time named Cheddar who didn't like the fact Slim switched sides. He made Slim get with the program or he couldn't come back to the hood, a place Pimp sent him back to busted.

That alone infuriated Slim, 'cause he felt played. And being that Pimp was an out-of-town nigga made it worst. He would get what was coming to him today and get robbed for his stash.

They follow closed behind, but not too close. His heart rate in a panic, Poncho just looked stone-faced. He was used to this kind of stuff, had to be used to it.

Gun in his lap, palms sweaty, Slim was not ready, but he refused to tell Poncho that. Right then he just wanted out. He just wanted to be the 14-year-old kid he was and nobody else. But right then he had to show face, show he was down or the hood would treat him bad. And bad he wasn't going out. It was Pimp who had to get it, and that was that.

\*\*\*

## Savarous

He peeped the white Honda when they first left the condo, yet he didn't say nothing. He didn't wanna scare Yummie, so he listened as she talked and talked, ears open to her, but eyes in the mirror.

It was two guys, he knew for a fact, but didn't know who. They didn't look like cops to him. Both were too small to be Rod, so the last person who came to mind was Slim. The more his eyes focused in the mirror, the more the driver looked like Slim. But who was his company?

Pimp pulled his 19-shot DE .357 from his waist, Yummie eyes went straight to the gun.

"Savarous, put that up."

She turned the Benz into a food joint twenty minutes later. When she parked, the white car also pulled in, but went to park around the front side of the food place.

"Baby, pull off. Go to that gas station across the street. When you see me run past you, just wait a moment and drive in that direction," Pimp said, getting out of the car. By now Yummie was scared for her life.

"What's going on, baby?" she wanted to know.

"Just go. I'll explain later," Pimp shot back, eyes looking for the car to round the corner.

"Ok, ok." She put the car in reverse. Pimp got down between two more parked cars and waited until he saw the white Honda. One thing was for certain: Pimp was not about to go out bad, and he had not one problem showing his ass to no nigga or bitch.

Neither Slim nor his friend really knew what was going on and who they were dealing with, but they soon would find out it wasn't a game. Pimp stayed low as the Honda crept behind Yummie in her Benz. As soon as the Honda passed, Pimp raised up, aiming and squeezing the trigger of the 357 19-shot.

It erupted loudly on the busy street, taking everyone by surprise, even Slim and his friend. Pimp ran up on the Honda.

*Boom! Boom! Boom! Boom! Boom!*

Glass shattered and flesh got hit. The Slim tried to desperately speed away, but was caught so off guard that the bullets did damage first. Slim and his friend didn't survive the shots.

Pimp ran right across the street through screaming traffic and over to the gas station where Yummie waited. As planned, he ran right pass her car and out the other side of the gas station on a side street.

Quickly Pimp dashed down the road and into darkness. Moments later Yummie's Benz pulled up and he jumped in.

"Oh my God!," was all Yummie could say as she sped down the street.

"Just drive, baby. Pay attention and drive," Pimp urged her while looking around himself for cops. This wasn't his plan. This wasn't supposed to happen so fast, so quick.

Pimp had just murdered two niggas in the middle of town, in daylight, on a busy street full of people in Texas, a place he knew nothing of nor knew anyone but Yummie. One thing about Pimp, he was quick on his feet and very thoughtful, so as Yummie drove, he formulated a plan.

Later that night Pimp sat in the SUV in the gas station parking lot, waiting on Dino. It'd been 30 minutes already. He thought maybe he was moving too fast, but fuck it, he was ready to leave. So the quicker he hit, the better. He came to Texas with plans to hustle the bricks he had, but shit didn't go right. All he had done the two weeks he'd been in Texas was lose three bricks and spend too much money, so he had to make up for the loss.

Dino pulled an F-150 pickup truck to the side of Pimp. When he saw Dino, his heart rate sped up, because there was no turning back now. This would be Pimp's second meeting with Dino. He was yet to shop with him because he already had bricks, but he needed a plug, so their first meeting Pimp and Dino just went shopping while feeling each other out.

It was now or never. Dino got out of his truck and climbed in the SUV. He was around 40 years old with smooth, fair skin, 5'11" with an 180-pound beer belly.

"What's up, young blood?"

"What good, yo?" Pimp pointed to the bag on the backseat with the bread inside for the five kilos Pimp set up to buy.

The plan was to meet in one place with the money and drive to the next to get the dope. When Dino reached in the back to grab the bag, he felt something in his stomach.

"Move and die," was the only thing Pimp said.

"Man, what the fuck!" Dino looked down at the gun pressed to his stomach. He was in a bad position. The mug Pimp wore let him know he could killed at any time, so Dino sat back upright in his seat.

"See, what you gonna do is grab them cuffs out the side of your door and nicely cuff yourself to the door," Pimp demanded. Dino was looking dumbfounded, but did as told because he had a feeling if he didn't, he would die.

Once he cuffed himself, Pimp pulled off with a smile on his face, glad he didn't have to bust this old nigga out in public.

They ended up at the brick house right outside of Fort Worth, Texas. Dino told him he had a couple hundred grand stashed there. He also let Pimp know his wife stayed there, so they had to creep in and out. She would be at work, though.

Pimp didn't like the sound of the creep-in and shit. It was going down his way whether Dino wanted to or not.

"Get out." Pimp kept the gun pointed at Dino and slid out of the SUV, also, once Dino got out of the cuffs and got out. He walked behind him a few feet as they approached the door. He saw Dino pull out the keys and stick them in the lock. The door came open and they both stepped inside. The living room was very neat, flowers everywhere, art pictures on the wall, fish tanks, and a piano sat in the corner. Dino led the way through some double doors, then down some steps, where a den was.

"Man, why you wanna ro—"

"Pussy-nigga, shut up and get to the money. This shit all in the game, son. You knew that, or didn't you?" Pimp let Dino feel the barrel of the DE.

The safe was behind the bar in the floor. Dino bent down to open it as Pimp stood over him with the gun pointed at his head. There were three clicks, then the safe came open.

When Dino turned to look up at Pimp, all he saw was fire, but felt nothing as the bullet hit his temple, knocking brain matter all over the floor, the bar, and the money. Blood was everywhere.

Pimp pulled Dino's limp body from covering the safe, then pulled a black bag from his pocket along with his gloves. Within three minutes he had the safe cleaned out. He looked down at Dino one last time, then left the body there so his wife could find it.

Outside, Pimp realized he had blood on his white shoes. He quickly jumped in his SUV and pulled off. "Damn."

\*\*\*

A couple of days later

*Yummie*

Pimp answered the door in his boxers with a bottle of water in his hand. He smiled at her, then moved to the side.

"Hi," Yummie said.

"Sup, ma?"

"Miss you," she replied and walked through. Pimp closed the door behind her. They hadn't seen each other since the shooting. She saw on his coffee table money – red money – and his gun. It wasn't a pretty sight. He was standing right behind her and put his arms around her.

"I miss you, too."

"Really?"

"Yup, really, really bad." Pimp turned her around in his arms and leaned down and kissed her lips. He brushed the hair out of her face, then asked, "How was work?"

"Crazy." Yummie took a seat on the sofa. For some reason she would not stop looking at the money on the table with what looked like blood on it.

"This lady's husband tried to pull her out of the casket. I had to re-do her makeup, then a body came in today a white girl. I was working on one body and all of a sudden the white girl sits up."

"What!" Pimp was shocked.

"It was just her nerves and gas build-up. That happens almost all the time."

"Damn," Pimp replied and took a sip of his water. Yummie looked up from the sofa to him. That was one of the many reasons she loved this man, because he paid attention, he listened, he wanted to know. She just never told him how she felt because she didn't wanna run him off. It had only been a three weeks now. She liked Pimp, but he also scared her with the shooting. It was all over the news, and he acted normal about it, which had her thinking.

"Savarous, I don't mean to be nosy, but is that blood money?" she asked, then pointed to a stack.

"Yeah, I need you to help me count it, too." Pimp also took a seat. He picked up some latex gloves, passed her a pair, and put on a pair.

"Did you hurt anybody?" Yummie wanted to know.

"Yup."

"You did?" Now she was shocked to hear him answer with the truth. Pimp laughed at the way she was looking.

"Yup."

"Sav—"

"Baby, help count the money, li'l nosey self." Pimp still was laughing.

She shook her head while picking up a stack. Never in her wildest dreams would she have thought to meet someone like Pimp. All of the men she'd dated had college degrees, good jobs, and was white. Now here came this beautiful black man into her life who showered her with love. A drug dealer who used guns, and she was in love. She had to be in love, because not in a million years would she agree to count blood money, but she did, and it was all for her man.

Yummie glanced over at Pimp and wondered if he felt how she felt. And if not, then how did he feel? She was scared to ask because she didn't want him to say the wrong thing, but she wanted to know the honest truth.

It took them an hour to count half of the money. Pimp said he wanted to get something to eat. She was glad because the last thing she wanted to do was be in the middle of some street war about this money. She really wanted to go back to her place and make love. It'd be much safer there.

\*\*\*

## Savarous

Once he counted 270 grand and still had a lot more to count, he knew he was rich, so Pimp dropped the stack in his hand onto the table, looked over at Yummie, and smiled.

"Stop, boo. Let's go get something to eat." Pimp stood up and grabbed a duffel bag that contained a few kilos.

Yummie also put her stack down on the table. Pimp had just noticed her tan skin. It looked good on her. The more and more they spend time together, the more he liked her company. It wasn't love, it was just a great deal of emotion. He loved Yalonda and still had no problem leaving her in the wind, just like Yummie would get left when it was time to go. He took the kilos into the room and put all the money in another duffel, taking it into the room as well before leaving.

He walked behind her as she strolled toward the parking lot. Yummie had a walk out of this world, something that would capture attention wherever it was seen. It was a sway in her hips, the glide in her walk, the way she held her head up just was perfect.

Yummie caught him looking at her hard and she smiled, he smiled, too, and bit his bottom lip. She did the same, then winked while going out of the lobby door.

*Damn, girl, you fine as fuck,* Pimp thought while still watching her ass move in the pants she wore.

She hit the alarm on her Benz, then looked back at Pimp. That was when she saw somebody coming up behind him with a gun out. He wasn't paying attention. Yummie couldn't help but scream.

"Savarous, behind you!"

Pimp turned in time to see three dudes running up on him. All three had guns out, held down while running up on him. Pimp quickly reached for his gun while pushing Yummie out of the way.

Everything seemed to happen so fast, but so slow. The shots just rang out from everyone's guns. Pimp was lucky to get behind one of the cars as bullets struck it. He busted back, catching one of the shooters in his chest, which made the other two hesitate. That was all the time Pimp needed as he rose up, busting more shots at the now-ducking niggas.

Pimp stood up straight and looked to the guys, and that's when he noticed one of them trying to run. Pimp aimed and caught him twice in the back, dropping him face-first. He was now looking for the last shooter, but at the same time backing up, heading toward Yummie's Benz.

The last guy rose up and aimed toward Pimp, but wasn't quick enough. Bullets rushed from Pimp's gun into the boy's neck and chest, and he fell against a car and slid down. Pimp ran over and stood over the dude with his gun aimed at the nigga's head.

"Fuck wrong wit' you stupid niggas in Texas? What's up? Who sent y'all niggas?" Pimp asked while looking around, then back down to the dude. He knew he was pushing his luck 'cause the police had to be on their way.

"Nigga, you killed my brother, and my uncle won't stop 'til you roasted. Big Derick, nigga. Remember that name."

Pimp hushed him with two shots to the face. He had heard enough. Quickly he jumped in the car with a shaky Yummie.

"Pull off, baby."

# Chapter 11

## *When the Move Must be Made*

### *Yummie*

This wasn't the life she dreamed of having. Pimp wasn't the man she envisioned herself with. Yummie had never experienced such drama, violence, and death. True enough she was the owner of a funeral home, but she had never saw a person killed until she met Pimp.

At first she just knew he was perfect. He carried himself like a gentleman at all times, and he looked so innocent. Yummie was more confused than anything because she was scared, but she was intrigued and hesitant.

Pimp had her take him to her house, a place she'd never brought him. Neither spoke words on the ride over. They both just listened to music, embraced in their own thoughts.

They both got out and Yummie used her keys to enter her beautiful home. Once inside, Pimp took her from behind by her waist; he pulled her into his arms

"Sorry, baby. I know this too much for you. Trust, this is not me. I don't know what's wrong with these Texas guys."

Yummie turned in his arms. She wanted to look him in his eyes. She was good at reading people, so she faced him.

"I've never went through this."

"And I know this, and I'm truly sorry." He kissed her forehead.

"So now you'll have to move, huh?" Yummie asked, one of her hands on his flat chest.

"Matter fact, I need you to call your friend. Tell her to creep into the condo and grab that money." Pimp had over 400 grand in the condo and 800 stashed in a drop spot. He had to make a move and make it fast, and he needed her help, Yummie agreed and made the call.

Yummie called her best friend, Ivory. The phone rang a few times before her country voice boomed through the phone speakers.

"Hello."

"Hey, friend, what are you up to?" Yummie asked.

"Oh, you wouldn't believe out of all these years I've stayed here, today is the first I have ever seen any action. Three guys was killed right before I got off work. Honey, I got home and saw all these cops, I didn't know what to think," Ivory said. Neither girl was used to this kind of action, though it was a turn on.

"I need a quick favor, girl, 'cause me and Pimp, we in Augusta. Look under the rug in front of his door, there's a key. Go inside and grab that gym bag for me." Yummie hoped like hell it worked, but she felt it wouldn't.

"Police questioned me about Pimp, girl, I'm not going nowhere near that apartment. Yo' best bet to leave him alone, too. Word he is no good," Ivory informed her, but Yummie didn't like it and quickly defended her man.

"However it go, Pimp doesn't have anything to do with those murders. We both have been out of town. I was just asking you to get my bag, but that's OK, you right, you don't need to be nowhere near him." Yummie was mad.

"It's not like that at all, sister. I just want you to be safe."

"And I will. I'll call you back in a few. Love you."

"Love you, too."

They ended the call and she turned to face her man while setting the phone down

"Ivory is trippin', and she said the police asked about you." Yummie really didn't want to tell him that.

"Ok, don't worry 'bout that." Pimp pulled his own phone out and dialed a number.

"Hello?"

"Money, what's up? You busy?" It was the stripper he had been kicking it with lately. Come to find out she was OK peoples that Pimp could mess with.

"Not really, what's up?"

"Man, I need you to go to my crib and grab something for me. Cops all over the place looking for a nigga," Pimp stressed.

"Whea you at? I'm on my way."

"Just pull up on Green Street, you'll see my car," Pimp quickly told Money, then they disconnected the call.

"Baby, I'm scared," Yummie said once he hung up the phone and had met her eyes. She wasn't used to this type of stuff at all.

"I understand you are, baby, but I'll never bring harm your way."

"We was just in a shootout a few hours ago. Us both could have been shot, baby."

"But you didn't, right?"

"Doesn't mean me or you are unharmed though, baby, is all I'm saying. And that shit scares me, that's all, boo," Yummie replied with honesty.

"I got you, baby, I promise," Pimp said while leaving to meet up with Money so she could get his stash. Before he left Ivory had called back saying the police was still out there looking around, so Pimp knew his face couldn't be shown. He listened to the news radio and heard them talking about the triple murder with no witnesses, no killer.

That was the good thing about it, but still Pimp knew to play it safe. He repeatedly cussed himself for slipping like he did, leaving his drugs there and his money. That was a mistake he wouldn't make anymore in life. Every mistake he'd ever made he'd learned a lesson and never made it twice, so this one was on him.

Money met him two blocks from the condos. He really didn't know the stripper like that, but she seemed cool. He kind of felt some type of loyalty from her, but still Pimp didn't trust deep.

He waved her over to his ride. She jumped in the black truck with him. Money was a dark-skinned, pretty female who wore her hair short and no makeup. Like most strippers, she had an banging body and juicy ass to match.

"So, what's the plan?" she asked once the door was closed.

"Look, some shit just happened over at my spot, but I left a bag of money in that bitch. I'll break you off if you slide in and out with it. Police there as we speak, so we gotta be on some sneaky shit, feel me?"

"Ok, just give me the apt number and a key. I got you, boo," Money said, looking unfazed, and Pimp liked that part of her. He gave her the key to get inside and the door number.

Money wasted no time jumping back into her ride, heading to the condos. What Pimp wanted was a simple task she didn't mind handling, even in the midst of the danger.

It was only right down the road, so she got there fast to find police everywhere. With crime scene tape all over the place, she went around to the back as if she stayed there. The cops let her pass through and she did, glad to not be stopped and questioned.

Money made her way inside and walked right past the white girl at front desk, there were a couple of cops inside asking questions to people. Money kept going toward the elevator, not trying to be one who got stopped.

She pressed three on the panel, not worried or looking scared. All she wanted to do was help Pimp out because he was cool. He was quiet, calm, and more handsome than a lot of niggas. Money wanted Pimp as her man, there was no denying that, and she was willing to put effort into anything she had to do to get him to agree to them being a team.

She was 28, no kids, no man, just herself and her small family. Money stripped because it was a mean hustle game up here in Texas, and hustle ran in her bloodline. Her entire family hustled hard. She wasn't one of those strippers who did drugs, drank, or even partied. Her mission was different; her aim was at the stars, not the sky.

When Money got off the elevator and headed toward the door, she saw three guys walking out of Pimp's condo — three guys she knew from the club. Money acted normal, walking past them until, like always, Rod stopped her.

"What's up, Money? So this where you stay, huh?" Rod always tried to get her to come home with him, always flaunted his money in her face like he was truly the man of the year.

"Actually, my dude stay out here. What's up, y'all?" Money waved to Skip and Bobby, his other two friends, and they spoke back. Money noticed that same gym bag Pimp told her to get and another he said would be there. She played it off quick and began walking off, heading in a different direction than the three guys.

"I be calling ya line, you never bust back. What's up with that?" Rod said as Money walked away. She turned, looked over her shoulder, and mouthed *I'll call you.*

When she rounded the corner and couldn't be seen anymore, her heart dropped into the pit of her stomach. She quickly called Pimp, who picked up on the first ring.

"Yo"

"Three dudes just left yo' spot with them bags. What do you want me to do?" Money asked. At the same time her mind was working overtime trying to figure something out to help him.

"Huh?" Pimp didn't wanna hear right. He wasn't trying to hear what he thought he just heard. It wasn't possible.

"I'm headed back out to see, could I follow them?" Money said, knowing Pimp was in shock, and right now they had no other choice.

Pimp agreed to her following them. At the same time he cranked up the truck and headed the direction the condo was located. He wasn't about to lose all that money to some weak-ass niggas. He'd rather die first.

Money made it downstairs fast and didn't see Rod or his boys. She walked out and looked left and right in the parking lot, but saw nothing but cops. She went back inside. Something wasn't right, because the police would stop three guys with bags, no hesitation.

She remembered Rod saying something about her coming down to his spot, meaning he had a condo somewhere in the building. A condo where, though? She called Pimp again to tell him what she thought.

"So you know these niggas?" Pimp asked.

"Yes, only from the club, though, nothing else. I got one of their numbers, too," Money said, hoping her information helped him out rather than made him think she was down with them niggas.

"Ok, well, call them niggas up, see where they at. Do you know what either one drive?" Pimp asked.

"Never paid attention," Money replied.

"Damn. Ok, well, we need to find out where they at, 'cause like you said, I don' think they left yet with all them motherfuckin' police out there," Pimp added.

"Ok, let me call him right quick."

"Call 'im on three-way," Pimp cut her off. Money did as told and clicked over so Pimp could hear the conversation.

"Yeah, who dis?" Rod's deep voice asked.

"Money. Dis lame-ass, so-called boyfriend of mines, his ass isn't even home," Money said.

"That's his loss and my gain then, beautiful." Rod felt confident.

"You right. Well, I'm 'bout to leave, but you with yo' friends, so guess me and you will catch up later." Money tried him with weak game, and he went for it.

"Oh, my partners, they'll leave once shit here in the condos calm down, 'cause some dumbass wanna-be thug killed three guys in the parking lot. That's why we got that nigga, but anyways, you can come chill down here if you want to."

"Yeah, what's the door number?" asked Money, ready for this to be over, said, and done.

"C13, second floor," Rod replied.

"Ok, I'm on my way," Money said, then hung up the phone completely even knowing Pimp was on the other end. She didn't wanna take no chance, so she quickly called Pimp back.

"Yo, go ice them niggas. Just text me like I'm yo' homegirl or something while I come up with a plan. Don't let nobody leave without me knowing," Pimp told her while his mind raced through which route to take.

"Ok, I'm headed there now," Money replied and they disconnected the call.

*** 

## Diamond

Diamond looked left, then right before pulling her mother's BMW truck into traffic, coming from school. She had to leave early today because something didn't feel right. She couldn't eat, could hardly sleep, she was always down, and she blamed everything on Pimp.

The first man she truly loved broke her heart without answers. She had yet to figure out what happened, what went wrong, and why. All she knew was one day he was here and the next day he was gone, no goodbye, no 'I'll see you later,' no fair warning, just vanished into thin air.

Not only was she mad, she was hurt and overly confused at the situation. It'd been two months almost and still no phone call, no pop up. None of the other girls had heard from Pimp since the last time they all saw him.

True enough, he left them with money in the bank, two cars to drive, and their rent paid up a year, but he still left them all shattered and baffled. Diamond was the one who took it harder than anyone else. Keyantay didn't really care; she was all about the money anyway. Honey was pissed off, plus it hit her hard, too. And Ke-Ke was just mad 'cause she felt played.

All the girls eventually parted ways after things just didn't seem right. Diamond was thinking about going back to dancing, but decided against it and moved back with her parents where she enrolled back into school. Everyone took something from the house except her. She didn't care about the car, the house, or the money. She only cared for Pimp; nothing or nobody else mattered.

The other girls felt some kind of way about how Pimp just up and dipped, so they all masked their hurt by taking from Pimp what he left for them to have. Ke-Ke kept one of the cars, Honey kept the other, and Keyantay kept the house since rent was paid up.

Honey was the only one Diamond kept in touch with out of the three girls. She'd heard Keyantay had E-bo living with her, running a drug house. Ke-Ke was back dancing at clubs and stealing expensive clothes, and Honey was raising her daughter and in a relationship with some dude she met at the club. He was a business owner, and a successful one at that.

It took Diamond over an hour to get home. Her mom and dad were in the living room when she entered the house. Just the smell of the house made her sick to her stomach. She felt like she had to throw up, her entire body became hot, and she got dizzy.

She closed the door and had to brace herself on the wall to break her fall. Her knees buckled and she couldn't stand any longer.

"Baby, are you ok?"

"Diamond! Diamond, baby, are you OK?" her mom and dad asked, concerned for their child. Diamond looked up to the faces of her parents and realized she was on the floor. She had fainted.

"Ma, something is wrong with me," Diamond finally spoke while being picked up by her father

"Come on, baby, we got you," her father said.

"I'm calling the doctor," her mother added, and Diamond fainted again.

\*\*\*

## Savarous

Pimp was now parked in the condos around back. The police were still there, but not as deep as earlier. He and Money had been texting back and forth for the past hour she'd been in the condo with the dudes with his shit. Good news was nobody had left. They, too, were waiting on the police to dip so they could leave, but Pimp had other plans, and it wasn't them leaving.

Pimp had made a promise that when he got his money, when he got his drugs, he was gonna get far from Texas. They ran him out of this state, plain and simple. His phone vibrated with a text from Money.

*Two of them leaving out to get something to eat.*

*Bet.* Pimp sent a reply back, and moments later he noticed two dudes come out and get into a caprice classic. Pimp was glad to see what they were riding in so it would be easy to follow them.

*He trying to fuck.* Money sent another text.

*Bait 'im up. I'm on my way up.*

His mind clicked fast. True enough the cops were out lurking, but there was only one nigga to deal with versus three, so Pimp decided to make his move now rather than later. He climbed out of the whip, tucked his gun, and closed the door. He was careful not to be seen by the white girl at the front desk as he headed to the elevator.

Pimp didn't have a plan at all. He was just going head-first, whatever happened would happen, and fuck it. He got off on the second floor and headed to the condo with murder on his mind.

Not one time had he thought about who the niggas was who had his shit, how did they know him, how did they get into his spot, and most importantly, how did they know about his stash? These were all questions he asked himself as he approached the door.

Without thought, Pimp pulled the gun from his waist and walked into the condo, catching Rod by surprised. He was so caught up by Money the stripper. He turned around slowly, thinking it was his friends, but when Money pushed him off her he realized there was something going on.

"Where my money, pussy-nigga," Pimp asked, at the same time pulling the trigger, hitting Rod in the chest, stomach, and face. He couldn't even help it. He had totally forgotten the police were outside still, and somebody other than them had to hear the five shots he let off.

Money snapped him back to reality. "You know the police is on the way, boy, what's wrong with you?" She pulled his arm toward one of the bedrooms where two bags sat on the bed. She grabbed one, he grabbed one, and they both made their exit out of the condo to the elevator.

"I'm tripping," Pimp spoke his thoughts out loud.

"You damn sure is," she replied.

"Lets just get the fuck out of here while we can."

The elevator stopped on the first floor. They both walked off and were happy to see no one looking crazy or, better yet, the police. The white girl at the front desk looked up and saw Pimp as he eased his way out of the door into the parking lot, where a few more patrol cars had pulled up.

Side by side, he and Money walked like a couple toward his Escalade, but the police stopped them.

"Excuse me, sir and ma'am, may I ask a few questions?"

"We have already been questioned, sir, when we first got home and saw what was going on. That's why we are packed up and ready to get out of here. We are done here." Pimp had cut the officer off with the greatest lie in the world. He was nervous because of the money and drugs they had, but still he was thinking and quick on his feet.

Money agreed with a shake of her head as the officer looked at them both.

"So you wrote statements and talked to whom?" the officer asked.

"I don't know, it was some white man. A woman, too, had us, but like I said, we are out of here for a few days. My wife, she's pregnant, and killings are stressful to our first child," Pimp lied with a straight face.

"Oh, sir, I surely understand that. Well, y'all have a nice night, and if you hear anything, then call us," the officer said.

"Will do." Pimp and Money jumped in the truck, both their hearts beating a million miles per hour, both happy to be safely in the ride. Pimp cranked up and pulled off fast, slipping through the cracks.

He drove to a storage place that took them a hour to get there. Money watched him go inside and come back out with a duffel bag, then put it in the backseat. He came back again with another duffel bag, a bit smaller, and climbed back in the truck.

"I really appreciate you looking out. I'ma break you off for that," Pimp finally said.

"It's all good. I just like you like that. So, what's the plan?" she asked, and Pimp was surely about to lie, but decided against it. He felt like he owed her a little loyalty.

"I'm 'bout to get the fuck out of Texas."

"Going?" Money looked disappointed.

"I don't even know, baby."

"So you leaving me to fight them other two dudes?"

"Who?" Pimp asked, baffled. He was so happy he got his shit back that he totally forgot about the other two niggas who was with Rod.

"The other guys who knew I was in that condo with Rod, They know where I work, they know where I stay, you know," Money spoke.

"Say less, I got you. Do you know where they stay?"

"I know where they hang."

"Bet I'll handle them before I leave. I can't let nothing happen to you," Pimp assured her.

"So, can I stay with you tonight?" Money wanted to know. She wanted to sex him and he knew it, she looked at him with lust in her eyes, a lust she couldn't control, one she wanted to let out, let loose.

"I got some business to handle for you tonight, then I gotta put all this stuff up. Tomorrow night we can stay together, but right now what I need you to do is explain all about these two niggas."

Money took a deep breath and started talking, telling Pimp everything she knew about the other two guys, where they hung out, where they stayed, and what they did. It took her ten minutes to explain to him as they rode.

Pimp knew he couldn't send her home; that would be going into a death trap, so he took her to a hotel room to chill while he went to drop off the money.

# Chapter 12

## *A Million in Cash*

Pimp rented a Honda Accord LX. He stuffed the trunk with all his kilos and his million dollars in cash. He then drove to a super Walmart, where he parked the rental, then proceeded to call a cab, where he got dropped off at his escalade.

When he climbed behind the wheel, he only had one thing on his mind: to get rid of two lames so he himself could get the hell on out of Texas. Pimp pulled off into traffic, gun laid across his lap, knowing he had to move fast because the police were slick onto him, and once they found out he was driving the truck, it would get even deeper.

Pimp also knew the niggas were already on point, 'cause seeing their partner dead let them know it was on and popping. Money said the guy named Skip stayed with his li'l brother and baby mother, and Bobby spent the night most times. Everyone didn't know about Skip's baby mother, but Rod ran his mouth to Money about it on some boasting shit.

When he pulled up to the address given, he saw the door to the house was open, but still protected by the screen door. Pimp got out smooth on the quite street and entered the yard. He had the gun down by his side as he walked through the yard, up on the porch, and peeked into the house through the screen door, that's when he saw a little kid playing a game with Bobby, which confirmed Money was right about Skip's little brother, Cris. Skip had to be in the back with his baby ma. They'd been ducked off for a couple hours now, probably thinking they was safe, but little did they know it was about to go down. Pimp tapped on the door.

Bobby paused the game when he heard a knock on the door. Skip's brother got up to get it.

"Bobby, it's for you."

Bobby then got up and grabbed his bombs of dope. He knew it had to be a junkie who wanted a fix.

When Bobby got to the door, he was facing his fear. Pimp had a gun pointed to his head.

"Don't say shit, nigga. Step back inside." Pimp forced him back into the living room, making sure not to touch nothing. Li'l Cris was stuck in one place, not knowing what to do.

"Listen—"

"Shut up, nigga, and walk me to yo' boy's room so we all can talk business." Bobby saw a death look in Pimp's eyes. He knew it was over, he just prayed now that God came down to save him. He walked to the back and pointed to the door of Poncho's room. Pimp told him to enter.

Skip was getting head when the door came open, as soon as he looked up, Pimp shot him in the face from a distance. The girl tried to scream too, but also caught a slug to the face. Bobby saw the blood and brains pop out of his people's heads and he fainted. Pimp looked down at him and put two into the side of his skull.

The little boy was gone when Pimp came back into the living room. "Damn," he knew he should've killed the kid, too. That was another slip-up. When he jumped in the truck, he saw the little boy balled up on one side of the house. Pimp got back and strolled over.

What's up, shorty?" he asked, then looked around before he snatched the little boy up.

\*\*\*

*two months later*

He pulled up to the Federal Pen in Atlanta, GA. Fed agents were all over the place. This was one reason he hated to come visit his father, because he hated everything about the police. He parked in the visitors' area as instructed by an officer. Then he was led up to the main entrance of the building where he had to be searched, which was one of the other things he hated.

Once inside, he passed the desk lady his ID and asked to see his father when he noticed the DA and two more people walking past. Pimp wanted to kill the cracker because no matter how many appeals his father put up, the cracker found some kind of way to stop 'em.

After about 30 minutes of waiting, Pimp finally saw his father walk through the door with two officers on each side of him. His father was around 5'10", 200 pounds of solid muscle with a bald head. He always wore a mug on his face like he hated everything he saw. Pimp stood up to embrace his ol' man.

"'Sup?"

"'Sup?" his father replied, and they took a seat.

Savarous moved the table that was between them and leaned up. His father did the same. Forehead-to-forehead, nose-to-nose they began to talk.

"Where you at now?"

"Miami," Pimp replied and smiled.

*At the age of 24, he was where he wanted to be in life: rich and well respected. Miami has been good to him. He was the man down there at the bottom, and it seemed it all happened overnight.*

*When Pimp left Texas, he left everything in it except his drugs and money. He landed in Miami and, by luck, linked up with a nigga named Murder Black, a well-known ex-jackboi who recently got out of the feds.*

*Pimp was in the club when they met through a bartender both guys were trying to get at. Half the night they watched each other.*

*"What's up, my nigga, you know me?" Murder Black finally asked he had approached Pimp at the bar while Pimp talked to the pretty bartender. He looked Murder Black over and shook his head side-to-side.*

Jerry Jackson

"Naw, I don' know you, brother. but you gotta know me how you keep looking. And seems you bothered by something for even interrupting my conversation with insecure questions to a real nigga," Pimp replied, unfazed.

"Insecure? Better ask about me, dawg. I eat 'round here, nigga. Better ask Stacy right here," Murder Black pointed to the girl.

"Black, excuse us," Stacy pushed him with a blush, then introduced them to each other. "Pimp, this is Murder Black. Black, this is Pimp. He's new 'round here."

"Ok, ok then. What's up, my nigga? It's no beef. Welcome to my city," Murder Black said, extending his pound.

"No pressure." Pimp gave him pound.

"Shid, I'ma let y'all have ya li'l conversation. Yo, Pimp, so when you done, come over and chop it up with me over at the booth," Murder Black said and left them both. Pimp instantly asked Stacy what was up with Murder Black.

"Oh, Murder just got out 'bout two weeks ago. He did, like, ten years for extortion of a federal agent. He's from Pokey Bean Projects. He's well known and feared most out there. Ah, he got two baby mamas out there, he's known for having a graveyard under his belt. Anything else you need to know?" asked Stacy.

"What kind of hustle he got?" was the big question.

"He's a jackboi."

It'd been two months down in Miami, and he and Murder Black had the Pokey Bean Projects on lock. Stacy was right, Murder Black had the entire project shook and respecting him. Pimp used his brain and Murder used fear to stamp the projects with some of the best dope money could buy.

Pimp was smart enough to lead Murder Black to thinking he was only getting five kilos at a time from a plug. He knew to stay one step ahead of the game when dealing with Murder, 'cause he knew the dude has more bad intentions than good, and Pimp wouldn't hesitate to kill him.

# Chapter 13

## *A Beautiful, Wrong Love*

### *Icey*

Icey Smith was 28 years old, no kids, a successful businessperson who owned an art school and art store in downtown Miami. She was a college graduate with her head on her shoulders. Very reserved and humble, and amazingly beautiful with an even finer body to match her look. She had the money, she had the look, but she would never boast or brag. She hid her beauty as best she could by wearing only ponytails, no nails done, hair fixed, or tight clothes. No makeup, no nothing because she didn't like the attention.

Icey was single because it took a certain type of guy to move her. It took a man on her level: a smart, driven man. It took a man of power and respect. She didn't really care for looks at all, though she didn't want no ugly dude, either. It was hard finding these types of men these days, so Icey didn't bother with them. Plus she still had a life to get in order.

She was in her back office inside the store when Tomeka, one of her students, walked in.

"There's a guy out there that's interested in buying that big painting you did, but I told him it wasn't for sale, though he insisted that everything had a price."

"Oh, really?" Icey smiled and wondered what old, rich, white man wanted her painting. It was only a painting of a woman burying her heart. Or could it be Brad, her best friend, just dropping in on her? She followed Tomeka out front into the store and was surprise to see a kid standing out front. He was clean, dressed in a lemon and blue polo outfit and crisp, white sandals.

When they made eye contact his gaze spoke serious, but she wondered his age and why would he want her painting?

"How are you, sir?" Icey asked.

"I'm great, Miss. I'm tryna buy that." He pointed to the painting.

Icey looked, then added, "Sorry, that's not for sale."

"You the owner of this place?"

"I am, yes, sir."

"Whoa, you look young," he said.

"Look who's talking," she shot back.

"I'm 24."

"Sure don't look it. But yeah, that painting's not for sale."

"It's yours?" the guy asked. He pointed again.

"Yes, it's mine."

"Ok, tell me where you got it from. I want to buy one."

"Let me ask you this: why are you so interested in this particular picture?" Icey wanted to know.

"To be honest, 'cause I wanna go find that heart, dig it up, find that woman, and give her life back."

When he spoke those words, he instantly did something to her. She was stuck for words. She had never heard someone say that, and one day she hoped someone would understand her outlook in the painting, because he just hit it on the head.

"Wow." She was stuck.

"So, where can I get me one at?"

"You can't. It's the only one," Icey finally said. "'Cause I painted it."

"Wow, ain't no way! How old are you? Oh, I most definitely wanna cop this now. What's your name?"

"I'm Icey."

"I'm Savarous Jones." The guy stuck his hand out to be shaken.

"Nice to meet you, Savarous."

Icey shook his hand, still looking at his baby face and youthful look. His hands were soft to the touch, something men's hands weren't.

"So, can I dig that heart up and give it back to you?" he smiled with that question a nice smile she notice.

"Now if you could find where it's located then yes I'll take that heart back but it's nearly impossible to so you're out of luck"

"Nearly made it possible, but you good with this art stuff, I must say. Well, I'm looking for the perfect picture to sit on my living room wall, and since I have a mission to that spot, I'll let you keep your picture and purchase something else."

Savarous had made her day, and he really did buy two paintings worth nine grand each. He left his number and asked for her number, but Icey wasn't as easy as some females, even though she was attracted to him and liked his swagger.

*** 

## Yummie

The plane landed in Miami, and her heart was beating faster and faster as she left the plane with her best friend. It'd been two months, and finally she found Savarous through a P.I. in Dade County. She needed answers to why he left her like that and what went wrong with them.

She really thought they were soul mates. Yummie's life hadn't been right since he left her alone. Everything had been going downhill, and she wanted her man back. Maybe he was scared to go to prison for the murders, or maybe he thought she would fold on him, but he was wrong. Pimp was wrong about her because love wouldn't let her harm Pimp in any way possible.

Love would make her protect him in every way possible. She just wanted him to realize that.

She and Ivory were led to the rental car with their luggage. Ivory was the one who talked Yummie into taking a trip to Miami, saying she needed a break from Texas and they could kill two birds with one stone.

"Girl, it's real hot," Yummie said, tossing her bag into the trunk along with her best friend's. She had one thing in mind, and one thing only, and that was to find Pimp and see what was on his mind.

"Hot and beautiful with some sexy-ass men down here, oh my gosh." Ivory watched a group of guys climb out of an SUV. Yummie just shook her head at her friend.

"Come on, let's go. You driving," Yummie said, giving her the keys and going around to the passenger side.

For the past two months all she did was worry something bad had happened to Pimp, but then reality set in and she realized he had just up and left.

Leaving like that had broken her heart. It made her become depressed and hateful at times, so hateful she lashed out at her friends and family, and the only one who knew what was wrong with Yummie was Ivory, because she was always the one Yummie vented to. She had gone into a shell that Ivory tried to pull her out of, but nothing seemed to work. Even her business was slowing up because she was messed up in the head. Nothing would make her feel better but some understanding, some knowing.

They made it to the hotel safely. Both girls were hungry, so they found a place to eat. Yummie chose a burger place, and Ivory agreed. They took the rental car through downtown Miami. Ivory couldn't contain herself; seeing all the sexy men without shirts did something to her.

Yummie, on the other hand, couldn't see any of the guys her friend saw. Her heart and mind were on one man, and one man only. Miami was a beautiful place, she had to admit, and being as it was their first time out of Texas, she would try to enjoy and not be a bum. Ivory wouldn't let her not turn up at least once.

"Why don't you call Pimp? See if he answers," her friend said when they were seated in the restaurant dining booth.

Yummie picked up the menu, prepared to order her food. "I've tried already. It's not the right one," Yummie replied, looking at the many different meals they had.

"So how you know the address is right?" Ivory had a point to her question.

"'Cause the P.I. has been following him. I have seen pics, too," Yummie said with confidence.

"Well, I'm happy to hear that. I'm so sick of seeing you walk around like you have lost your first Barbie doll," Ivory finally got a chance to pick at her friend. Pimp did a number on her, and Ivory needed to bring her back.

Both girls ordered and waited on the good-smelling food.

\*\*\*

*Five hours later*

*Savarous*

Pimp was standing in front of the pool hall with Murder Black, one of their hangout spots. They both were dead fresh, draped in diamonds. Hos came and went, niggas hung on their nuts like pubic hairs, but it was nothing to them anymore. The fame had played out long ago.

"Steph still try'na hook you up with her cousin, nigga," Murder Black said and tried to pass Pimp the blunt. Like always, Pimp slapped it out of his hand.

"Yo, I'm cool, son. I'm tired of hos," Pimp replied, and his eyes focused on the car that pulled up next to his Benz truck. His eyes grew wide when he saw Yummie step out, along with her best friend. Murder Black also saw the girls.

"Gotdamn, look at that thick-ass white bitch, bruh." Murder Black grabbed Pimp's shirt while never taking his eyes off of Yummie.

Pimp was shocked. She looked even better than when he last saw her. They locked eyes as she walked toward him with that same walk he loved. Her friend was steps behind.

Murder Black tapped Pimp and said, "Watch this fly shit." Murder Black walked toward Yummie, blocking her way. "Marry me and I'll give up the game right now." Yummie stopped, then looked over his shoulders at Pimp, who was stuck. How did she find him, he thought.

"Savarous, we need to talk." Murder Black moved to the side and let her pass when he heard his partna's name. He then went at the best friend.

"What you doing down here?" was all Pimp was able to say.

"Look'n for you. Why you leave me, Savarous, like that?"

Pimp just looked at her. He didn't have no answer for her. It'd been almost two months, and she was just now showing up.

"I thought we was in love, at least I was and am." She reached for his hand and Pimp pulled back.

"Look, Yummie, we two different kinds of people."

"I don't care! I don't care! I'll do anything, Savarous, please don't do us like this. Please, it's not right without you." tears rolled down her face.

"No, Yummie, it ain't gon' work. Don't you see it's been two months and you just now coming around? Shit has changed. I done changed."

"You're just afraid, and I understand, but know I got your back fully, Pimp, for real, for real." She reached out again.

"I got something going on that I can't let nobody stop, and being with you will stop it. And truth be told, baby, it's far more important than you. Don't get me wrong, you are perfect. You are just right, but life calls me in another direction." Pimp could be sweet as cake, but sour as month-old milk.

When he spoke those words, all of Yummie's true emotions came out to the forefront. She broke down crying right in front of the pool hall while everyone watched. Pimp was a playa and didn't do drama. He knew he was the cause of her actions right now, so he pulled her into his arms.

"Stop crying like a big baby, you making me sad." Pimp spoke those words in her ear. He rubbed her back up and down and kissed the side of her face also, saying, "I miss you so, so much."

Hearing those words softened her cries. She only sniffled and said "I'm sorry for whatever I did, baby. I just don't wanna lose you."

"Just chill, boo. Where are y'all staying?" he looked over at Ivory and asked. He noticed her give him an disapproving look.

"The Hilton." Ivory passed him one of the hotel card keys. Pimp took Yummie's phone and put his number in it. He looked at Yummie hard and long before saying.

"Listen, I got business here, so I need you to go to your room pack your stuff and call me. I should be done here by then. We will talk then, ok?"

"Ok, Pimp. Please don't—"

"I promise I won't." He knew what she was talking about.

When he said that, she took a step back and looked at her phone and back up to him. She slightly smiled and took another step back.

"I hope you keep your promise." She walked off with her best friend and got back into the car she was driving.

"Man, who da fuck was that?" Murder Black asked once Yummie and her friend left.

"Li'l shorty from Texas."

"And you turnin' that down? Nigga, I ain't never seen a cracker that fine." Murder Black laughed at his partna.

Jerry Jackson

\*\*\*

*Icey*

Icey was relaxing at home after a good day at school of working with the youth. Every Monday she took in sixth graders to help them with their art. Usually she dealt with college students and highly advanced students, but made time for the kids. Her wine was on the table, laptop rested across her lap on Facebook, liking pictures and making posts.

Her doorbell rang three times back-to-back, meaning it was Brad, her best friend, with his silly ways. She shut the laptop, placed it on the table next to her wine. She got up in her loungewear and slippers, her long hair down her back. Icey opened the door and was surprise to see Jimmy, Brad's partner, with him. Both guys walked into the house and hugged her.

"What's up, princess?" Brad said.

"Relaxing. What's up with y'all?" she asked and went back to the sofa, but instead of laying down she sat up. "Oh, I'm being rude. Do you want anything to drink, Jimmy? Brad's second home is in that kitchen and you're company, so I'm only talking to you." She got up, smiling.

"Yeah, I'll take a hen, no chase."

"And I'll fix it," Brad added with a wink of his eye.

"Oh, Brad is being nice. What happened at the job? Y'all must've got promoted?" Icey laughed because at all times Brad had something to say.

"Since you asked, me and Jimmy here are going undercover."

"Brad, you wasn't suppose to tell her that," Jimmy warned his partner.

"Man, Icey just like one of us, bro. Our secret safe with her, trust me," Brad said as seriously as possible because that's how he felt. He told Icey everything, holding nothing back, and she did the

120

same. Brad returned with two glasses and a bottle of hen, no ice. It's how he drank.

"I'm just saying."

"I'm just saying we're going undercover in the Pokey Bean Projects posed as the plug. Shit is about to be so much fun, I swear," Brad boasted. He loved a challenge and excitement. Things like this were amazing to him and funny to Icey, but crazy to Jimmy.

"Undercover?" Brad and Jimmy were two FBI agents, Brad being the senior. He had been with the bureau eight years now and was good at what he did. He may be white, he may be dingy, but he was good at taking out the bad guys. He knew his job inside out.

"Yes, in the next couple of weeks." Jimmy decided to add his say into the matter.

"Ok, this sounds fun," said Icey, looking from one man to the next.

"So how is working coming along? How is Ms. Smith?" Brad asked while taking a sip from his hen.

"Mom is fine, and work was good, I must admit. I see work is good with you, though."

"As always, princess, as always. So, I was telling Jimmy about your new studio that's about to open in Atlanta. His daughter, she loves art, and she's in Atlanta. I was telling him you're the best."

"I'm blessed, I can say that much."

"Wonderful. I was thinking put her in training first, then art school. What do you think?" Jimmy asked Icey, also drinking from his cup.

"Depends on her age and her talents, but like I tell any child, you can do whatever you tell yo' mind to do."

The two guys sat over through one more cup and they finally left, leaving her to clean and get back to her Facebook page. Her mind couldn't help but wonder 'bout the guy she met last week at the shop. He was cute, too cute if you asked her, but something about him spoke loud to her.

Jerry Jackson

Sexy and young-looking, he seemed like a boss. He carried himself like he ruled everything around him. He walked and talked like a grown man about his business. She was still scared to pick up the phone and call him. She had been holding that number for a whole week, thinking about what to do and how to do it.

It had been so long since she had even considered a man in her life, and as bad as she wanted that part of life, she as bad wanted to stay away from it, because men these days just didn't have it right. But then again, was Savarous different?

\*\*\*

*Savarous*

The sun was coming up through his wall-sized window into the master bedroom as he lay on his king size bed. The clock read 9:30 a.m., and he could smell food in the air. He leaned over on his nightstand and pressed a button on his phone.

"Mr. Parks, I'm up."

Minutes later an old man entered the room and went to the closet. It was large, like a small room. Pimp stayed in a beach house, seven-bedroom, that overlooked the beach. He had three maids: Mr. Parks, one who cleaned and cooked (which was Mr. Parks' wife, Mrs. Parks), and one who washed cars and tended to the house work. Mr. Parks dressed him, took his phone calls, and ran errands when needed. Pimp loved the rich life. Miami had been good to him and Murder Black. Now all of a sudden Yummie wanna pop up from nowhere, acting in love and shit.

Yesterday he had to smooth things out with her 'cause she was about to get stupid in public, and he didn't want that at all. Plus she had the nerve to have her friend there, who Pimp didn't trust. He knew he had to play it safe with Yummie and her friend because they knew too much, and he thought he had escaped Texas. Last night he popped up on Yummie at her room. She and Ivory were up talking. He kicked it over for a few hours, then left with promises to see her the next day.

Mr. Parks pulled out a gray Gucci suit with white-gray gators to match. He pulled both of Pimp's chrome 9mm twin Berettas out also, with the shoulder holster to match.

Mrs. Parks' voice boomed through the phone. "Mr. Jones, your food is ready, sir."

Pimp slid out of bed. It was so high off the ground he had to use steps. He put his bare feet into some leather bedroom shoes and headed downstairs. His plate of food and the morning paper were on the table along with juice and water. He thanked Mrs. Parks and started to dig in. On the table were four message cards. He picked up the first one, and it was from Murder Black saying everything was a go on the drop. Pimp only brought out five kilos at a time, making Murder Black think he had a small plug. The next call was from a stripper named Temptress, one from his father thanking him for the money and birthday card, and the last one from a unknown number. He also had mail from Yummie. He re-read the card twice and wondered how she got his address. How did she find him? It wasn't looking good right now. He had come too far to slip up and fall now.

Later that day he met up with Murder Black over at Black's house. Steph, Black's wife, opened the door big-as-a-house pregnant with their second son.

Pimp gave her a hug and stepped inside. "'Sup, big girl?"

"Hey, Pimp. He's downstairs playing that game, like always."

"Check."

"Pimp, Monica said call her, too," Steph said when he walked off. He turned around and smiled at her.

"Why you always trying to hook me up?"

"'Cause I wanna see you happy, and I know Monica is a good girl."

"I am happy."

"Yeah, whatever, nigga."

Pimp just shook his head and went downstairs to holla at his partna. Just like Steph said, he was knee-deep in the TV with a hen glass in front of him.

"'Sup, nigga?"

"'Sup?"

Murder Black didn't even look up from the TV. He was captivated. Pimp took a seat next to him and grabbed a joystick. "Start this shit over"

# Chapter 14

## A few hours later

*Never will it be the same*

*Honey*

Honey and her boyfriend Rodney made a pit stop in Miami to get gas and use the bathroom. It was night out, but the Miami heat was still blazing, causing her to want an ice cold drink. When she laid eyes on Pimp inside the store, she couldn't believe it.

She was holding her daughter's hand as she walked toward the store, in awe at the sight she saw. It'd been so long since she last saw him, and it was nothing like she expected it to be. At first she was mad at Pimp for just leaving her like he did. She didn't give a damn about nobody else's feelings, just her own, but then she quickly got past it and moved on. Plus Pimp didn't leave her fucked up, he made sure he left her straight.

She walked into the store just in time as Pimp was leaving the counter. He was super fresh. He looked better than before. He looked up in life and without a care in the world. Pimp smiled when he saw her and her little girl, two people he didn't expect to see.

"Ah, man, what's up, Honey? Long time, no see. Hey, little lady." He bent down to Honey's daughter, then looked up to Honey.

"Hey, Pimp. What you doing in the south?" was the only thing she asked him.

"I'm king of Miami, baby."

"Oh, really?" Honey smiled. He always made her smile.

"Hell yeah. What's up wit' you, though? How's the team?"

"Broke up, broke down. I'm moving. Me and my baby and boyfriend, we going to New York for a while," replied Honey. She picked her daughter up and looked out to Rodney, who was pumping gas, looking into the store at her talking to another man. Honey knew she needed to get out of there.

"Take my info. Y'all keep in touch, though. Need anything, then hit my line." Pimp peeped her looking over his shoulder to her nigga. He slick slid her a card with his number on it. Honey pocketed the card.

"Ok, I will," she said and went to grab drinks and snacks, knowing Rodney was about to be heated up with her and she would have to explain exactly what was going on and who Pimp was, 'cause one thing about him was he was a very jealous man, and she knew this.

Overall Rodney was a good man who took care of her and her daughter without questions asked, and the last thing she wanted was to make him feel disrespected in any way. She had great intentions when it came to her relationship, and with this one in particular she wasn't about to mess up.

Once Honey got what she came for and paid for the gas, she went to face her boyfriend. By the way he stood she knew he was pissed off now and wanted answers.

"That was Pimp, the ex I was telling you about. It's nothing though, bae."

"Bae, my ass. I watched how that nigga had you smiling and shit. Don't come bae me wit' that fake-ass shit." Rodney snatched opened the door and got in, cranking the car and slamming it shut.

Honey rolled her eyes and put her daughter inside the car and in her car seat. She then got into the car herself and calmly said, "Baby, trust me when I say I love you and only you. I was not expecting to run into him, but I'm not hateful of the boy, either. Plus remember I was telling you about my friend Diamond? She pregnant by him. That's the only reason I took his number, so I can give it to her, 'cause he don't know. I'm 'bout to text it to her now and toss this shit out the window and erase it out my phone. You can do it yourself, baby. I don't want you mad at me."

Rodney pulled off from the gas station. He looked at Honey and said, "Give me that phone and that number. I'll text and erase it myself."

She passed it to him without hesitation, and he did as he said and tossed Pimp's card out of the window and into the streets while pulling into traffic. Right then and there Honey promised herself to remain loyal to this man at all times. She considered herself lucky to have met Rodney, 'cause she did so much wrong in the past that she deserved nothing like this.

One thing Honey regretted was being the helping hand that killed Big Pop months ago. He was a good dude, and she had kept having second thoughts about setting him up. Her love for Pimp was greater, but his love wasn't at all, and as soon as Big Pop was murdered, Pimp vanished into thin air.

Now that she had another chance at a better man, she planned on doing the correct things, because life was getting short and all she wanted was to live it as good as possible. She relaxed in her seat as the music played. Her mind was on loving the man who was driving, not the one who left her behind.

\*\*\*

*Pimp*

Pimp couldn't believe he ran into Honey with her sexy ass. She still had it going on and still knew how to wrap a sucka around her finger. One thing about Honey that Pimp liked was her heart. If she fucked with someone, then they had themselves a rider. But, like always, Pimp's mission was bigger than a bitch's loyalty, and that was as real as it got.

Yummie was waiting on him at their hotel with her friend Ivory when he pulled the Benz up to the curve. He was pushing a white 650 on chrome wheels and heavy tints, tints so heavy he almost always got stopped for it, but he never cared.

She was looking so, so good in her summer dress and flip-flops. Ivory wore shorts so short he could nearly see her pussy print, which made Pimp want to fuck something. Yummie got in, followed by her friend. She was blushing 'cause Pimp kept his promise like a man.

"Hey," Yummie settled in her seat.

"What's up, baby?"

"Nothing much, boo. Glad you came."

"Didn't I tell you I would?" he asked.

"You surely did."

"Hello, Savarous," Ivory spoke, closing her door.

"What's up, Ivory?" he spoke back and pulled into traffic.

Yummie reached across and took his hand into her own. At first Pimp was about to pull away, but decided not to be so mean because he was running the G when it came to the game. He was just trying to get the girls comfortable so he could really see what was going on.

He took them to his beach-front, seven-bedroom house where he had the place laced with some of the best furniture money could buy, with the equal entertainment. Pimp turned on the music and had dinner being made. He allowed both girls to settle in their rooms as he went to his own to change into something more comfortable for the taste of the night. They all met at the dinner table. Yummie and Ivory were having drink after drink, getting loose. Pimp only had water; he wasn't a drinker at all. The food was served and they all ate and talked about everything.

"Do you still stay in the condo?" Pimp asked Ivory as they talked. He wouldn't remove his eyes from Yummie, though.

"Honey, I moved soon as yo' butt killed them boys. Lawd, it was all over the news," she replied, and it made Pimp look at Yummie funny 'cause she had no business running her mouth.

"That wasn't me. Hell, the murders ran me away. That's why I left. Did they have pictures of me and shit?" Pimp wanted to know. He took a bite of his steak.

"Obviously no, 'cause it would be on CNN," said Ivory.

"Nobody knows it's you, baby, but they do have questions," Yummie added.

When Pimp had killed those dudes for Money, he only stayed in Texas long enough to trade his truck back in, break his lease, and set Money straight with a couple grand 'cause she helped him out with getting his shit back. He left soon after jumping into the rental car parked in the parking lot. He rode to Miami with over a million in cash and 27 kilos of pure dope.

He had left everything behind, even the good girl he had in Yummie. She had proved to be loyal and down, but he couldn't and wouldn't take her with him, so he left without explanation and thoughts of never being found by nobody in Texas. But he was surprised to see Yummie and her knows-to-much-ass friend.

"Well, to clear the record, it was not me who killed those dudes." Pimp wanted to get that out of Ivory's mind, though he knew it was seemingly impossible to do so.

"Pimp, being a killer isn't so bad. But now, killing how Yummie says she witnessed is another thing." Ivory burst out laughing like what she said was so funny.

"Ivory, hush, will you?" Pimp could tell Yummie was uncomfortable. Pimp was getting pissed off by the second. Ivory caught the hint and decided to switch the conversation.

"So, why you leave my girl like this?" She pointed at Yummie and smiled.

"Important thing is that we are here, 'bout to settle this thought of his. With that being said, will you please excuse me, friend, and let me holla at him?" Yummie spoke, not taking her eyes off Pimp's. She was still in love, she was still captivated by everything about this man, and no matter what happened in the past two months, she didn't care. She just wanted to belong to him and only him.

Ivory picked up her glass and plate and stood to leave. She blew them a kiss and walked off toward the bar. Pimp focused his eyes on Ivory's ass, seeing it had gotten fat.

"What's up, pretty?"

"What happened? What did I do wrong?" were the questions asked by Yummie.

"There's just too much going on in Texas, babe."

"We're not in Texas, Pimp, and I am a part of you, not of what Texas seems to be, I know you been through hell, but I'm willing to take some of that fire, too. I'm in love, and I want to stay like that. I'll give everything up for you, baby." Yummie spoke from her heart. She was telling the truth. She was in love like no other, and all she wanted was Pimp.

Pimp couldn't lie, he liked Yummie as well. He knew she was near perfect, but it was something that made him not trust, her no matter what she said. Maybe it was her friend, or it could just be she knew too much of his dirt. Either way, Pimp left Texas for a reason and vowed not to bring anything with him, and he was a man of sticking to his words. He took both of Yummie's hands into his own.

"I love you, Yummie. And baby, you right. I'm just fearful of prison, that's why I left. And I'm not gonna lie, I thought if I did go that you wouldn't stay down with me, so before I could get hurt by you, I just left," he lied.

"I'll never give up on you though, Savarous." Tears of joy were in her eyes.

"Baby, I got a question. Has Ivory been telling people about me and what she thinks of me?" Pimp wanted to know.

"No, baby. Ivory be only joking around. She just be joking with you," she lied.

"Cool. Well, you need to tell her to stop that."

"And I will," said Yummie and kissed his lips.

"So, I got a business meeting to attend. Then later we'll find something to do. We all will meet up here and leave, 'cause my partner wanna meet Ivory anyway. Love you." They shared another kiss, this time a deeper one.

Jerry Jackson

# Chapter 15

*Something Like Home, Nothing like Family*

Pokey Beans Projects was the best spot in Miami to buy and sell crack cocaine, and Pimp was glad for his investment into the business. He had the whole block of NW 63$^{rd}$ Street and NW 15$^{th}$ Street on lockdown, selling only dime rocks to the junkies and seven grams to the hustlers. Money poured in from many crack sales, and shit stopped 'cause Murder Black was back.

Pimp played the background and let Murder Black's name get out there strong in the streets. He just supplied the work and watched the money grow. Certain people knew the real deal, knew Pimp was the plug, and that's where the respect came in at. Niggas respected the baby-faced, light-skinned, skinny Pimp, but they feared Murder, and that was the plan.

Pimp was always on top of things, always one step ahead the next nigga and his plots. Already he didn't trust nobody, and staying in Texas those months proved to not put anything past no one. He led Murder to believe he was getting fronted the work by a Mexican dude out South Beach. No matter what Murder would or could think, he had to believe what Pimp said 'cause he had never exposed his hands to Black. He wasn't that foolish.

"Listen, I'm not from down here, my nigga. You is, and you don't got no money, and I do. You don't got no work, and I do. So, I tell you what we gonna do. We gonna use yo' fear and my brains, my money, my drugs, and both get rich. Listen. Listen to me good. I went through hell for what I got, so any slick shit, I'm not gonna play wit' you or no nigga. I just want the money, my nigga," Pimp remembered telling Murder Black when they had met and finally sat down and talked. From that day it had been going down major in the city of Miami.

Pimp drove down NW 63$^{rd}$ and made a right on 15$^{th}$. He eased down the block as kids played in the summer heat and young dope boys stood posted as fine-ass chicks walked by. He pulled the Benz up right in front of the blue store and jumped out fresh, wearing a pair of Dsquared2 jeans, a Givenchy Cuban star polo shirt, and a white pair of Giuseppe Zanotti with the golden zipper. The store was where he and Murder Black met up at most times.

Pimp made his way inside the store. A few niggas who were sitting out front followed him in. They were some young niggas who looked at Pimp like he was God.

The owner of the store was one of the hood's most-feared project niggas. His name was Queen, half white, half Jamaican, and crazy as fuck. He and Pimp pounded each other while walking to the back where business got handled. There were stacks of money on the table and a few guns. Queen pointed to it.

"Murder still haven't picked this cash up yet, and my street dry. Shit in high demand."

"How much that is?" Pimp pulled out his phone to call Murder. His phone went straight to voicemail. He wondered where he was, because they were supposed to meet up here.

"Like, 120 grand or more, I got it wrote down, though," Queen said. Pimp called Murder's number again to get the same thing: the voicemail.

"Ok, bag that up. I'm 'bout to make a run to grab something from Migo. What's up? Have anybody seen Murder today?"

"I haven't," Queen shot back, knowing something, but not telling Pimp.

Pimp came from the back calling Murder Black's phone again, and it was the same thing. He talked to a few of the young niggas and waited on Queen to come with the money. As he posted up, he paid for all the kids' snacks and drinks like always.

One little girl ran into the store. She was a black, skinny little girl, but pretty and too grown. She put her hand on her hip, rolled her neck, and said, "My sister, Taylor, said come see her before you leave." She then turned and walked away, making Pimp laugh at her little gestures. She was a handful, and her sister was a mess.

Pimp paid the money and took the bag from Queen. He was followed back outside to his ride. Taylor was one of the hood's baddest hos, and she liked Pimp. Every chance she got she let it be known, and most times it was funny to him.

He had yet to find him someone nice, but in due time he would, so for now all Pimp did was meet females, smash them, and keep it moving. Now, the girl from the other week at the art store, she was his type, but she didn't give him a call and he wasn't into chasing hos, so he let her be. But at the same time he always thought of her and wished she would be on him like every other girl in the world.

Taylor was standing by the Benz. Pimp remoted the trunk opened and placed the bag in it, and before closing it back he looked at the fine Taylor and said, "What's up, wifey?"

"Boy, why you wanna keep playing? I can't tell I'm wifey when I don't even got yo' number. I just don't understand that at all. What's up? Why you lie, saying we was going out two weeks ago?"

"Baby, you know Murder Black be working me to death. Gotta keep boss man happy, that's how I get paid. What's up tonight? I hear it's a block party or something going down," Pimp shot back, closing the trunk.

"What's your number, Pimp? Or do I gotta wait in line like the rest of them hos?" Taylor was a sexy, pretty girl. She had a banging body and the swagger to match. Every nigga in Miami that ran across her path chased her like she constantly chased Pimp. She had two kids by a known kingpin named Devil. She was set for life, but she and her sons' father just didn't get along at all.

Pimp smiled at how aggressive she was, at how she wouldn't never give up. She was like men on females when it came to him, and the shit was funny. Pimp gave her his number and jumped back inside the Benz. He had business to handle. He called Murder Black again and again, but the phone went straight to voicemail. He pulled off down 15$^{th}$, tossing the phone on the passenger seat. He was gonna cuss Murder out when he caught him.

\*\*\*

## *Diamond*

Diamond looked at her phone. She had her finger over the send button, about to send Pimp a text. She had gotten his number from Honey a few days ago and was surprised God answered prayers fast and quick. She was just praying God linked them back up, because she didn't want to go through the pregnancy alone. She was almost four months pregnant with Pimp's child, and she wanted him to know it.

At first when she found out she was pregnant, she would have liked to have died. But once she thought about it she realized she was pregnant by the man she was in love with, her dream man, her everything. And even though he left her, he left her with the perfect gift: a child. Her mother and father showed their support, and most of her family and friends. All everyone wanted was for her to find Pimp, and the moment was here.

She decide to erase the long-ass text and just send one saying who she was, but then she decided against it. She just sent a text saying his real name in hopes he'd hit back fast. She went ahead and sent it along with a prayer he would reply back. Not only did she miss him, she needed him around now more than ever, and that was all everyone was saying. She was at home after a long day at the doctor, and school had been long and boring. She had become drained and wanted nothing more than some ice and her child's father in her life.

Diamond didn't want to raise this child alone. She didn't want to be alone, either. She needed Pimp, plain and simple.

She stood her small frame up, placing both hands on her growing belly. Diamond smiled and admired her glow. Would Pimp be as happy as she was? Would he drop everything he was doing to be by her side? Would he come running? She sure hoped he would.

Diamond still was at her parents' house with plans to move into her own place for the sake of her child. Her parents both agreed to help her out in any way possible. They just wanted their daughter to succeed in what it was she was doing, and that was a big reason she loved her mom and dad, because through all her mistakes, they never changed and always stood by her side.

When the phone vibrated on her bed, it scared her. She instantly started shaking and became nervous. For the longest time all Diamond did was stare at the phone, hoping it was Pimp, the love of her life.

\*\*\*

## Savarous

Pimp was fresh out of the shower in his silk linen. He held in his hand a cup of water. Yummie was in the bed, looking heaven-sent in an all-white sheer top and silk panties, her hair flowing down her back, looking extra good. It was late and there wasn't nothing in the streets but jail and hell, and tonight Pimp didn't want either. He sat on his end of the bed and picked the phone up. When he read the text, it was just his name. It had to be Honey.

*Wassup*, he texted back.

*It's Diamond.*

His heart dropped when he saw her name instead of Honey's. First, how did Diamond of all people get his number? Was he that easy to find? Then again, just reading her name in the text message made him miss his li'l lady with her sexy self. Pimp had almost forgotten about her and wouldn't mind seeing her. He sent a text back: *What's good?*

Pimp felt Yummie's arms wrap around his body. She kissed his neck, then his shoulders. He missed her affection. She was good at what she did. She made him feel good as a woman should to a man, and that was important to him. He got another text and opened it.

*Call me.*

*Can't I'm busy I'll hit you later*

Pimp sent his reply and tossed the phone to the side, but it quickly vibrated and he picked it up. His heart dropped when he read the message.

*I'm pregnant.*

*And?* he replied.

Pimp was now confused. What the fuck was she telling him this for? He hadn't seen or heard from her in so long.

*And it's yours, Pimp, I'm almost four months. She text.*

*I don' know what kind of game you playing, but you need to stop it. What's up?*

He had to stand up on that one. He now stared at the phone, waiting on a reply.

*I'm so serious. I have been looking for you high and low.*

*Why didn't you get rid of it?* he texted.

*Was waiting on you.*

*Ok what you need the money?*

*I need to know what you want, she replied*

*I know what I don't want and that's a child, it's not in my plan at all baby girl. Go get rid of it. I'll pay the ticket no matter the price.*

"Everything ok, baby?" Yummie asked as he started pacing the floor back and forth, looking lost, looking thoughtful.

*Ok.*

Even though those were the words he wanted to read, he wasn't sure Diamond got the picture, Pimp turned around to Yummie. "Excuse me one second." He walked out of the room and called Diamond's number. It rang three times before her voice embraced his ears, sounding as sexy as ever. Now he could really put her sexy face to it. Diamond reminded him of Nevea, the one-hit singer who appeared and disappeared. She was pretty cute, and that was something he missed.

"Hello."

"Baby girl, listen, listen good. Let me pay for that abortion. I'll send my aunt to go with you, and I'll be down to visit in a few weeks. Just so much shit going on 'round here. But go handle that, like today. I'm 'bout to hit my aunt up. You still in the north?" Pimp acted cool, but on the inside he was mad as fuck. He could've slapped half the bitch's face off.

Diamond knew what she was doing, and really Pimp wasn't feeling that. The bitch knew she was pregnant and didn't say anything because her stupid-ass wanted the baby, if there was a baby. Was there a baby? Was this a big, fat joke on him? Pimp didn't joke like that. He didn't play games. He wasn't a kid.

"I got the money," was all Diamond said in a humble, respectful way. He could hear the hurt and defeat in her heart, but he didn't give a fuck. Right now he needed her to listen.

"Ok, I'll have my aunt ride—"

"I got it. My mother will go with me. We have already discussed this, so when and if I found you, I would know what to do. And now I know, loud and clear." Diamond was crushed

"Ok, so when you going?"

"Don't worry, I'm going. You don't gotta stress nothing. You don't want your child, fine. I will handle this ASAP, trust me," said Diamond.

"Ok, say less. You at your mom's house?" Pimp asked.

"Yes."

"I'll be up there to fuck with you." Pimp hoped like hell Diamond was faking it. He'd be so happy. He wished it was a joke, but something told him she wasn't joking and she was indeed pregnant, and she planned on keeping it. He made a mental note right then and there to pay her a surprise visit just to see. He would give her one week to rid herself of that baby, and if when he saw her she didn't handle her business, then she would surely die a Painful death, her and her unborn child.

He walked back into his master bedroom and closed the door behind him. Yummie was waiting on him, lust written all over her face. He could tell she was horny; her nipples were hard through her top.

Pimp turned his phone off and placed it on the nightstand. He went into the drawer and slick pulled out a razor. He slipped it in his mouth and got into the plush softness of his bed next to a beautiful white woman he really couldn't trust.

Yummie moved over closer to him, the man she loved, the man she wanted so badly to just be with. She wrapped her arms around him. Pimp turned to face her, their eyes locking, both minds moving in two different directions, two different intents. One love, one nothing.

With one motion Pimp spit the blade out of his mouth and slit Yummie's throat, not giving her even a second's thought to recover. She choked a few seconds as blood poured from her gash, but within seconds she was dead and his bed was bloody.

Pimp got out of the bed. He wiped his hands with the sheets. Inside his bathroom, he took out a silencer, then found his Glock under the bed Yummie just got murdered in. Pimp walked out of his room, down the hall, and into the guest room where Ivory was drunk, asleep without a care in the world. All this was her fault, though, because if she would've never opened her mouth, then maybe Pimp wouldn't feel the bad vibes. So, with that being said, Pimp aimed the Glock and was about to shoot from a distance, but didn't. He walked over to the bed. He towered over her and aimed directly at her face. He pulled the trigger, killing her instantly in her sleep. Pimp shot her face two more times just to make sure she was dead.

"Punk bitch," Pimp said, leaving the room and going back to his room, where he wrapped Yummie's body up in the sheet and the plastic he had under the mattress. Once he had her body wrapped, he went to do Ivory the same way, then he took both of the bodies down to his Benz and tossed both in the trunk. Pimp felt not one bit of remorse because people like them didn't deserve to live life when they ran and talked too much. It was Yummie who told Ivory all this gangsta shit, and Ivory couldn't hold water, so he had to get them hos before they got him.

Pimp pulled up on Murder Black's house with his kids and wife He hadn't answered Pimp's calls, and Pimp wanted to see what was up, 'cause it wasn't like Murder to not answer. It was late, but Murder's wife let Pimp into their home, He was surprised to see her up. They embraced at the door. She was big as a house, ready to go into labor at any time now.

"Where's your old man?"

"Honey, I was hoping you knew something I didn't. I haven't heard from him all day," Murder Black's wife said.

"You called and checked the jail? The hospital?" Pimp wanted to know.

"Now that you said it, that's what I'm going to do."

"Ok, bet that. Just let me know. Hit my phone when he show his face," Pimp replied. And just as he came, he left the same way: with two bodies in his trunk.

Jerry Jackson

# Chapter 16

## *Let Me Find Out*

It was almost 5:00 a.m. when Pimp finally found Murder Black in the club King of Diamonds, posted in the parking lot with a group of niggas from the projects. He was leaning across his Benz truck with a cutie in his face, fresh like always.

Pimp pulled up and parked. He jumped out with a mean, but cool expression on his face as he went straight to Murder.

"Where yo phone at, nigga?"

Murder Black reached in his pocket for his phone, but didn't come out with it. He then leaned up and patted his other pockets, looking for his phone, but still found nothing. Murder stood up and looked over to one of his li'l homies and said, "Yo, check the whip for my phone." He turned back to Pimp. "What da hell going on, though? You out late, huh?"

"Yeah, looking for you and shit. Had them hos, the white bitches, too, but you was nowhere to be found. I had to murder them hos myself, but look, come take a ride with me."

They both jumped in Pimp's Benz. He pulled off, made a few turns, and mashed the gas down Martin Luther King Boulevard. He made another turn and ended up at a cleaners just down the streets from the projects. For the ride over, neither one said anything.

Pimp was feeling a bad vibe. Murder was acting unlike himself. Pimp wondered why as he parked the Benz on the side of the building and killed the engine. He turned to look at Murder Black. Murder looked at him back, also trying to read what was on Pimp's mind.

Pimp opened the Benz door. Murder did the same.

"I need a spot to bury these hos," Pimp said.

"Huh?"

With the remote, Pimp popped the trunk. Both guys walked to the back, and Murder jumped when he saw the two dead white girls balled up, stuffed in the trunk bloody. Pimp closed the trunk back up. He faced Murder Black and instantly saw the nervousness in his so-called partner.

"The hos knew too much, bro. Fuck them bitches. This yo' city, my nigga. Take me to a place these hoes won't be found," said Pimp.

"Lets go. I got a spot," replied Murder Black, and they jumped back in the Benz. Murder Black couldn't believe Pimp was capable of such acts. He thought Pimp was just some pretty, boy-ass nigga who had a hustle. Yeah, he felt Pimp would bust his gun, but he didn't think he'd go this far in the murder game.

The next day Pimp made his way down to the art store where he first met the beautiful girl Icey. He was hoping she was at work, not busy, so he could get some time to talk to her. It was very rare to see Pimp chasing females, and the ones he did get, he used as stepping stones to get where he was going, but with this woman he didn't have them wicked intentions. He really wanted to know this female. She was so much the ideal woman for him. She was the perfect size and shape, had the beautiful face, and was soft spoken.

His type was the reserved, humble, smart kind. The ones who were beautiful, but didn't ponder on their beauty. He liked business-minded females and driven females who didn't just lie there and wait on a nigga to give them a handout. Strong-minded females who weren't scared to take a chance in life. Someone who could match his fly.

He pulled into the store parking lot and got out of his old-school car, fresh as always, looking like money. Pimp held in his hand a single rose as he walked to the store, he begin to open the door, but it shot opened as two dudes walked out. Pimp and one of the guys grilled each other in passing; the dude was white, his friend was black. Inside the store, Pimp quickly forgot about the two guys when he laid eyes on Icey.

She had on a summer dress and flip-flops. Her hair was braided to the back and she wore no makeup. She could only be five feet even, 'cause Pimp towered over her, and he was only 5'7" himself. He walked up on her while she had her back to him, helping an older lady. For a moment all Pimp did was stare in awe at her grace and charm. She was super bad in his eyes.

The lady she was helping looked over Icey's shoulder to Pimp, which made Icey turn to find him standing there, holding a single rose.

"No disrespect, no pressure, but I had to come see the only woman in Miami that I'd date." He reached the rose out toward her. Icey smiled and took it.

"Aw, thank you, sir."

"Savarous," he corrected her fast.

"Oh, yeah. Well, thank you. Its not every day that a guy comes into my store and gives me flowers, you know," Icey said.

"Well, I have the other eleven at the table."

"Table? What table?" She was lost.

"Downtown Miami. I have reservations for us, so if you don't mind, could I take you to this table so I can feed you? Probably haven't even had lunch yet," Pimp said with a hopeful smile.

"Actually, my friend just brought me some lunch." Icey pointed to the hot wings platter.

"Oh, you got a dude. Damn, my bad." Pimp started taking a step back.

"No, I didn't say that. I said my friend. I don't have a man in my life, sir. If I did, I would've never took this." She held up the rose.

"Oh, ok. I didn't want to pry, but I most def want to know you."

"And that's fine with me, but I'm sorry, I can't leave. Work is an overload, and I already have food. But take my number, text me, and we will see to it that your reservations don't go in vain," Icey said.

"Cool. I can deal with that."

Icey went to grab a pen and paper to write her number down. Pimp looked on in admiration at how she carried herself. She walked nice, she moved gracefully, and she was more beautiful than she realized. Pimp knew in his heart he wanted this woman, and her being single was just perfect for him. He knew there was a reason for everything that happened, and him being in Miami was reason to meet Icey with her sexy self.

She came back into the storefront where he waited and gave him the number folded in a paper. This was the closest they ever got to each other. She smelled good, she looked good, her eyes were even colorful, he noticed. Pimp put the number in his pocket.

"I get off at six. Just hit me anytime after that, ok?" Icey said.

"Bet that. I'll holla at you later, then." And with that said, Pimp left the store with hope and feeling good about today. He felt no type of remorse for murdering Yummie and Ivory last night. The only thing he regretted was killing them both in his beds, beds he had to get rid of this morning.

Last night he saw something in Murder Black he didn't like, plus there was something fishy going on with Murder that Pimp couldn't really put his hands on, so from then on he would keep a close eye on him and his moves. Pimp wasn't sold by a long shot. He was always 'bout his steps in life, and right now his steps seemed uncareful, and he wasn't with that.

Pimp jumped back into the rental and pulled off with hopes to talk with Icey later that night.

# Chapter 17

*Everybody Not Solid, Everyone Isn't Real*

He ended up over at Taylor's house, the girl from the projects. She was happy he came over, 'cause when he knocked on her door, she almost jumped in his arms, smiling from ear to ear. Pimp needed a place to duck off for a while, and he knew he was welcome at her place. He was in the rental car, so nobody knew he was out here, and that was the plan. He wanted to see how things moved, 'cause there had to be something going on he didn't know about.

He was kicked back on her sofa, flipping through the TV channels while she was in the shower. Little did she know her shower had just begun, because he was finna fuck her all over the house. She wanted to fuck him, Pimp knew this, and he planned on using it to his advantage

Pimp put the remote down when he heard the water cut off. He got up and walked into her bedroom, where she came out of her shower in a yellow and blue polo towel. She jumped when she noticed him standing at her mirror.

"Boy, you scared me!"

Pimp turned around to face her. Her body was still wet when he walked toward her. "I hope you know you finna get back in that shower, right?" He pulled on the towel.

She held on and smiled. "Uh-oh." She smiled and walked around him.

Pimp walked up behind her and placed one hand on her stomach, the other on her hip. He kissed the side of her neck. She leaned her head to the side and moaned. Pimp pulled the towel from her naked body, then let his hand move down to her pussy. She stopped him then, turned around in his arms. She looked up at his face while going for his belt.

"That's what I'm talking 'bout," Pimp said.

"Come on," she replied and led him to her bed, where she stripped him naked. Taylor wasted no time dropping to her knees and started giving him head. She was a pro, taking his whole dick into her throat, coming up slow, then going down fast. She gripped his dick at the base and looked up at him while sucking and jacking him until he felt he was about to cum. Pimp grabbed her head and started fucking her mouth, and she took it like a champ. After Pimp came in her mouth, she told him to lie on the floor. He was confused at first, but got off the bed and lay down. She straddled him sideways and rode him until he came again. Boy, Murder Black didn't lie when he said she was the truth; he now saw she was a sex pro.

They shared a hot shower, then got dressed. In the living room he grabbed his .45 and cellphone.

"So, you leaving?" Taylor asked, watching him after coming from the bathroom, looking lovely in her panties and t-shirt. Pimp was looking out the window to the blue store and the niggas posted in front of it. Queen was among them, Pimp liked Queen. He was a nigga about his business, never showed a flaw or weakness.

"I'm not going nowhere too fast. Might want me another round or something. Look, what's up with them, though?" Pimp asked and points to three dudes he'd never seen. Taylor made her way over and stood in front of him, her booty brushing his dick.

"Oh, them some peons. They ain't nobody but some hot boys. Them same niggas got Black caught down bad day before yesterday," she said.

"Black?"

"Yeah, that's how he got caught by two unmarked cars. He had some cash and drugs on him," Taylor said, not knowing what she was doing, so Pimp played it cool.

He quickly rocked her to sleep with a lie that was gonna make her open up rather than peep him and change up. "Yeah, I made that nigga bond. He acting like he didn't get caught with much work, though." Pimp threw that lie out there, hoping she took the bait.

And just like almost all hood females, they love the gossip, so Taylor shook her head and said, "I sat there and watched from my window when them folks rolled up on that boy. He had some work on him, and cash, too. He tried to get Beko to take the charge, but the folks weren't going for it. His ass probably just don't want you to know how bad he went out. Know he just did ten, too."

"Beko? Who da fuck that is?"

"Oh, that's the dude under Queen. Li'l young boy, bad as hell," Taylor answered.

Now Pimp knew Murder Black was on some fuck shit, 'cause he never even said anything about getting knocked with some work. What was this nigga's motive? Who all was down with him and his slick ways? Pimp remembered giving Murder half a kilo to bust down with Queen. Was that the work he got popped with? If so, then how did he jump out the next day, so fast, so quick? Was Queen with the bullshit? Was it time to leave Miami before some fuck-shit pop off?

So far Pimp had pumped 20 kilos in sacks through the projects. He had the love and respect of niggas, but Murder Black had the fear. He didn't want to leave. He wanted to get off the last 10 kilos he had and find a plug to keep pushing work for a few years, 'cause things went good unexpectedly and fast, so he wanted to stay in position. Pimp needed to talk to Queen and Beko. He needed confirmation that this shit was true.

He grabbed his gun and cellphone and car keys. "You gonna be waiting on da kid when I get done, right?" he asked, looking Taylor up and down with lust in his eyes, in her eyes, but really determination in his outlook. He wanted badly for what she was saying to be untrue, but his gut feeling told him it was so true, so real.

"I'll be waiting, babe," she joyfully replied.

Pimp left her apartment and walked directly across the street where a group of niggas were posted up, slanging crack and talking trash to each other. Everyone acknowledged Pimp when he strolled up. Some gave him dap, some gave him head nods. He walked into the store and found Queen stacking sodas in the soda box.

Queen was a big dude with a face full of hair and long dreads down his back. He was a nigga with green eyes, which was ugly as fuck to Pimp, no homo.

"Come stroll with me one second." Pimp went straight to the back of the store where they did business. Queen stopped what he was doing and followed him back there. As soon as Queen walked in the room, Pimp questioned him. "Bruh, what went down with Murder and the cops?"

At first Queen just looked at the smaller Pimp, a small dude with big nuts, big heart. He was also lost as to what was going on, but he was there, so he told Pimp. "Folks caught bruh with the half and, like, 30 racks. They booked him, but bruh got out the next morning and gave me a whole."

"Whole what?" Pimp asked.

Queen turned and walked to the locker on the wall. He opened it and pulled out a kilo of coke. He tossed it on the table.

"He told me to make sure y'all business good, and to bust the other between me and him," Queen replied.

"Oh yeah?" Pimp was at a loss. He didn't know what was going on. He was shocked, and Murder Black was suspect. Niggas didn't get knocked for a half a brick and get out the next day, let alone pop up with a whole instantly unless they had a plug. Did Murder have a plug?

"Bruh ain't told me shit, though. That's crazy."

"Real shit, that nigga Murder cutthroat, my nigga. I just play my cards with the nigga. You know everybody scared of him and shit, so he be thinking he can do whatever 'round here," Queen told Pimp.

Pimp left shortly after that with his mind going crazy with thoughts. He was so caught up thinking that he almost forgot to text Icey. He pulled out his cell and sent her a text telling her to call him, then he tossed the phone on the passenger seat while cranking up the rental. Now pimp would run to his dark corner and plot his win against niggas he couldn't trust. By the time he made it to his condo, Icey had called him. The conversation was smooth and quick. Really Pimp couldn't talk right at that moment. He was on a mission, but he did ask to call her back.

Almost two millions dollars in cash and at least 10 kilos. He wasn't ready to leave Pokey Bean Projects just yet. He wanted to get at least another million before leaving, 'cause he knew to get it while the getting was good. He knew to stay down, but be slick.

Murder Black scared people, and that's why people followed him. They followed through fear. Pimp was followed by hos 'cause of his baby face and swag. The niggas followed 'cause he was Murder Black's right hand and his heart was big, he had nuts. Pimp needed to take over. He needed to be different, though. He needed to instill fear to these same niggas Murder Black had shaken, and Pimp only knew one way.

As soon as Pimp pulled into his crib, his cellphone rang. The caller ID read unknown caller. He picked up while steppin' out of the Benz.

"Yo."

"What's up, playa?"

It was Murder Black. He sounded joyful, which made Pimp stop in his tracks. He pulled the phone away from his ear, looked at it crazy, then spoke into it.

"What's good, son? Why it took you so long to hit me? Nigga, you been acting lame every since we dumped them hos." Pimp used his keys to enter his home.

"Man, hell nawl. You know Steph is pregnant and shit. I gotta play the family role, that's something yo' ass don't know about. But good news, though. I got us a plug on the work. I gotta link up with these niggas later tonight. You can role if you want," Murder Black said.

"What time?" Pimp knew he was flexing 'bout being with his wife

"'Round nine."

"I may make it, I don' know. What they talking like? What's the numbers on the bricks?"

"Sweet. They got good prices, but best thing is whatever we buy, they front, too," Murder said, and even though it sounded good, Pimp had in the back of his mind that he couldn't trust this nigga.

"Yeah, that is sweet. I'll hit you up later, fool. I gotta take this call," Pimp said once he saw the call was from Icey.

The cleanup crew was just finishing up his room when he walked in and laid across his new bed. He clicked over.

"Beautiful," he answered.

"You busy?" Icey asked.

"Never busy when you call. Wassup, boo?"

"Nothing much, just wanted to rattle your brain a bit, if you down."

"Is I? Yes, I'm down baby girl." Pimp kinda laughed at her.

"Ok, so first, where are you from?" Icey asked, laughing back with him.

Pimp always lied when it came to his personal life, but he decided to be as open and honest as possible with her, 'cause he really liked her. She was his type from her looks to just the li'l of her personality. "I'm from North Carolina. And you?"

"Here. And your birth name is Shavarous?"

"Savarous," he corrected her.

"Where are your parents? Your siblings?"

"My mom was never around, and my father is in prison. I'm the only child," Pimp replied.

"Well, both my parents are married still, and I'm also the only child. Do you have kids?" Icey asked after her statement.

"No kids. You?"

"None. Do you want any?"

"Not right now."

"Wow, that's how I feel as well. I never thought I'd meet someone with so much in common with me. So, the big question is why are you single? Hold up, are you?" she chuckled.

"Yup."

"Why?"

"'Cause every female isn't for me, and it's a certain type that moves me," Pimp shot back. He sat up on his bed, then stood up to walk into his closet where he had stashed his drug supply.

"Exactly. I think you're too good to be true. I think you might be running a game, honey," Icey said.

Pimp pulled the duffle bag out. He reached inside and pulled out two clips and a folded chopper. He tossed it on the bed.

"I don't get as far as I would telling a lie rather than the truth, especially with just meeting you. What can I gain from a lie? Nothing. But what I can gain from the truth is a forever, some respect, and plenty of love, feel me?"

"Goodness, yes. I get good vibes from you."

"So when can I see you?" Pimp pulled out two bricks, tossing them on the bed, also.

"When do you want to see me?" Icey asked.

"Shid, right now," he shot back.

"Oh lord, I was hoping you said that, but hoping you wouldn't. You gonna come over here?" she said.

"Hell yeah. Text me the address so I can put it in my GPS."

"And what time should I expect you here?"

"Give me 'bout an hour." Pimp had a master plan he had to set in motion before he went to cuddle. It was business first before anything else.

"Ok, that's good. It gives me time to get this home of mine cleaned up. I'll just text you the address, so I'll see you in, say, an hour?"

"Facts," replied Pimp.

With two kilos and two guns, Pimp jumped back into the rental car. He drove over to Murder Black's crib to see if he was home, and just as Pimp turned on his street he saw Murder getting into his Benz. It was perfect timing, 'cause he wanted to follow him for a while just to see what was what, peep the signs with this nigga and the games he played.

Pimp knew Murder was a street nigga, so he was careful not to follow too close behind, but close enough not to lose him in traffic. He played it fair, and within two or three miles he saw Murder Black pull into a restaurant. Pimp pulled into the gas station across the streets from him.

He watched as Murder Black got out of his Benz and shook hands with a white dude. Pimp looked harder. The guy looked familiar. Then another dude got out of the black Charger, and he too looked like someone Pimp had seen before. He just couldn't put a place with the face.

Pimp watched him and the two guys walk into the restaurant. That's when he made his move and drove over there to the Charger. He wrote down the tag number and pulled off. If those two guys were the plug, then something was wrong. They looked like some bullshit. Though he wasn't supposed to judge a book by its cover, Pimp did 'cause he had common sense. He pulled off back into traffic. He had seen enough already.

Pimp put Icey's address into his GPS. She stayed 45 minutes away, he saw as he hit the highway. He couldn't wait to see this beauty and to see what she was really talking about.

\*\*\*

*Icey*

She couldn't ever remember being this nervous, never thought a man could make her feel like a kid again. Even through her nervousness she was excited and joyful. It was like she had finally met her match, and hopefully she didn't have to wait it out a few more years to find him again. Hopefully Savarous was the one, and not the two.

Icey skipped around her three-bedroom townhouse, making sure everything was in place and neat, because first impressions were the best. She had music playing and a meal on the stove. She texted Pimp telling him not to eat anything because she had made hot wings, and he agreed via text.

Icey was loving the feeling of joy, something she hadn't had in a while now. No man really had a chance anymore with her because of her career, for one. And most men in this lifetime weren't ready for the type of woman she was. Only once had she been in love and gotten her heart broken. That was college, that was years ago, and she promised not to get played anymore. So her next two relationships dealt with trust issues. She couldn't trust a nigga as far as she could see them, and ultimately it led to a bad relationship that couldn't be fixed.

She did want love, she did want affection, she did want to belong to someone, but at the same time she wasn't in no rush because men weren't really ready. They would quickly say they were, but reality showed their true colors in the end, and that was something she didn't want. Pimp just needed to be that guy she prayed him to be and nobody else, because she really was feeling his vibes. She liked his respect level and his charm. It wasn't everyday a man brought a woman flowers, showed attention, and was consistent in his approach.

Icey had finally gotten the house in order, and now she relaxed on her soft leather sofa. She picked her phone up and sent him a quick text, asking how far he was. It took only a couple seconds for him to respond, telling her he was only ten minutes away. Not enough time for a shower, but just enough time to for her to finish the food.

She became nervous again all of a sudden and smiled through it as she cooked and pranced around the kitchen. She could only hope he liked her cooking, 'cause she wasn't the best, but she was trying, definitely trying. She wasn't a drinker, nor did she smoke, and she was hoping he didn't, either. But if she had to choose one to go, it was the smoking. She'd rather deal with a drunken fool than a high one.

Her heart dropped when ten minutes passed and she heard a car pull into her yard. Icey raced to the window, pulling the curtain back. She saw Pimp pull up into her driveway. She smiled harder and bit her lip when he stepped out with his super cool swagger.

Icey was at the door, opening it before he could even knock. Pimp stood there, fresh in a polo and crisp white Air Force Ones. His hair was cute in a low-temp fade with his deep waves of curls brushed down. She stepped to the side, allowing him into her warm household.

Pimp passed her 11 more roses as he entered. "Here you go."

"Thank you. So, welcome to my world," Icey said and waved her arm around her colorful living room. She had her own paintings hung up, and mostly everything inside was art and just different, which impressed Pimp as he walked further into the living room, taking notice.

"Nice spot," he finally said.

"Thanks. Are you ready to eat now, or would you rather wait?" she asked, then added, "'cause the food is ready, but if you wanna just chill we can always warm it."

"Shid, I'd rather eat fresh, hot food. I'm just hoping you can cook," Pimp joked and laughed.

"I'm pretty sure I can. I just hope you like it rather than not," she replied, then led the way into the kitchen, directing him to the dinner table laid with all sorts of beautiful dishes. Pimp took a seat and adored the sight of her.

Icey was the perfect size for him, the right type of pretty, the just-right swagger. He could only hope she was the one to make him settle. Not settle to marry, but to really, truly hold down. Something like having a relationship, like Yalonda again, but better. See, Yalonda was fine as fuck, built like a brick house, and had the altitude to go with it where Icey was sexy as fuck and humble with it, like she didn't even realize her beauty. Yalonda was hood with a business mindset, but never reached her goals, where Icey was big business and not a hood chick at all.

She put the wings and fries on the table with some water before taking a seat across from him. She smiled and picked up a glass of water. She took a sip from the glass and said, "All I drink is water. Hope you don't mind."

"I don't. I'm no drinker either, baby girl. No alcohol, no drinks, no smoking, anything at all. It's not my thing," Pimp replied.

"Now that's so amazing to me. Oh my God," she exclaimed, still smiling. She put the glass down and grabbed a wing, taking a tiny bite because it was hot. Pimp followed her lead, but picked up a fry. They ate and held a conversation over the meal. He did most of the talking, telling her things about him he felt she needed to know. And everything he told her was real, from him growing up without his father and mother to him selling drugs and robbing people as a kid. He told her about school, his goals, his likes and dislikes. Pimp was presenting himself to this woman because she was someone he wanted to be with on a high level.

Icey also shared things about herself with him: about her parents, about her not having brothers or sisters, and having a white male as her best friend. She showed him pictures of her family and of Brad. Pimp looked, but he really wasn't paying attention to the pictures. It was her body he was adoring at that moment. She was so beautiful to him. Pimp just had to have this woman. His mind was made up, and he wouldn't give up. He could tell she liked him, too. It was plain to see. He just needed to play his cards right.

Pimp had stayed over until 11:00 p.m. They embraced at the door. He kissed the beautiful Icey on her cheek and made plans to see her soon.

He still had business to handle tonight. Looking at his phone, he saw Murder had called and texted: *Get@me.*

Pimp called Murder Black, who picked up on the third ring. There were some females in the background, laughing.

"What's up, bruh? Where you at?" Murder Black said when he picked up. Pimp could tell he was tipsy on the hen he always drank 'cause he was talking loud into the phone, making Pimp have to pull the earpiece away from his ear, looking at the phone as if Murder could see his facial expression.

"On my way to the spot. Wassup? Whe'e you at?" Pimp shot back, looking down the streets he rode.

"I'm at the hotel wit' a room full of hos, I called you to let you know the plug wanna meet you, my nigga. They talking good shit, bruh. You should've came out and had dinner," Murder said.

"As long as you handled it, it's all good. Ain't no pressure. You got the right prices, right? You trust these niggas, don't you? Then we should be good," Pimp replied.

"Oh, we locked in, bruh. So, you coming over or what? We got plenty of pussy to pass around."

"Nah, bro, I'm good. I'm 'bout to head in. I'll rock with you tomorrow."

Pimp ended the call, making it to his house 30 minutes later with Icey running through his mind non-stop. He wasn't focused on Murder Black and his slick shit. He wasn't thinking about Diamond being pregnant or about Yummie being dead. His heart was cold, but only one person held a warm spot there, and that was Icey.

Jerry Jackson

# Chapter 18

*Amazed at How Love Calls Your Name*

*two weeks later*

For the past two weeks all they did was spend every chance they got with each other, getting to know each other better. She was loving all the attention she got from Pimp, and he enjoyed her, too. Neither could get enough of each other. Every time both of them got together they had fun on date nights, understanding one another's thoughts.

Pimp had opened up more to her about his life. The only thing he lied to her about was him slanging drugs. He refused to tell her he was one of the biggest crack dealers in Miami. He led her to believe he was trying to open up a paint shop and club. When she asked where he got that kind of money to start a business, he told her a lawsuit his father won, which got him a pass for the time being.

Both of them were at her house, chillin' after a dinner date and movies. Pimp just wanted to be under her as much as possible. He wanted to lock her in. He knew she liked him and she knew he liked her, but what she didn't know was Pimp was in love with everything about her. He wasn't rushing. He didn't even really care if she felt the same. He just wanted her as his own.

Last night over the phone they both agreed to get into a serious relationship with each other. Today was their first kiss, first passionate kiss, that blew her mind when Pimp's lips and tongue embraced her own.

Pimp was down to six kilos and had a major stash of cash. He was loving Miami, but he was hating the niggas around him. He closely watched every move Murder Black made and still had to meet the so-called plug Murder wanted him to meet.

Pimp no longer had any type of trust for the niggas in Pokey Bean Projects. He didn't feel none of the love he felt when he first moved out there. Pimp knew it was only Murder Black he wasn't feeling, but the niggas in the projects were so scared of the nigga that it was like they turned on Pimp also, but his mind was only thinking that.

Queen was the only nigga Pimp had rolling with him. He kept Pimp on point with what Murder's moves were. He and Queen made money under the table, right under Murder's nose. Pimp allowed Murder to buy from the so-called plug, but he refused to show his face, 'cause Murder was suspect. Every nigga he had with him was suspect to Pimp.

As he and Icey sat on the sofa kissing and touching each other, a knock came at her door. Icey got up after one last kiss. It was late, and she knew the only person who came to her house this late was Brad. And the only reason he came at this time was when he'd had a fight with his wife.

When she opened the door, there he was looking pissed off at the world. Without the exchange of any words, he walked into her house, but stopped in his tracks when he saw Pimp. He and Pimp looked at each other, then Brad spoke.

"What's going on?" Brad asked, turning back to his best friend. "I'm not interrupting anything, am I?"

"Brad, this Savarous, my boyfriend. Baby, this is my best friend Brad, the one I'm always talking about," Icey introduced both men.

Brad reached out to shake Pimp's hand. Pimp reached back out.

"So don't believe any of what she's told you of me. How you doing? Nice to finally meet the man she's so secretive about," Brad joked.

"Ah, hush up. Do you want anything to drink?" Icey asked as she wrapped herself in Pimp's arms.

"I'm good. I just needed a moment 'cause me and Pam are at it again, so I'm just going to my li'l black corner to grab me a little peace before I face her again," Brad had shot back with a wink of an eye to Icey. Then he patted Pimp's shoulder while walking into one of her guest rooms.

Pimp's mind was stuck. It was like he knew this guy, like he'd seen him before other than on the many pictures she had of him. It was like they had met before, somewhere other than through Icey. Murder Black came to mind, the plug came to mind. Pimp had not gotten too close, so he couldn't really say.

Pimp didn't say anything, he just held her from behind and kissed her neck.

She giggled and said, "Please don't do that."

"Why?" Pimp did it again.

"'Cause just don't, unless—"

"Unless what?" He attacked her neck. Icey laughed and wiggled out of his embrace. He was hitting her spot, and as bad as she wanted him, she would never have sex so fast with a man, nor disrespect her best friend's presence like that. She and Pimp went back to the sofa.

"Just know you're lucky Brad is here," she replied to his question.

"Don't he got a job or something? A wife, some kids?" Pimp asked. He wanted to know because he wanted the pussy and Brad was in his way.

"All of the above. He's married, got two kids, and works for the government," she told him. Icey never really shared Brad's business with Pimp, so it was new news to him.

"Government?"

"Yes, he's an federal agent. You can't even tell, huh?" she asked.

"I would've never knew." Pimp's heart dropped.

"I could've went into the force as well, but I decided to follow my dream as a artist, I just let Brad handle the shoot 'em up, bang-bang stuff," Icey said.

"How long bruh been feds?"

"Since we finished college," she replied.

"Oh, that's what's up, I thought about being an agent once, but my father was so against it. Plus the streets had me by the ankles, held down, you know," said Pimp.

"I understand that, but as long as you turned your life around, that's all that matters. You are now an amazing man that I've come to adore as a friend first, I'm glad we met, Savarous. Really, I am."

They shared a deep kiss. Pimp found one of his hands between her legs, and to his surprise she didn't stop him as he used his fingers to rub her pussy.

"You lucky yo' friend here," Pimp said once they broke the kiss. He stood up to leave.

She stood with him. Icey wrapped her arms around his neck. She kissed him again, then said, "No, you lucky."

She walked him to the door. They promised to see each other the next day and shared one more deep kiss. Pimp jumped in his rental and left. He wasn't feeling the fed best friend of hers. He hated cops with a passion, but he would never tell her that. He just knew not to let that white boy see shit.

*** 

He was on the G4 the next day, and he couldn't get his mind off of Icey. She was down to Earth, smart, kind, beautiful, and funny. They had a lot in common.

Last night when he got home he wanted to call, but didn't. While he was in bed he wanted to call, but didn't. Now there it was, 9:30 p.m. and he wanted to call, but didn't. He really needed and wanted her to make the first move.

He had just recently landed in Atlanta, GA. Atlanta was the place to be, the city he loved and could adapt to at any given notice. Pimp wasn't in the city to stay, he was just handling his business.

School had started back and he wouldn't waste a moment's time. He stepped off his $1000-a-day flight, one-way ticket to Atlanta where he attended Clark University. He went twice a week for 12 weeks, starting today. He was dressed in Prada light-wear, the shoes and shorts matched his sports Prada shirt. The Atlanta air was just right as he stepped down and jumped off the jet. He was met by Montay and one of his hos. Montay stood in front of the new Benz wagon. He smiled bright at Pimp.

"Wassup, bro?" Pimp said, dapping Montay with a shoulder-to-shoulder embrace. It had been a minute since they last saw each other, but they still kept in contact after the first business they ever did. Montay was a solid cat that Pimp could fuck with. That's why every time he was in the city, Montay scooped him up. They did business together on a daily. Montay was the one person Pimp had reached out to when he had gotten low on the bricks, and instead of buying the bricks, Pimp just let Montay eat with him, and Montay agreed.

They rode to one of Montay's cribs and Pimp got one of his cars to hit Fair Street, where Clark University campus was located. Pimp also had a stash of kilos in Atlanta because he would make plays to certain niggas he had linked with since visiting the school campus. Pimp had a nice spot downtown where he would go when he wasn't at school. It was a spot he took hos to get freaky and count up the money he made while down there.

Pimp made it to class just on time. He found a seat between two females and got comfortable. He wasn't there to mingle; he was there to finish school because he had started it. He was there to get money because his mission was far from over, and he needed all the money he could get his hands on. Nothing else mattered to him. If it wasn't money, then fuck it. He had Icey, too, which was a plus to his journey. He liked the woman so much that he constantly thought about her.

She was the only woman who had ever made him feel the way he was feeling at the moment. Pimp wasn't the lover type, he just knew how to make females fall for his game, his charm, and he just used them for whatever they were worth. But with Icey, he had other plans. She was now a part of his mission. He wouldn't let this one go. He was in love for the first time ever. Not because he said so, but because that was how he felt. There was no denying it, no faking the truth; it was just facts.

School was completely over in a few hours. He left the college and headed to College Park Airport. He had missed calls from Taylor, Murder, and Queen; all of them had called minutes apart from each other. He wondered why, but didn't hit anybody back. Whatever it was, he would deal with it when he got there.

Pimp had a plan he was putting together – a take-over plan. Take over Pokey Bean Projects with the niggas he knew and had faith in. Pimp trusted no man or woman, but he did have faith in a select few. When he pulled Montay's whip up at the airport, he saw his li'l homie posted fresh as a first-day-of-school kid. Donte didn't know what whip was what, and the heavy tint hid Pimp until he rolled the window down and blew the horn.

Donte's 6'3" frame smiled as he picked up the bag he carried. He made it to the whip and got in, instantly pounding Pimp. They hadn't seen each other since Pimp left the north, and from the looks of things Donte seemed to have his shit together like Pimp told him, and that was something Pimp liked.

"Wassup, my nigga?" Pimp asked, pulling off. He had reached out to Donte as well when shit started moving wrong in Miami. He needed a different breed of niggas with him, and that was that.

"Good to see my big homie," spoke Donte. He had gotten grilled out a little bit bigger and looked like he was doing his thang in the streets of North Carolina.

"Told you two players was gonna meet again, didn't I?"

"You said it," Donte agreed.

"So, what yo' check like?" Pimp wanted to know.

Donte flexed his watch; it was a iced-out Frank Muller. He had the chain to match, as well. He looked at the watch and smiled. "I'm workin' on my first 100 racks."

"Well look, that's good, but I got better. Six months down here you'll see a million. I got this shit on smash, li'l homie, but them niggas sour at the same time. I need my team wit' me instead of some hating-ass fakes that don't even like me."

Pimp told Donte about everything going on in Dade County. He shared everything but the bankroll, and even though Donte had his stamp put down in North Carolina, he was still in awe with what Pimp was saying.

"I'll show you better than I can tell you." And with that said, Pimp headed to Hartsfield Airport, back to the G4 headed to Miami.

When he parked and walked up the steps to his door with Donte, it came open. He had one housekeeper as of now. She smiled at him as he strolled into the plushed crib. Ms. Mae led him into his second living room, where Montay was having a drink, deep in conversation in his cellphone. He threw his hand up to Pimp, then started back into the phone.

"Ms. Mae, get me a glass of water and, um, refill his cup," Pimp said, then took a seat on his sofa, which felt like clouds. Montay hung up the phone, then sat up.

"What's up, shawty? I see you doing it big, huh?" Donte also took a seat and looked around the spacious living room.

"Tryin' to, anyway. Look, I need—" Pimp stopped talking as soon as Ms. Mae walked in with their drinks. He waited until she was gone be for he said, "I need to clean some money up."

"How much?" Montay took a sip of his Grey Goose.

"Six."

"600 grand?"

"Six million," Pimp replied and sat up. He knew if anybody could help him out, it was Montay.

"Damn, shawty, you been on the grind, huh?"

"Li'l some," Pimp replied. With his money and the money he planned to take from Murder Black, it would put him over eleven million dollars, which was way beyond his goal.

"Shid, lemme holla at my peeps. What you try'na do?"

"Club or something. Something that gon' make paper."

"You done went big business, huh, shawty?" Montay said, laughing.

"You don't even wanna know what I been going through."

The maid walked back into the living room. "Mr. Pimp, um, there's a lady outside of the gates demanding to see you," Ms. Mae cut him off.

Pimp turned his attention to her. "What's the name?"

"She wouldn't give it," Ms. Mae said, looking concerned.

"Let her up. I'll be outside." Pimp got up from his sofa along with Montay. He went to his hall closet and grabbed a Glock and tucked it at the small of his back. Montay cocked his own chrome and followed Pimp outside.

He saw the car stop, then the driver's door came open. It was Taylor. Pimp closed his eyes and put his hand over his forehead. "Why me," he said under his breath.

Taylor wore some jeans and a tank top with Air Force Ones on her small feet. Her hair was in a ponytail. She looked good as always, but Pimp didn't want nothing to do with her right now.

"Can we talk?" Taylor asked, stopping in front of Pimp.

"What's up, Taylor? How you know whe'e I stay? What the fuck you got going on?" Pimp wanted to know.

"Murder Black. I stole it out his phone. I'm not gonna lie. I let the nigga come over at the house to count some money, and I'm glad I did, but at the same time I hate I did. But anyways, I crept his phone went into the bathroom and got yo' info out, but thing is I saw some sucka shit in his messages," Taylor said.

Now she had his full attention. "Sucka shit 'bout me?"

"No. I mean sucka shit like fucking with them folks that sideways shit, and that's the only reason why I found you like this. I think he think I took his phone, but he really don't know. That's why I came to you."

Taylor had just been spared and Murder Black had just been slaughtered.

"Don't be showing nobody else my crib. Lemme introduce you to my partnaz from back home. This Montay, and that's Donte. Y'all, this Taylor, my li'l loyal wifey-to-be one day," Pimp did the introductions.

"Hol' up, hol' up. Excuse us, li'l buddy," Montay said to Taylor and pulled Pimp off to the side. "Man, who is she talking 'bout? I heard some fed shit if I'm not mistaken."

"Remember I was telling you how me and this cat took over an entire project? Well, it's him she talking 'bout on some fuck shit. I told you 'bout this nigga anyways, how sour he was?" asked Pimp, then went back to Taylor. "What kind of info he got in his phone?"

"I just read his text. All I know is one text was about setting someone up on a buy. You know word was out that it was a nigga 'round town getting other niggas popped left and right," Taylor added.

"Fuck going on down here, big homie?" Donte cut into the conversation after listening the entire time.

"Told you, I don' trust these niggas."

"These babies need some killing, huh?"

"Fuckin' right." Pimp laughed because that was the initiative about to be taken. Pimp also had Shaw on his way from the north. He had a delay to handle his issues up there before linking up in Miami. He felt better knowing there were some solid niggas around him.

"Where that nigga Murder at now?" Pimp asked Taylor, looking her dead in the eyes.

"He was posted at the blue store last I seen him," she replied.

"Ok, I'ma need you to get that nigga over to yo' spot when I hit you and tell you so. Can you make that shake?"

"Y'all must finna whack him?" Taylor asked, which was the wrong question, but she didn't know it, so Pimp laughed.

"Nawl, I'm just about to expose this nigga for what he really is, that's all," he assured her.

"Oh, yeah, I can do that."

"Bet."

Pimp sent her back to the projects to wait on him. The three guys came up with a plan how Pimp would get at Murder Black. It wasn't about to be pretty, but well worth it. Pimp was locked in more than ever now because everything was on the line, and it was up to Pimp to make it better or worse.

# Chapter 19

## *Lies Turned into Light*

### *Icey*

She was a total wreck, running around her house trying to find the right outfit to wear tonight. Nothing that Icey put on she liked; it was either too short or too ladylike. Tonight she wanted to present herself as a simple woman, yet with the young look. Whatever she was gonna do, she needed to do it fast, because Savarous and her had plans tonight. Icey was glad she got her hair, feet and nails done that morning. She also took some time to spend with her mother and father for their 32$^{nd}$ anniversary; she was proud of them both.

Icey heard a knock at her front door, breaking her train of thoughts. She didn't want to leave the closet, but the knocking didn't want to stop, and she knew who it was. Icey hurried downstairs and snatched the door opened. Brad rushed in and took her by both shoulders.

"I gotta tell you something." His look was so serious she knew he wasn't joking at all. Even knowing her best friend played too much, she knew right then he was being real.

"What?" He had her scared now.

Brad walked over to her sofa. He sat down and looked at her, searching for the right words to say and how to put them. Icey stood there nervously, waiting on him to tell her what it was that had him so frantic.

"It's about Savarous."

"What about him?"

"That so-called smart guy you thought he was? He isn't. Savarous Jones is the man himself, the big-boy dope dealer from North Carolina. The informant I got is willing to sell your boy out."

"A drug dealer?" She couldn't believe her ears. It could have been a rumor. It could not be true.

Icey's heart shattered when Brad said, "Yes, big time. Serving the entire project."

Icey was heartbroken. She was crushed and wondered why Pimp lied to her like he did. Brad stood up and hugged her because he knew she liked Pimp a lot. She hardly ever opened up to men, and the very time she did jump out there on a leap of faith, she got hurt.

"Lord," was all she could say.

"I'm sorry to have to be the one to tell you this."

"Thank you, Brad. I appreciate it. I'm just shocked, that's all," Icey stated.

"Murder Black has exposed Savarous, everything about him. The man has a mansion out in South Beach."

"Really?"

"Yeah, he got a seven-bedroom pad," Brad added.

"Wow."

Brad had just messed her entire night up with this news of her so-called boyfriend. *Why did he lie?* She kept asking herself that question. He could have told the truth and still she might have dated him because overall he was her type, and in reality Icey saw good in everyone. She could've worked with him on changing or anything, but he didn't have to lie. Tonight they had a date. She couldn't even look at him right now. She didn't want to see him right now. Brad wasn't playing; he was serious, and she knew it.

Icey walked her best friend to the door. They hugged before he said, "Don't say nothing just yet. Let's see if Murder Black got us chasing our tails. I wasn't supposed to tell you, but you my ace, and I know you thought different of him."

"Don't worry, I will not say anything," Icey promised with a broken heart. She watched from the door as Brad climbed into his car and left.

\*\*\*

*Savarous*

Pimp had called her twice and still got no answer. They had a date night tonight, but plans had changed, and he wanted to let her know verbally that he couldn't make it. But since she wasn't picking up, he sent her a quick text. Donte was on the passenger side, riding shotgun as Pimp drove the Miami Streets. Montay was already in position after Taylor made the call saying Murder Black was at the blue store.

When Pimp pulled the Benz up on the block, like always a few kids eased over 'cause they knew Pimp was gonna buy them something. He and Donte jumped out. Nobody had ever seen this guy Pimp had with him, so everyone who was out there looked as the two guys walked over to Queen and Murder Black, who were posted on one of Murder's rides.

"What's up, my main guy?" Murder had asked. He was smoking a blunt. He got up to dap Pimp.

"Shit, coolin' this way. Yo, this my nigga, Donte," Pimp pointed to the bigger kid, then added, "This Queen and Murder Black," he introduced them.

"What's up, my guy?" Murder spoke first.

"What's good?" replied Donte.

"Bro look like a football player. What's good, my nigga? If you with Pimp, then we don't gotta question you at all. Welcome to a million-dollar trap spot," Queen was the next to speak.

"My li'l nigga ain't no football player. My nigga a baller, though," Pimp added.

"So check the mojo, baby boy." Murder Black waved Pimp to follow him. They both walked into the store and into the back room where Murder had ten kilos laid out. He waved toward them.

Jerry Jackson

"Shipment came in. The plug say it's pure, but they want us to pay for these with our own money. But the price cheap this time. He only want 15 a brick," Black told Pimp, who just listened. He said no words, made no moves. He just looked and was all ears.

Pimp looked at his watch. He had five minutes to get into position, 'cause it was about to be a show.

"Ok, so, we'll deal with—"

"The plug on his way, bro. Told you he wanted to meet you. It's the only way he's gonna fuck with us on the money tip," Murder Black cut him off.

"Didn't I tell you I wasn't with meeting him, bro? You forcing me to meet this man?" Pimp already was feeling played. He had three minutes, so he asked, "How long before he pull up? I'm 'bout to go holla at Taylor across the streets," Pimp told him, and Murder agreed.

"He should be here another hour or so. Just don't get lost," said Murder Black.

Pimp and he came back out and posted. Pimp went to Taylor's house as planned, and she was waiting, looking out her window. So when he got to her door, it opened.

"Hey."

# Chapter 20

## *The Double-Triple Cross*

### *Donte*

Donte watched Pimp and Murder Black come out of the store, and just as planned, the alarm went off on his phone, meaning it was time to handle business, Pimp ran across the street like he said he would. Donte got out of the Benz. He had the gun out, held down by his side as Murder Black had his back to the kid. It wasn't until everyone went into panic mode that Murder Black turned around and saw Donte raising a gun to his face.

He heard the shot before he saw the flame. He felt no pain, just as if he got pushed in the face as the bullet tore through his forehead. People were screaming and running as Donte stood over the body, pumping slugs into its face and chest. The streets were in a panic, all but Donte and Queen. Queen just stood on the porch of his store and watched Murder Black get gunned down. Donte emptied the whole clip into Murder Black's body and face, then walked back to the Benz and got in to wait on Pimp.

Pimp walked up behind Taylor, who was looking out the window at Donte killing Murder Black. They were up in her living room, talking when the gunshots erupted and she ran to the window. Pimp already knew what was going on and didn't bother to rush over there. Instead he quickly sent Montay a text telling him to go.

When Montay received the text, he was right around the corner from Murder Black's house. He cranked up the car and pulled up minutes later, using the code Pimp gave him to get into the gates. Murder Black stayed in a large home surrounded by expensive cars, pretty grass, and palm trees. Montay jumped out normal-like. He was the worker of Murder Black. All Montay had to do was follow everything Pimp told him, just don't do nothing extra.

He walked over to a old-school Impala sitting on chrome wheels and skinny tires. Pimp said the passenger door was open at all times. He would find some keys and a remote under the driver's seat. Montay did it, and there were the keys and remote. The remote was for the car garage, the keys for the side door to enter the house without being seen. Montay crept through the six-bedroom pad, following the direction Pimp gave him. Pimp said Murder Black had two kids and a pregnant wife who stayed there.

The kids slept in the last room, while Murder Black and his wife slept in the first room on the hallway, which was the master room that held the safe behind the bed. Montay had the silencer on the berretta nine, ready to pop shots. He tried the door. It cracked open, and that's when he saw Murder Black's wife sleeping peacefully. He eased into the room, gun aimed, and walked over. He shot her twice in the face, killing her without her even knowing.

With gloves on, Montay pulled the bed out of the way. He removed a small tote bag from his waistline and pulled some tools out to crack open the safe. Pimp told him there was no security around the house, so he was good on that, and the only ones to worry about were the kids, and they were little teenage girls that better stay in their rooms. It was late, anyway.

\*\*\*

*Savarous*

Pimp pulled out a hunting knife, and with one powerful swing he stabbed Taylor in the top of her head. She dropped instantly to the floor. Pimp snatched the knife out of her skull as blood shot out everywhere. He walked out of her apartment to the street where

Murder Black was laid out, shot to death. Pimp walked out, looked at the body, and climbed into the Benz with Donte. He pulled off.

*** 

Pimp, Montay, and Donte were in VIP, enjoying the naked girls dancing to Li'l Jon and the Eastside Boys. Montay assured him he had a spot for a club, and yes, he could turn his six million into good, clean cash. He put other businesses on the table also, which Pimp refused.

While this dark brown female danced, Pimp felt his phone vibrate. It was Icey when he saw the caller ID.

"What's word, ma?" he picked up.

"Hey, we need to talk."

Pimp took a sip of his water while looking at the naked girl in front of him. "Ok."

"Well, come get me, then," Icey replied.

He sat up, looked at his Jacob before saying, "Eight o'clock, I'll be there."

"Okay."

He hung up the phone, giving his attention back to the girl in front of him. His thoughts were still with Miss Pretty Eyes. What would they do tonight? It really didn't matter to him what they did. As long as he was with her, he'd be alright. Pimp hadn't felt like this since his first girlfriend when he was only eleven years old. He knew Icey was the one for him. It seemed so perfect.

He reached into his pocket to pay the female for the dance, then he stood up, looked down at Montay, and gave him some pound.

"Tomorrow, my nigga, we'll get together." The lick they made tonight was three million in cash and some bricks. Pimp knew the streets were in an uproar and were riddled with fear, and that was exactly what he wanted.

"Okay, folk. Think about what I told you, though." Montay replied.

"Bet," Pimp shot back, but his mind was already made up. He only wanted to open a couple businesses and make this Icey girl his main thang. Montay wanted him to join a bigger drug ring, but Pimp was done in Miami. He had what he wanted and more.

He made it outside where the sky was dark blue, the air was warm, and the traffic on the street was light. An hour and some change later, he had to go get dressed, and he wondering what Icey wanted to talk about. Once inside his whip, his thoughts went back to his hometown. He came from nothing to now. Pimp knew his hustle game was strong and he thanked his father, Silky, and Bobby Gray. All those men mattered the most to him. Bobby Gray was dead and gone, Silky was still in the hood, and his father was locked up. Pimp had a li'l of all of them inside himself, so how could he be stopped?

That's how he slid through the cracks, being slick, on point, and up on game. Pimp loved his life and was not ready to lay back and enjoy all the sweat and tears. The pain was over with. It was time for joy now.

\*\*\*

## Icey

Icey and Brad watched Savarous leave the club. She had called and asked Brad to let her ride on a stake-out with him. Now this could get him fired, and Brad made sure she knew it.

"I can get in big trouble for this." But she needed to see for herself Savarous in action. Brad had her call him just to track his phone and see where he was. She didn't think things would take a turn for the worst, but when Brad got the call saying there had been a triple murder and Murder Black was one of the ones killed, Icey knew it was real.

"Damn, babe, I got to pull up on scene. It seems someone has killed Murder," Brad told her.

Pimp pulled off in his Benz. He was alone. Moments later she got a text, and it was him. Icey became scared.

"This Savarous here," she showed him.

"Ok, text him back. Go meet up with him, see what you can find out, I'm having your house bugged as we speak, so give it about an hour and make sure you take him there," Brad said and drove off in the other direction than Pimp. Icey was nervous, but she agreed to do as told.

How did she get caught up in this mess? One minute she was falling in love, the next moment she was running in fear. She didn't feel the same anymore, and most of all her feelings were hurt. What would she say to him tonight when they got together? She really couldn't mask how she felt, and she didn't want to let on to her knowing about him. She was confused and scared at the same time. Did he have something to do with those murders that happened tonight? Was he really some big-time drug pusher that the government wanted? Icey had so many questions and not enough answers.

When Brad dropped her off at her car, Icey sat there and texted Pimp back and forth. He wanted her to meet him at his crib, but she told him she was out at Ruby Tuesday, an upscale restaurant, waiting on him. She lied, but she didn't want to meet him nowhere if it wasn't a public place. When Pimp texted and said he was on his way, she went to the restaurant she told him she'd be at. She had to fix her nerves quickly, 'cause he wasn't far away at all.

Not in a million years would she have thought she'd be in this predicament. Not in a million years had she thought she would fall so fast for a thug nigga who was really thuggin' it. Icey pulled up to the restaurant and made her way in, making sure to sit at the bar around people, and waited for Pimp to get there.

\*\*\*

## Savarous

He walked in and gave the place a glance, looking for Icey, and spotted her at the bar, looking amazing. Pimp smiled when he saw her and made his way over. He was fresh like always and looking so innocent. It made no sense how he had so many people fooled.

Pimp stopped in front of his girl. She stood up and hugged him. He kissed her once on the jaw and twice on her lips. Pimp couldn't help but notice Icey was tense, and he wondered why.

"Do we have a table?" he asked her.

"Right here is fine with me, that's if you don't mind?" Icey replied, hoping he wouldn't.

"Here is cool with me, baby." They both took seats at the bar. Pimp got comfortable and looked at the woman he was willing to do right. "So, what's on your mind, boo?"

For a moment after the question Icey just looked over the menu, battling her thoughts, trying to get her words right. At that point Pimp knew something was going on that didn't add up to him.

She finally looked him in the eyes and asked, "Have you lied to me about anything? Ever?"

Pimp wanted to know where that question came from. What would she do with the answer? "Not that I know of, baby. Wassup?" he wanted to know.

"Savarous, are you dealing drugs? I mean, I just would like to know," stated Icey, and as bad as Pimp wanted to lie, he also wanted to tell the truth because he needed her in his life.

"Was I? Yes. But am I now? Hell no. I know that's not something you like in a man, and that's nothing you don't see in me. I'd rather have you over the streets and money. I don't need no more, no extra. So, to answer your question, baby: no."

"Why am I hearing different?"

"Who telling you this? Your friend?" Pimp hoped like hell the feds weren't in the picture. He did not have the time to be fooling with them, and if anybody knew something, it would be her.

"No, Brad could never tell me his job business. I have a homegirl that swears she knows you. Said you be in Pokey Bean Projects everyday, all day," Icey lied, and Pimp found himself believing her lie.

"Well, she got it mixed up. True enough, I fucks with them cats out there because they welcomed me in their city fresh from another state. Them niggas always treated me like family, so yeah, I go out there sometimes and post just to kick it, but I'm not selling dope, I promise."

"Or killing people?"

"Most definitely not killing nobody, 'cause I can't do the time," Pimp quickly replied.

"Savarous, I surely hope she doesn't know what she's talking about, 'cause I really do like you. I really do want us to be together, but if you have lied and I find out, I'ma be hurt."

"I'm not worried 'bout that, baby," Pimp cut her off with reassurance.

"I like that."

"Me too."

Outside he walked her to her car and held open the door for her to get in, like always. She got inside and put on her seatbelt. When Savarous leaned down into her car, they kissed. Then Icey asked, "You coming over?" She needed to know.

"Shid, I can, baby, if that's what you want. I'd love to end my night next to you and begin my day with you being the first thing I see," Pimp shot back.

"Yes, I'd like to see you there," replied Icey, but she lied.

\*\*\*

Pimp's Phone was blowing up with all kinds of text messages and calls from niggas from the projects, but only one caught his eye. A text came through saying the feds were walking around asking about him with his picture. Feds also were looking for him and his unknown friend, and were looking for Queen, too.

He had already weighed his options before this even popped off and had his alibi down pat, plus a few good lawyers. Pimp didn't answer no calls as he drove to his condo in downtown Miami that no one knew about. Montay and Queen were in the living room watching the news while Donte slept, lying across the sofa. Money was everywhere when Pimp walked in and closed the door.

"Boy, it done got ugly," Queen said and pointed toward the TV, looking at Pimp, who was unfazed by what the news showed. Queen was straight. It was the plan for him to witness the murder of Murder Black, 'cause Pimp needed his statement.

"They wanna holla at you, and you the one who gonna save me," said Pimp to Queen.

"Huh?"

"They only want you for questions, so I already got you a lawyer who gonna be there with you. You write the statement that's needed. That's gonna free me, 'cause I know them pussy-niggas snitchin' on me. All you gotta do is describe Donte and the nigga who pulled off in the Benz. Tell them you know it wasn't me, that you know me from anywhere, and I'm good. My lawyer got the correct statement needed, so give him a call," Pimp explained to Queen, making sure he understood his role.

And he did. "Ok, bet," said Queen.

"In order for this shit to work as we plan, we gotta do our parts. And guess what? So far, so good. We'll all be rich in no time," Pimp added

"What we doing with this money? It's three mill," said Montay.

"Queen, how much paper Black had stashed?"

"Probably half mill, might be a little more," Queen answered.

"We stash it, we off these bricks, and take over the projects. Give it six months and we split out million dollars, niggas," Pimp told them both.

He looked at his phone and saw a text from Icey. *You're all over the news smh.*

He texted her back. *Headed to police station now as we text. Wrong man, baby, trust me.*

Pimp sent the text back. He looked at Queen and said, "Showtime. Go ahead and link up with the lawyer, 'cause I'm 'bout to turn myself in so I can get out through your statement."

"Turn yourself in?" Montay asked.

"Fuck yeah. Gotta play my part. I don't got shit to hide or run from. Gotta show them I'm clean," Pimp replied.

"Ok, my nigga, if you say so."

Pimp's phone vibrated with another text from Icey. *Really are you turning yourself in?*

Pimp replied, *Yes, baby, 'cause I'm innocent. It's not me that did no shit like that, so I'm headed there now once my lawyer gets here.*

Pimp had it all mapped out. He had to beat them at their own game. He was just hoping Queen did his part.

*Ok, call if u need me.*

Icey sent another text with a frowny-face emoji, which made Pimp smile and send one back. Queen left to handle business and Pimp got dressed so he could go meet up with his law team. His plan was in motion.

Jerry Jackson

# Chapter 21

## *There is a Time and a Place*

Shaw landed in the Miami airport and was picked up by Queen. He had just left the police headquarters, writing his statement for Pimp. Shaw saw Queen standing there by the phones, like he said he would.

"What's up, bruh?" asked Queen.

"I'm just making it. You Queen?"

"Yeah, that's me. Let's get out of here."

Queen helped with the two bags Shaw had with him. They made it out to the ride where Queen had parked. Once both the men were in the ride, Queen pulled off and out of the airport. Pimp was already in police custody, and Queen's lawyer said he was being processed by a bonding company to be released, so that was a good thing. The statement worked.

"What's going on with Pimp? He in or out?" Shaw asked, 'cause he also knew the plan, but didn't know it had taken affect yet.

"He on his way out" Queen told him.

Right then Shaw knew his role was next. It was his time, so he asked, "Where we headed?"

"I was told to drop you off with Donte."

Pimp was smart. He knew he and Shaw favored each other, so he had it set up for him and Donte to ride back to the projects and shake some niggas up. It didn't take them long to make it to the condo. Pimp knew this move would free him all the way, 'cause both killers would show their faces while he was still in county.

When they made it to the condo, Donte was already there. He tossed Shaw the Benz keys and got inside. Shaw caught them out of the air, and just as planned by Pimp, he jumped behind the wheel. He cranked up and Donte passed him a gun. He took it and pulled off. This was just a pass through to shake some niggas up and get out of Miami. Leave it up to Queen and Pimp and Montay to handle Dade County.

Montay had trap spots in Atlanta for both Shaw and Donte, and a team of city niggas willing to ride for them. Pimp had a loft up there also for them as a duck spot, but each had an apartment to themselves. All they had to do was show up and play their roles.

Meanwhile, Pimp remained in the county jail awaiting his paperwork to be processed. It was his first time ever stepping on this side of the jail, and his last. Coming to jail was all in his getaway. It had to happen so he could be clean, so when he showed his face back in the projects he would have that fear Murder Black once had. All Pimp could think about was Icey and what she was doing. He had to get her trust and show her being in the streets wasn't so bad. Or should he keep it away?

Her best friend was an FBI agent, so how would this work? He couldn't tell her anything real about him being in the streets; she may panic. Or better yet, she might just not fuck with him. Pimp had to figure some shit out when it came to having this woman in his life.

He looked at the time and realized he'd been in the system too may hours waiting to be released to the streets. They needed to hurry up and do it fast.

Donte and Shaw rode down 15th Street in the Benz. It was 1:00 a.m. and the streets were still alive with crack sells and junkie moves. Murder Black being killed the day before didn't stop nobody from doing them. As soon as the cops left, the trap started back jumping. The only thing the murders did was give the hood something to talk about, and everyone from the hood – that hood preferably – was talking about how Pimp crossed Murder Black out.

Shaw pulled over at a small corner store where eight or nine niggas stood posted. He and Donte jumped out and started busting shots in the store direction, and within seconds they peeled out down the street doing 80 mph. Only two dudes got hit in the process.

Shaw slowed the Benz down to make the turns. Donte leaned out the window at some females posted at the bus stop. Shaw looked at them as well as Donte shot in their direction and Shaw pulled off. Donte shot over them as planned, 'cause two of the four girls were down with the plan Pimp had put together.

Shaw made a couple more turns, then both guys switched cars, jumping into a pickup truck with tints. Shaw pulled off as Donte reloaded both guns. Now all they had to do was make it to the highway and get out of the state of Florida. But if need be, they'd go out in the fire of glory with the cops. But so far, so good. Shit was going as planned.

***

## Savarous

Pimp had been out two days now, his case dismissed, and Pokey Bean Projects was in total shock when they all witnessed Pimp, Queen, and Montay post up at the blue store for hours, just kicking it. Nobody dared say anything, like they didn't like what had happened. Niggas that did walk up and kick it with the three were niggas who wanted some money, who wanted to be down, plus the niggas who were already on Queen's side, who also sided with Pimp in fear of what he would do to them, and that's what he wanted.

Today he was with Icey. It was their first time seeing each other since he turned himself in. She came to his condo when he had called that morning. He had cooked breakfast, and all for her. Icey was in the living room while he stood in the kitchen on the phone, talking to his father.

"Yo."

"What's good, son?" It was his father; a smile came to his face.

"Yo, it's good out this way, Pop. How you holding up?"

"Coolin'. So what's word? What yo' next move is?" his father asked, which made Pimp look over to Icey.

"I'm about to do the club thing and finish school, plus I think I found my son's mother." Pimp smiled when she looked at him.

"Word. What she lookin' like?"

"Righteous, Pops. Super right. I think I'm falling, and I don't wanna get up." Pimp joked, but at the same time he was dead serious.

"Dat's word. When I'ma see you, son?"

"Sat and Sunday. I was gonna stay in Atlanta Thursday when I land and just stay that weekend," Pimp replied.

"Love, den. I'll see you, son. Be careful. One," his father spoke.

"One." Pimp clicked off and slid the phone back into his pocket. Everything he told his dad was almost real. It was real when he said she was right. He was in love, but he was not feeling her to the max-max, 'cause her friend just made Pimp feel some kind of way. Yet he wondered how she felt.

Pimp gave her a plate once the food was ready. He pulled her chair out and joined her with his own food.

"No one has ever treated me like this," Icey said, impressed.

"All this can be me and yours when you decide you wanna be my wife."

She took a small bite of food, chewed it, and looked into his eyes before saying, "Why you playing with me?"

"I'm for real."

"Me too, but don't you think we should get to know each other?" Icey asked, still chewing.

"I know enough," Pimp shot back and took a bite from his plate.

"Well, I don't."

The Heart of a Gangsta

"What you wanna know? I'll tell you anything about the new me. My past is my past. I hate to relive it."

"And that's what I want to know about," she replied.

"Why?" Pimp looked at her for answers.

"Because I wanna know who I'm dealing with and what I'm getting myself into, that's why."

Was he ready to reveal his past to her? Or to anybody, for that matter? Inside the kitchen, under all the bright lights, he got a good look at the beauty queen in some jeans and Timbs. Damn, she looked good to him. He could just hold her all night. It was like her small frame was just right for him. It was like they fit perfectly together. Pimp knew he had to have this woman on his team. It just seemed so right.

"In due time, you'll know everything you need to know," Pimp said.

"That's fine by me. So, I didn't know you could cook. This food is pretty good," Icey said, changing the subject.

"I'm nice with everything I do," Pimp bragged through a smile.

It took them a couple more minutes to finish their breakfast, and they ended up back in the living room. Icey and he both sat on the floor in front of his Blu-ray and DVD collection.

"Love, drama, action, or what?" Pimp asked.

"Huh?" At first she was lost.

"What movie?"

"Oh, um, it doesn't matter," she replied. Icey looked like a light-skinned Meagan Good with colorful eyes. She was the same size, just a little shorter, but she did have those same sexy-ass lips and a right frame.

"Follow me."

Pimp led her into his bedroom where his 80-inch TV was mounted on the wall. He saw she was amazed with his room. He climbed up on the soft bed and took the remote. Icey kicked off her boots and climbed up, also.

"So, is you gonna tell me?" she asked.

"Tell you what?"

"About you."

"After the movie you tell me about you, because if I could recall, I've already told you about me." Pimp searched for the right movie.

"Not about how you, of all people, got caught up in them murders, how you got this condo, all those cars and stuff like that. I thought you was in college and worked or something," Icey said.

"Why do it matter so much?" Pimp spoke in an irritated voice.

Icey gave him a look, then turned her face to the movie without saying anything else.

***

*Savarous*

She was lying back on his chest. This was their second movie, which was going off. The woman felt so damn good next to him. He didn't want it to end, but it was over with. Pimp kissed the top of her head.

"You ready?"

"Yeah."

She tried to sit up, but he pulled her back. Icey turned around, and that's when he kissed her. She kissed him back, but pulled back when he was trying to stick his tongue in her mouth. She gave him a quick peck and got up.

Pimp just laid back and looked at her as she put on her boots. She was running from him for some strange reason, and he wondered why. Shit, he was horny. He wanted her and no one else.

"What's up, baby?"

"Nothing."

"Get back up here with me, then," Pimp said.

"Nope, I gotta go. I got to work tomorrow."

"Be my wife and you ain't never gotta work no more."

"I'll be yo' girl, yo' woman." Icey climbed back between his legs on the bed. She kissed him. "Yo' lady and more, but I'm going to work tomorrow."

"So, you my girl now? We going to Vegas this weekend?" Pimp asked while kissing her again.

"Nope, 'cause you gotta see your pops, remember?" She reminded him what he told his father.

"Oh yeah. Well, the next weekend. Until then, you my one and only girlfriend."

"And you're my man. All I ask is that you don't lie to me or hide nothing, because we gotta be able to trust one another."

"That's a bet."

Once Icey got dressed, she left, and he left shortly after because he had to meet Montay at the club he just paid for. Things were looking good as of now and couldn't do nothing but get better as it went. Pimp jumped in his BMW 745. He cranked up and placed his favorite album in the CD player.

As soon as he pulled out of his gate, two unmarked cars pulled him over. Pimp wondered what the fuck was going on as he pulled to the side of the road. He knew it was the FBI, yet they didn't have nothing on him, so he wasn't stressing. He was cool.

Four white men with vests and guns jumped out of the two cars. Two came to the passenger side and two went to Pimp's side, where he had the window down.

"How y'all doing, sir? What's da problem?"

"Savarous Jones?" one white male asked him.

"Yeah, dat's me?"

"I'm FBI." The man showed ID. "I need to ask you some questions. Could you follow me downtown?"

"No problem, sir," Pimp said, then pulled out his phone. "Just let me call my lawyer."

"Ok, go ahead," the agent told him.

One car in front and one car behind, they rode to the FBI building. Pimp also called Montay to inform him about what happened and where he was headed. The lawyer was on his way also.

It took them fifteen minutes to make it to the building, then another twenty minutes for his lawyer to get there,

There was an old, white man sitting at the table alone inside the room he and the lawyer were led into. Pimp took a seat and let the games begin.

"Savarous Jones, I'm sorry for my assumptions. Okay, the reason you are here is because I need to ask you a couple of questions. You're not in trouble. You don't even have to answer if you don't want to."

"Okay, shoot," Pimp said.

"Do you know a female from Texas named Yummie Greene?"

"Yeah, that's my ex," Pimp replied.

"Ex since when?"

"Two months ago."

"Well, are you aware she is missing?" the agent asked.

"No, I wasn't. Damn!" Pimp covered his face with his hands.

"She was in Miami with you when she came up missing. She and her friend came to find you. She had an private investigator who found you. This was just some weeks ago, and you are saying it's been two months?"

"That's exactly what I'm saying, sir."

"What if I told you we have photos of you and Yummie? Video?" the agent asked.

Pimp stood up, because he knew the agent was just talking shit. He was too slick to leave pictures and shit lingering.

"If I'm not under arrest, then I'm leaving."

The agent also stood. "Fine. Just know that you are being watched, Savarous. because you're not slick at all."

"Check," was all Pimp said, and he and his lawyer got out of there.

Jerry Jackson

# Chapter 22

*The Father Talk*

*One week later*

"I got a letter from Yalonda last week."

"About what?" Pimp asked his father and wondered why that girl was writing his dad. Was she that crazy?

"What she said was you have a girl pregnant that you running from, that you just left her hanging, and everyone else."

"Man, that girl front'n you."

"Well, get the blood test, son, and prove it. And I thought Yalonda was your boo thang?" His father smiled. He was a powerful-looking man that commanded so much fear. He was a bit taller than Pimp and weighed 100 pounds more than his skinny son. Pimp's father had killed so many federal informants back when Pimp was just a little boy. His father worked for a mob cartel. He was their hit man, and he didn't play at all. He was always about his business.

"That was then, Pops. This is now. I haven't heard from Yalonda's ass in six or seven months," Pimp replied.

"And go see that woman that's pregnant, though? What's up with this new girl, though. That got yo' nose wide open? I ain't never seen you like that. You over a piece of chicken."

"Man, Pop, she is everything I want. I can't wait 'til you bounce. Me and her been kicking every day. I just like her flavor."

"Word?" his father asked with a smile.

"Word is bond, Pops!"

Pimp and his father kicked it about a lot more, then it was time to go; visitation was over with. They gave each other dap. Pimp told him he wasn't coming back Sunday because he was about to ride to NC to see what Yalonda was talking about.

Inside the Benz he called Icey, who was, like always, delighted to hear his voice.

"Hi, baby!" she said with joy in her every word, which made him smile. They were just together yesterday, and he already was missing her.

"'Sup, ma? What's good?"

"You. What's up where you at?"

"Headed up north to handle something. I'll be back in a couple of days, though," Pimp said.

"Oh. Well, baby, I'm gonna miss you. Soon as you come back, come get me, okay?"

"I gotcha, boo."

Pimp clicked off his cellphone, feeling really good about himself. For the last week he and Icey had just been getting to know each other more and more. He was right about this woman: she was all that and then some.

He found out her last relationship was a lie; dude was married and had kids. He saw the hurt in her eyes when she told him about it. All this made him want her more and more. He also told her about Yalonda, the girls he had working for him and Yummie. He told her he used every female for his own reason. He just didn't go into detail about how he did things, and when she asked about what he was doing, he just replied, "Bad things," and laughed at the cute look she gave him.

"Have you ever killed someone?" she then asked.

"I've wished death on a person once, but I don't think I got the thug heart to kill a person."

It'd been a week of just talking and talking, going out, and having a good time. Pimp must admit he hadn't had fun like that in a while, and he had never been this happy being around a female.

Pimp left the jail and hit the eastside of Atlanta. He pulled up on Gleenwood where Shaw had a trap spot. Donte was in the yard with a few dudes, fixing a dirt bike and smoking weed. When Pimp jumped out of the Benz, Shaw was on the porch, just chilling. He was always the laid-back type.

"What's up, family?" Shaw met Pimp in the yard. They both walked over to where Donte was posted.

"Man, just passing through. What it do?" Pimp shot back.

"It's good this way. It's better than the north, I know that much. These young niggas keep some shit going on 'round here. I just be laughing at these clowns," said Shaw.

Pimp and Donte shoulder-to-shoulder dapped each other. Donte held a blunt between two fingers and asked, "What's up, big homie? You good?"

"Hell yeah. Just passing through, coming from seeing Pops."

"Ok, cool. He good?"

"Most definitely," replied Pimp.

All three guys walked off from everyone else, then Pimp updated them on what was going on in Miami. He told them the case had to be thrown out, that Queen and Montay and him got Pokey Bean Projects on lock. And just like he planned, they all should be rich in six months' time, no ifs, ands, or buts about it.

He didn't stay long 'cause he had to go catch a flight to North Carolina. He needed to catch Diamond's stupid-ass and kill the bitch, because he told her to get rid of the baby. And for Yalonda to know anything about Diamond being pregnant was Diamond running her fucking mouth like a jackass. As far as Yalonda went, he didn't care about her reaching out to his father. It wouldn't change nothing.

Yalonda was a great girlfriend, but he was in love with this other woman, and nothing would come between them. His father told him to handle his business, so that's what he intended to do. Go talk with Yalonda and go murder Diamond. If she was pregnant for real he might just murder the bitch.

\*\*\*

## *Yalonda*

She pulled her SUV up to her sister's new home to find Yasmine, her niece, playing on the porch. Yavonda was standing between her husband's legs as he sat on the hood of the car. Yalonda was very proud of her sister's new-found love. She and Tyon make a great couple. Yavonda was content and happy, that's what mattered the most. Tyon waived to Yalonda as she climbed out of the tuck. She waived back and wished like hell he had a twin brother with his black, sexy ass. Her sister turned around with a big smile and a fat stomach. She was expecting her second child in a couple months.

"Hey, big girl," Yalonda said while embracing her twin sister.

"Hey, boo."

Yasmine was almost across the yard when she saw her auntie. Yalonda picked the small child up into her arms. Yasmine couldn't stop smiling.

"Hey, auntie!"

"Hey, pookey bear," Yalonda said and kissed her sister's four-year-old daughter, who was getting bigger and bigger seemingly by the day.

"How was yo' first day on the job, Yalonda?" Tyon's deep voice asked.

She kissed Yasmine's fat cheeks again before saying, "Good. It was very good. I like it." She was no longer working at CVS. Now she worked at the new spa in downtown NC. Her money was low and she could not mend with all the bills and a new car note. Things were hard, which made her hate Pimp even more for leaving her. He couldn't even be a man and tell her nothing. He just left, and it didn't sit right with her at all.

It had gotten to her so much how he ran from this situation until she wrote the one person she knew he'd listen to. She poured out her heart to his father and prayed over the letter before sending it out. Now she was praying for an answer.

It had been two weeks now, and she still hadn't heard anything from Pimp or his father. Yalonda wasn't going to give up because love won't allow it. She decided to go ahead and head home. She had a lot to do with not a lot of time on her hands. She only had stopped by her sister's in passing from work and needed to get home to check her mailbox, hoping to get a letter from Pimp's father.

"Girl, call me tonight, okay." Yavonda leaned inside the SUV and kissed her twin sister on the cheeks. Since Pimp left, Yalonda has gotten even closer to her sister. That was the only way she was gonna make it through college.

"Okay, girl, I'll do that," she replied and waved to Tyon while pulling out of the driveway of her sister's nice home. Thoughts of her and Pimp came to mind. If only he could've been that man. If only he would've kept it real with her and not allowed her to play the fool. But in the end everybody did except him and Donte.

Yalonda really began to hate Pimp because, her trust wasn't 100% with nothing or nobody anymore. Pimp had her whole heart, she kissed the ground he walked on with no problem, and he took her for granted. He took her love for granted and crushed it. Tears forced themselves to her eyes, but she refused to let them fall. She'd been too strong for that over the months. Her emotions were under control.

On the highway, she fumbled with the radio and found *Street Talk* by Cash playing. She cut the music up because that was her jam. She needed something to get her mind off Pimp, and right now Cash was the man.

An hour later when she pulled up to her condo, she didn't expect to see Pimp sitting on the hood of a white, brand new Benz. He wore a blue velvet Sean John outfit with snow-white Timbs and blue trim. He even had a Rolex with blue diamonds and the necklace to match. She'd always expected him to look good, but not so rich with a rich glow. He didn't see her pull up three cars down as he ran his mouth over the cellphone. She watched him for a second, then prayed a silent prayer.

Yalonda took a deep breath, then exhaled before opening the truck door. Pimp still didn't pay her any attention, now laughing at somebody on his phone. She looked once again, and this time made eye contact with Pimp. He said nothing, just looked and looked. Yalonda went to the passenger side of her truck to grab her work overnight bag. Pimp was already on his way over toward her.

She really wanted to act as if she never saw him, yet she knew that was impossible. She felt him take the bag from her hand. She allowed it, but didn't look to her left side where he walked with her to the apartment door. All these months she held her pain inside, she struggled emotionally, crying many nights because of the broken heart. And now he was here, back in her life, and she wanted to hurt him really bad. She wanted him to feel the pain she felt for those months. She hated Pimp more than anything in the world.

Yalonda used her keys to unlock the door. Still they hadn't said one word to each other. Pimp placed the bag on her black leather sofa, then followed Yalonda into the dinning room, where she put her new vase. Pimp leaned over to take a look, then turned to Yalonda.

She could no longer be strong. The tears themselves made her cry just knowing they were only seconds from falling.

"What's up, Yalonda?" Pimp reached up to try to wipe away the waterfall, but she slapped his hand down and tried to walk away. She wanted to hide the pain, but Pimp was on her heels.

He grabbed her shoulders and said, "Yalonda, we ain't gon' get nowhere if we don't talk."

She snatched away from him. "Don't fuckin' touch me, nigga!"

"Don't start this shit!" Pimp also yelled.

"Fuck you," she shot back while wiping her eyes with the back of her hand. She walked into the living room because she didn't want to be around him.

"Can we talk, or what?" Pimp asked.

"Shid. Talk," Yalonda replied while taking a seat on the sofa.

Jerry Jackson

# Chapter 23

*Meaning What I Say*

*Savarous*

He just looked at her for a moment. He understood her anger and pain, and that's the reason he hadn't snapped yet, because for once he was in the wrong. Still, whether wrong or right, she had better calm down.

Pimp took a seat next to Yalonda. He pulled his phone out to cut it off. He took the Glock 9 and placed it on the table. She looked different, looked finer, but still had that pretty brown skin and even longer hair. Yet her eyes said she was tired, and he understood what it was. Being back home, Pimp realized how much he missed the north and how much he missed Yalonda.

He finally turned toward her and took a deep breath before saying. "Yalonda, listen, I know you hot right now. There's no reason you shouldn't be, because a nigga played you for a fool. I used you for my own selfish reasons, then vanished. All I can say is I'm sorry about the pain I have caused over the years of knowing me, and by me just leaving without words. I really never knew love, Yalonda, until I hit these states alone and saw how I didn't have nobody, I have this certain mission in life to get my dad outta that slammer, baby girl, and I felt like I needed to do this shit solo, 'cause anything else will hold me back."

"Savarous." She paused to lock eyes with the man she once was head-over-heels for. "I've always had your back, wrong or right. You 'posed to be my man, and that's my duty."

Pimp smiled 'cause he knew she was right. "Yalonda, I know you don't trust me, but let me make this up to you. I'm not trying to be your man or none of that. I just feel like I owe you for what you have done for me." Pimp placed one of his hands on her thigh.

She didn't knock it away, just allowed it to stay there.

Yalonda and Pimp talked two whole hours. She told him about all he missed while being gone. Donte came up big in the projects, Keyantay got killed months ago, and Diamond is pregnant.

"That same li'l bitch put that hickey on yo' neck. You must been making love to the bitch, because you got her pregnant."

"That girl is lying, Yalonda." Pimp was sure.

"Not wit' no big-ass stomach, Savarous. She only a kid, anyways. What she gonna lie for? Boy, bye. That's yo' fucking baby."

"Fuck no," said Pimp. He wasn't going for it. He pulled out his phone and sent Diamond a text.

*I'm in town. Let's link up. Told you I was coming.*

He knew she was head-over-heels. He knew she lusted him badly, and Diamond would not pass up a chance to be around his swag. He knew within minutes she would text back and he would find out if she was pregnant for real.

Pimp got ready to leave. She walked him to the door, leaning up on his frame with her arms folded over her chest. Pimp turned to face her and smiled.

"What's the latest I can pop up on yo' crib?" he asked.

"Whenever. Just call to let me know when to open the door," she replied, then they both said nothing. Neither knew what move to make or when to make it, so Pimp nodded his head and walked away.

The first spot Pimp went to was Diamond's old stomping ground, 'cause he never knew where her mom stayed. He just knew her from the block. Nobody was really out, and Diamond had yet to text back. Pimp pulled off and went around the corner.

Niggas stood on what seemed like every corner. Some were shooting dice, and some were trying to get their mack on with the females who walked around in li'l shorts and tight jeans. Pimp pulled up in front of Silky's spot, his old school friend. Silky had two of his hos posted on the porch.

Cream was his bottom bitch. She was old, but looked young, still pretty and fine. "Pimp! What's up, boy? Yo', where you been?" She held a beautiful smile on her face.

"Getting to it. You know how I do. Yo, where Silky at? Tell that nigga I'm out here."

"Yeah, let me get him for you. Silky gonna love to see you looking all rich and shit," Cream said.

\*\*\*

## Diamond

Diamond got the text message and instantly felt something wasn't right. She all of a sudden feared Pimp and that he might hurt her. Hurt her 'cause she had refused to have an abortion when he said so. She couldn't let him see her like this. He would go crazy, and Diamond knew it. One of her friends and both her parents told Diamond to consider an abortion even when they were against it because of the stories they'd heard about Pimp.

Diamond was in Virginia at her grandparents' house, hiding out from Pimp 'cause she just felt in her heart he would kill her, no second thought, and she really, really wanted to have his seed. She wanted to forever be a part of him and to share his world. Some said she was crazy, most said she was insane. Diamond thought she was just in love and just wanted what she wanted.

She was almost at 5 months, only four months to go, and the baby soon should be in this world. Her plan was to enroll in school where her grandparents lived and raise her child for the next four or five years up in Virginia.

Diamond looked at the text message one more time. She wanted to text back badly, but knew to just stay away. Though at the same time it would be amazing if Pimp allowed her to keep the baby.

Should she try to ease him through the conversation? Should she just tell him the truth and tell him she wasn't gonna get rid of their child? Her mind battled her heart, and her heart battled her common sense. She picked the phone up, pressed reply, and began to send him a text back. She decided to just lay it out there.

*Hey, I'm 5 months. My parents wouldn't allow me to rid my child. I'm sorry, I am not in state 'cause I know u hate me for this, I love you I just wish you love me back. oh btw it's a boy. I am having your son in 4 months.*

Diamond sent the text and a prayer to God Pimp understood and accepted the facts.

\*\*\*

*Savarous*

When he saw his childhood friend Meeks' BMW sitting on chrome wheels, a smile came to Pimp's face. To see him doing swell was good. Pimp wanted all his partners to have something in life. He climbed out of the Benz and Meeks leaned on the grill of the SUV. He was one of the two guys who hit for diamonds with Pimp. He had a twin brother and cousin, too, and they all did licks together.

"What's good, son?"

"Yo, son, what's up?" Meeks shot back. They gave each other a big hug, then pounded each other before jumping inside the BMW. Meeks was dead fresh with the jewels on, repping his status in the streets. There was a lit blunt waiting on him. He took two puffs, then tried to pass it to Pimp.

"Nigga, you know I don't smoke."

"Oh, okay."

"So, what's the move? How has life been for you?" Pimp smiled.

"Shid, my nigga, I took the game you gave me and ran with it. I'm the man up this way, me and bruh. Word is bond, yo. These niggas don't like that, but respect it, and the hos loving ya boy swagger."

"That's cool, my nigga. Listen, though. All that's good now can and will come to an end, so when you feel like you done, then come down to my spot in Atlanta. I got a job for you. Everything and anything we've done is history. I don't speak on the past because it's just that, the past."

"That's a bet, yo," Meeks replied. Pimp gave him the small rundown on what was going on in Atlanta and Miami, giving him a picture so he'd see and could better explain to his brother and cousin what was what.

"Yo, where Diamond though?" Pimp asked when he thought about what Yalonda told him.

Two females pulled up in a Jeep, both fine as wine. Then they climbed out and approached them. Before Meeks could answer Pimp's question, one of the girls spoke.

"Where you been, Meeks?" She pointed a long nail in his face.

Pimp noticed she was beautiful, a honey-brown, round-faced dime piece with a short, fly haircut.

"Pam, get the fuck outta my face with dat stupid shit. You know a nigga been getting money."

"Yeah, and fuckin' Tameka's nasty ass. You ain't shit, nigga!" She rolled her neck and walked off. Pimp saw she had a phat ass on her back.

"Who dat, yo?" Pimp asked.

"My stupid-ass li'l boy momma, and Star, her homegirl, gold-diggin' ass."

"How many kids you got?"

"Two."

"Yeah, but what's up with Diamond, my li'l ho? Word on the street she knocked up."

"Yeah, by you, nigga."

Meeks' statement hit him like a ton of bricks. It was like everybody knew about this baby, like the bitch been posting this shit online. Meeks began to tell Pimp about how he ran into Diamond some months ago at the club, said she was showing then, and she was with Honey that night. Meeks said Diamond was telling everyone who asked about her being pregnant, that it was Pimp's child she carried, and Honey co-signed it.

Meeks didn't have whereabouts on Diamond, but did say her parents stayed on a Mirror Drive townhouse. He gave Pimp the directions to the crib. They kicked it a couple more minutes about Meeks joining him in either state.

"Don't wait until you get hot and come running. You need to run right now," Pimp said once they gave each other dap and another hug outside of the whip. Pimp also took Meeks' number to keep in touch. He hit the alarm on the Benz and watched the doors flip straight up, then the car came to life. His mind went straight to Meeks' baby mama's, Pam's, fine ass. He had to shake that thought ASAP, though.

When Pimp looked at his phone, he realized Diamond had texted back, and he was happy until he read the message. He had to read it two more times before tossing the phone in the passenger seat. She said she was having the baby. Pimp couldn't let that happen. He had to put a stop to that, and he only had 4 months to do it. He was heated that he knew she was in hiding, 'cause it would be hard to find the bitch, and he had too much other shit to do other than chasing a ghost. The bitch could be anywhere.

Pimp had to try another method. He sent her a text back saying he was disappointed she asked him what he wanted, then turned around and went against him.

*Diamond, as mad as I am right now, you're 5 months, meaning that baby already got its heartbeat and shape, I'm not gonna lie I feel trapped, but the good part about it is its a son you're having, wherever you at I hope u n my child is good. get@me when you ready for me to do my part.*

He knew that was the shit she wanted to hear, so he sent it. All Pimp wanted was the chance to kill the bitch and the baby. He meant what he said: no kids, point blank. And he was serious about that. Nothing or nobody could change his mind.

Pimp pulled up to the address given. He noticed two cars in the yard. He wondered if Diamond was in there or not. He wondered should he knock, or kick the door in, or should he even go in at all? Diamond needed to text back fast. He needed to get his hands on this stupid bitch.

It was 1:35 a.m. when he called Yalonda. She was asleep, but unlocked her door when he said he was coming.

Yalonda's door was open. He stood in the doorframe, just looking down at the woman he once loved. She held a peaceful look upon her face. Pimp realized he wanted to be with her just one more time, but thoughts of his girl Icey came to mind and he knew he couldn't be with Yalonda.

Icey hadn't called him today, and he hadn't called her. It was too late to do so now, but first thing tomorrow he was gonna call

Walking toward Yalonda's bed, he pulled his Glock 19 out and placed it on the nightstand along with his cellphone and car keys. Yalonda rolled over and saw him through lazy eyes. He smiled down at her.

"Can I join you?" he asked.

A weak, tired smile came upon her face as she pulled the sheets back and moved over. Pimp striped down to his boxers and climbed in beside her. Yalonda's body was warm. She cuddled next to him when he wrapped his arms around her thick frame, something he missed doing. For a good ten minutes he wondered what next move to make with her, but she didn't keep him waiting for too long. She turned around in his arms.

"Savarous, what are we gonna do?"

Pimp didn't expect that question to come about this quickly, but he had already prepared for the answer.

"Take this friendship one step at a time."

He could see her bright smile through the dark. She pulled him toward her some more, where the lips locked. The kiss was deep and hot, a long-awaited kiss. She slid one of her thighs up his thigh to feel his hardness.

"Can we?" she moaned.

"What?" he asked.

"Make love?" Yalonda replied while grabbing his dick, which was hard as a rock. She waited on no answer as she made her way under the sheets. She freed him and stroked it twice. Pimp ran his fingers through her hair while pushing her head down. She kissed his head, then did circle licks around the tip of his hard dick. She knew he loved her to first slowly bob on him, so that was what she did. Real slow, she gave him her warm, wet mouth. She sucked his balls just like he loved it. Then she took him in her throat, where she let him shoot his juice into her belly.

Pimp shook a good ten seconds. This was the part he missed about this woman. He pulled her up toward him and flipped her over. He slid her panties off and slip up in her with ease.

# Chapter 24

## *Is Love Really Worth It?*

### *Icey*

The cellphone woke her from a good night's sleep. The hotel clock read 10:30 a.m. She reached on the nightstand and took the phone. Savarous' number showed up.

"What?" She let it be known she was upset and it wasn't a front. Pimp had her mad for real, because his ass ain't call until now. It just didn't seem right to her, not when they was in a relationship.

"Damn, boo, what's up? Did I catch you at the wrong time or something? Because you don't sound the same," he said, which made her roll her eyes at the phone and sitting up in the bed.

"I'm tired, Savarous, that's it. How you doing?" Icey said.

"No good so far. Um, when I get back we need to talk."

"About?" she asked.

"I'll tell you when I get there," replied Pimp.

"Is it good or bad?"

"Icey, I'ma tell you when I get there. I'm leaving around three o'clock. Can we do dinner?"

"Okay, I'll see you at what time, then?"

"I guess around eight."

"I'll be home," Icey replied and hung up. She found herself blushing like she was in her teens again. Savarous was slowly doing something to her, and it felt good, like her first love or something.

Icey couldn't rest anymore, so she called Brad, telling him Pimp was on his way over. Brad had begged her to let him put a tail on Pimp's car, and she agreed 'cause even after Pimp beat the charges and the government closed the case, Brad was convinced it was still Pimp, so he had his own investigation going on. She got up out of the bed, then grabbed a quick shower. She needed to get dressed.

Icey was still confused, and as bad as she wanted to believe her best friend, it was hard doing so because she saw firsthand how the federal government dismissed the case against Pimp. Plus Pimp showed her a different side as to what Brad saw. She'd known Brad her entire life and knew he wouldn't lie to her. It was the only reason she agreed to let him put a tracker on Savarous' car.

She needed to know Savarous was telling her the truth and Brad was wrong about his assumptions of Pimp. She really wished her hopes and dreams came true, that Pimp was the man he said he was and Brad and him could find some form of a friendship, because she loved them both

*** 

Icey was making sure everything was in place at her house. She knew Pimp would be there in a couple of hours, and she wanted her home to be as clean as possible. Brad had popped up at the house with his partner, which she didn't like.

"Brad, what is you doing?"

"So me and my partner thought it would be a good idea for you to wear a wire tonight. That way we can listen in on y'all two. We need you to get him talking," Brad told her, which made Icey shake her head side-to-side.

"Brad, I'm not doing all of that. First of all, I think you are going over the top as it is, plus I'm not being paid. Also the man was dismissed, and it's like you're trying to rail him," Icey said.

"I'm only protecting you. I know he's hiding the truth. I just want you to see for yourself," Brad shot back, but Icey knew better. She knew her friend when he had his mind set on something. It was hard to make him see otherwise. She wasn't trying to see Pimp go to jail, no way. She only wanted to know the truth about him, and Brad was making it harder than it should be.

"I'm not doing it, and you need to leave 'cause he'll be here any minute now. So both of you air-heads get ghost so I can do what I gotta do," she said. It was bad enough she felt funny even allowing Brad to track Savarous, but now he wanted her to go undercover.

She saw her friend to the door with his partner and was happy when they pulled off. She got her phone and sent Pimp a text asking how long would he be.

Her hair was in a bun tonight. She wore a simple outfit for around the house: some gray tights and a black tank top. She didn't have plans on doing anything but chilling, but if Savarous had other plans she wouldn't mind changing real quick into something for the occasion.

Her phone vibrated a text: *One hour away.*

*Have you ate anything?*

*No wbu?*

*No, I'll cook.*

*Gonna make me fall in love.*

*You already are.*

*It's noticeable like that?*

*lol yes.*

Pimp sent a frowny face emoji. She sent a heart, and behind it she stated, *feeling mutual though, so you not alone.*

They both texted back and forth about everything and anything. He always said the right things to her, and when they were around each other he always treated her like a queen. What more could she ask for?

Icey had prepared burgers and fries for them to eat while texting him. Pimp pulled up into her driveway moments after she finish cooking. Icey met him on the porch with a hug and kiss — a kiss she missed.

Pimp didn't want to let go. She felt so soft in his arms. She smelled so good, but he finally turned her loose.

"Beautiful lady, I missed you," he said.

She smiled. "I missed you too, mister," replied Icey and led him into the house. Her paranoia was in overdrive, praying Brad and his partner did not leave anything around the house to indicate anything out of place. She was still battling her own thoughts of happiness. She wanted Pimp so bad she was scared of the truth, because she didn't want to be hurt by him

Savarous followed closely behind her into the house. He closed the door as she quickly scanned the living room. Nothing was out of place, which was good. Walking toward her room, she was hoping her luck there was the same.

"Icey," she heard Pimp call. She stopped in her tracks at the sound of his voice, frightened to turn to face him. She didn't know what was on his mind, what'd been found that she missed.

"Yes?" she answered, still not moving.

"I miss you. I love you," he replied, which made her spin around to find him looking directly at her. She walked back into the living room, heart pounding away in her chest. He was sitting on her sofa with a foot on the table, holding a throw pillow. It made Icey smile because she missed him, too. She just didn't know how to say it. No, she knew how to say it, but she didn't want to speak those words because they were true. She was slowly falling for a man her best friend was trying to put behind bars.

"Let's eat, baby."

"Always running, huh?" Pimp followed her into the kitchen, looking at his girl in lust. She started fixing them both plates.

"I'm not running from you at all. I just know me," said Icey over her shoulder.

"That's what your mouth say, but yo' actions show smoke on your toes," Pimp shot back with a joke they both laughed at.

"Ah, hush. And here, put these plates on the table so I can feed you." Icey passed him two plates, then went to fix them water like always. She was happy he wasn't a drinker, because it was a big turn off for a man's breath to smell like he'd drunk up the bar.

Pimp took the glasses from her when she made it back to the table. He kissed her again. "Thank you. The next cook is on me," Pimp said.

"I was thinking the same thing," Icey replied with a smile.

"You sure been showing out lately."

"How you figure that? If anything it's you who be showing their butts."

Like every night they spent with each other, their conversation was good and long. They talked a few hours about all types of things. Both of them enjoyed one another, and it showed in their actions. There was nothing Brad could say now that would make her believe Pimp wasn't the man for her.

After conversation, Icey excused herself to shower. That's what she told him, but really she wanted to see if Brad put the tracker on his car, in hopes he didn't. Pimp was good to her. He wasn't as bad as Brad said he was. There was no denying that he was street, but he was smart and driven. He was about his business, and that's what she adored of him.

Brad didn't text back. Instead he called, but she didn't answer as she ran the shower, deciding to get in and play her role on off. She didn't want to leave Pimp waiting too long, so she made it quick, in and out.

\*\*\*

*Savarous*

Never has he seen so much of her skin at once, and to see her smooth legs and bare feet, which were cute and small. She had her hair down, framing her beautiful face, which made him just wanna be next to her. Pimp realized this was his woman. He really was feeling everything about this lady was heaven.

"Why don't we just watch a movie?" she said while sitting down next to him.

Pimp pulled her frame closer and kissed her neck, then said low in her ear, "Whatever you want is fine with me, as long as I'm with you."

Pimp ran a soft hand through her silky hair, which made her eyelids drop and a low moan escape her full lips. He ran his hand down her neck slowly while looking into her eyes. *How can I not be in love?* he thought while moving down to her back. Icey's eyes came wide open.

It was like she knew his thoughts. Their eye contact spoke so many words without understanding that neither of them said anything. They shared a kiss. Being with this woman meant a lot to Pimp.

As they kissed, Pimp ran his hand between her legs. When he touched her middle, she clamped his hand between her thighs to stop his movement, then pulled away from the kiss.

"I gotta clean up from dinner," she said.

When Icey tried to get up, he pulled her back down across his lap. She was light to the touch.

"We got plenty of time for all that." He gave her a hard, long, deep kiss and looked for the reaction, but she said nothing. She just smiled and kissed him hard on the lips.

Savarous wanted nothing more than to make love to this woman right here, right now. One of his hands slid under her white t-shirt to her breast, which was without a bra. She stuck her tongue inside his mouth when his finger brushed over a nipple. The kiss went from hard to soft, from fast to slow. Pimp felt her body loosening up under his touch. Her nipples were small like rocks, ready to be sucked, licked, and played with.

They both broke the kiss for air. Pimp used the opportunity to pull her shirt up, exposing two beautiful, hard, light brown nipples on a pair of softball-sized breasts. He waited not another second to see what they tasted like. A moan found its way out of her lips when the warmth from his tongue embraced her flesh. Icey put her palm on top of his head so he'd know to keep going.

Pimp used his tongue to make circles around each nipple, a tender bite then he sucked one at a time into his mouth. With his free hand he began to pull her shorts down. She lifted so they'd come down with ease. Pimp stopped what he was doing to stand up. Her shorts fell to her ankles, and he pulled them all the way off to find no panties. He then pulled his shirt off. She sat up and went for is belt, but he stopped her movement.

"Your bedroom." His voice was low and lust was deep in his eyes. Without a reply, Icey got up, leaving her shorts on the floor. Her t-shirt was the only thing covering most of her ass, which was fat and almost clapped with every step she took.

He stripped inside the bedroom as she pulled the shirt over her head. They embraced each other. Her small hand found his hard dick. She stroked it while they kissed, both of his hands full of ass cheeks. Pimp slowly laid her back on the bed.

He placed the head of his dick between her wet pussy lips. Before he could push, she said, "Hold up, boo. Grab a rubber"

He stopped in his tracks, feeling the heat from between her legs. He knew it was good, and it took more than a male's willpower to keep him at bay. "Where are they?" he asked and moved inside her an inch.

"Don't you have one? 'Cause I d—"

Pimp pushed all the way up inside her, Icey arched her back and moaned loudly because it hurt, but it felt so right. She rolled her hips each time he pulled out, and when he pushed, she gripped his member as tight as possible. Both of his hands found her own as he stared directly into her eyes while making love. That made her roll even harder.

He let her hand go and grabbed her under both knees to put her into the buck. He pulled all but the head out of her and rabbit-hit the opening of her, which made her bite his shoulder. When the feeling got too powerful, Pimp pushed as deep as he could go inside her. He rolled his hips with her own and she wrapped both of her arms around his neck. Pimp knew she was about to cum because her pussy muscles wouldn't stop gripping him. He pounded at her pussy a solid ten stokes until she screamed she was cumming.

After her nerves calmed down, he pulled out of her. He turned her over and entered her pussy from the back. She quickly grabbed a pillow as he went to work, one hand full of her hair as he pounded.

She couldn't take that position too much longer, so she turned her head and said, "B-baby, let me ride it."

Pimp gripped both of her hips and pushed deeper inside her. He let a load go. She tried to move once she realized what was going on, but it was too late. Pimp fell on her back, tired. When he pulled out of her and lay on his back, Icey gave him a confused look. She also lay down on her side, facing him. Her small hand found his chest.

"I'm in love," was the only thing he could say, because it was true. His intentions toward her were pure. He just wanted to be with this woman.

"Me, too," Icey replied back.

*** 

*Icey*

She saw Savarous smile when she spoke those words. Icey also had to smile because it was true. She had fallen in love with this man and couldn't help it. If she could, she probably wouldn't even try. Pimp's only problem was that he was gangster. Icey was somewhat a nerd, a good girl with a nice background. She was happy she had found this relation like this, but why couldn't this situation be different? She asked herself over and over again. What mattered the most to her? Her career, her friendship with Brad, or her heart? She was truly in love, and right then and there she decided.

Savarous looked so peaceful, so right, and so cute laying in Icey's bed, like that spot had been waiting for him a long time.

She leaned over him and his eyes popped open. She remembered him saying he had something to tell her, so she asked, "Boo, what did we need to talk about?"

He closed his eyes once again and smiled. She playfully hit him in the chest, and he laughed and said, "Damn, baby, you gon' beat me up?"

"Yup." Icey sat all the way up, holding the sheet over her breasts with a fist balled up, trying to look for real. But being happy and in love, she could not hide her blush.

"All I wanted to talk about was us. I want you to move in with me. I just want to spend as much time as possible with you," he said while also sitting up. His eyes said he meant every word, and Icey saw why she fell in love.

"I wanna spend my time with you, too. And yes, I'll move in with you if that's what you really want," she found herself saying, but wasn't really, really sure.

The phone rang, which scared the life out of her. Icey jumped and reached for the phone so she could send Brad to voicemail, 'cause that's who she thought was calling, but to her surprise it was he mother. If Icey didn't pick up she would keep calling, so she told Pimp to hold up and answered.

"Hey, Ma!"

"Icey, why didn't you call me back last night? Girl, what you doing?"

"In the bed."

"The bed? I thought you had a show tonight and you in the bed?
"

"The show was postponed, so I'm just chilling with Savarous," Icey said.

"Sa – who?"

"Ma, the guy I was telling you about." Icey smiled, looking over at him

"And where is he?" her nosey mother asked.

"He's right here." She tried her best to sound normal. The short answers to her questions still didn't give her the picture.

"In yo' bed?" she asked in a shocked voice.

"Yes, Ma."

"You've had sex with this man, Icey?"

"Mama, I'll talk to you about this later. I'm tired."

"So you're for real about this dude, huh?"

"Yes, Ma. Lemme call you back."

"Bye, girl." She hung up in her daughter's face.

Icey knew she was mad because she didn't give her li'l nosy-self details. She always spoiled her mother with gossip, but right now was not the time to be talking about Savarous Jones with him lying right next to her.

When Icey placed the phone back on the nightstand, he pulled her toward him. She straddled his lap, placed both of her open palms on his chest, and looked him in the eyes.

"You wanna meet my mother?" she wanted to know. She wanted to see where they really stood. Was he for real about them, or was this all a joke?

He gripped both of Icey's booty cheeks and pushed his hardness up on her. Icey was getting wet just to feel him pressed on her pussy. "Yes, I wanna meet momma Duke. Wish I could meet all those who's close to you."

"Me too," she replied and bent down to kiss him. Icey felt him slide inside her with ease as their tongues found each other. After they broke the kiss, she leaned up and did her job.

The very next day she went over to her mother's house, the very spot she grew up from the womb to her years in college, and things still had not changed. Mr. Wilson still has six or seven dogs running around his front yard next door. Back when Icey was smaller, she and her friends used to throw rocks at those mutts because they stank and would never stop barking. Over the years she grew to hate those dogs until one day two of them saved her momma's life.

For some reason Mr. Wilson's gate was open, and her momma had just gotten off of work. Icey and her friend were in the den watching videos, so they didn't hear nothing. Two dogs out of eight attacked the man until he let momma go, and that was the day she grew respect for them thangs.

When Icey pulled up in the driveway and got out, she could smell dog poop all over the place. Her momma had the door opened, so she walked straight inside to find her coming out of the den. She looked shocked to see her daughter.

"Hey, Ma," Icey spoke.

"Hey, baby." She took her hand off her chest. They embraced like always with a kiss, then took seats on the sofa. Her momma was almost sixty years old and still looked forty, if not younger. She still had her silky hair, which was gray on the sides, and her skin was still flawless. She was also in great shape for her age.

Icey's momma was like a best friend, someone she could talk to about anything, no matter what it was. She always gave it to Icey uncut and raw, no matter if she wanted to hear it or not, and that's why she loved this woman.

"So, tell me what's going on, Icey. I know my daughter, so don't lie to me, girl," she decided to break the ice.

Icey's head dropped when she gave her that sorry look. Without making contact, she said, "Ma, I don't know what happened. All I know is I'm happy being with Savarous, and its confusing because it's like I'm helping Brad bring him down, but he ain't showed me nothing but goodness," Icey explained.

"You had sex with this man, Icey?"

"Yes." Her reply was low. Her momma shook her head and stood up. She walked to the picture of Icey that hung on the wall. It was a picture of Icey and her daddy.

"What is this guy like, baby? I mean, help me understand what you see in him." She turned around and they finally locked eyes with each other.

"Ma, he's very respectful. He listens, he gives good advice, he's a perfect man in the mind and body. It's just his soul – meaning his street ways – throws the picture off."

Icey's mother burst out laughing at her. She walked back toward the sofa. "You in love, Icey Smith."

"I know, Ma."

"So, what is you gon' do? Help bust the man or let him live?"

"I can't be his reason to fail, Ma," Icey said from her heart.

# Chapter 25

*Show Who's Boss*

*Savarous*

The next day Pimp pulled up in Pokey Bean Projects for the first time solo since the murders took place. Mostly everyone from the hood knew Pimp had something to do with Murder Black, his wife, and Taylor's deaths, but nobody dared say anything in fear of what the li'l dude would do to them. He pulled up in a brand new Lincoln Navigator with shining rims and wet paint. He wanted to stunt a little. He wanted to show them who was boss, who ran shit and who didn't.

Pimp pulled up at Queen's store and climbed out in skinny jeans with a huge pistol, its long clip hanging out, he was fresh as always and feeling good. He was feeling in love and happy he had Icey in his life, happy he stopped in Miami rather than Atlanta like he planned. He would've never met her, his soul mate, his true other half.

Queen was inside the store helping a customer when he and Pimp locked eyes. "What's up, my guy?" Queen stopped what he was doing to give Pimp some dap

"I'm just passing through. What's the mojo?"

"Ah, man, everything lovely, brother. I heard the good news, too. So, y'all opening the club tonight?"

Queen asked about the club Montay and Pimp had been working on. It was finally ready to open. It was a small sports bar/pool room Pimp named ICE.

"Yeah, grand opening tonight. Shit should be live. That's one reason I stopped by, so you can pass these flyers and t-shirts out to the hood, you know? We need our hood support. We gotta show who run the spot, feel me?" Pimp asked.

"Fuck yeah. Just leave 'em on the counter. I'll get to it when my help comes," replied Queen and started back with his customer.

Pimp went out to get the shirts and flyers. He walked outside and saw two young, cute females coming his way. They were the same girls who witnessed Pimp and Donte come through and told the police it was Shaw, as planned.

Pimp reached into the trunk as they approached. He came out with some flyers.

"Hey, Pimp, wassup? Can we come to the club tonight?" Ashley asked. The both of them were only 17, but had bodies like they were grown, and niggas in the hood sure treated them like they were. The other girl's name was Cindy.

Pimp passed Cindy the flyers and then pulled out an armload of shirts. He gave them to Ashley before saying, "Hell yeah. Y'all just can't drink. Asses better get lit before you come. And plus I'ma need y'all to do some selling of shot glasses, anyway. Y'all asses wanna be part of this team, ya ass gotta work."

Pimp grabbed more shirts and they took them into the store. Both girls were happy Pimp didn't say no to them coming to the club that night.

"Do we wear what we wanna?" Cindy asked.

"Nawl, I'ma get y'all something that match. Just write down your sizes," Pimp replied, and that's what they did.

Pimp had a thought and turned to Ashley. "Let me see your phone."

She gave him her cell after unlocking the screen. Pimp pulled his own phone out. He went through the contacts and, using her phone, dialed the number he was looking for. The phone rang three times and Diamond's baby-like voice picked up.

"Hello?"

"Baby, damn, you just not gonna respond to my last text? You that mad at me, boo? What's up?" He tried to sound as sweet as possible. He needed to find her ass.

Diamond didn't respond, so Pimp said, "You walking around almost 6 months wit' my son and you acting like you don't want me in his life. Ok, at first I said get rid of it because I had no plans to come back, but since you not gonna do it, then the least the both of us can do is take care of him. My first son, Diamond, and you not gonna let me in his life?" he pressed.

"I'm not saying that," Diamond finally spoke.

"Ok, what are you saying?" he asked.

"I want you in his life, Pimp. It's just I know you don't want the baby. And I know you, and I know I'm scared. So, to save my son's life, I'ma just wait 'til he's born."

"Diamond, that's crazy if you think I'll kill my own seed, let alone you. You ain't did shit to me but gave me love, baby girl. I'm not ruthless, and you know that. You never heard of me killing a kid, ma. Come on, don't try me like that." Pimp wanted her bad.

"I'm just scared, Pimp."

"Ok, I tell you what. I know where your mother stay, so let me give her some money for you. She can send it wherever it needs to go. I just want you comfortable and took care of. That's a start so you can see for yourself, but just let me be there when he's born."

"Ok, that's fine. I'm sorry, baby, I'm just–"

"Ain't no pressure, boo. And send me a picture of you. I know you fat," he laughed, fake kickin' it.

"Hush. And ok, I got you."

"Send it to my phone."

"Ok," she replied, and Pimp hung up. He knew he had to play her now and hope he could find her before she had the baby so he could choke the bitch out.

He gave Ashley back her phone, then dapped Queen before leaving the store. Jumping inside his SUV, Pimp sent Icey a text telling her the color to wear that night and what time to be at the club. He pulled off, headed to the mall to buy the perfect outfit for the night, and the two girls their outfits.

Pimp didn't know he was being tailed by Icey's best friend and his partner. They had successfully placed another tracker on his new ride while it was at the rim shop. Montay called him while Pimp hit the busy streets. He picked up Bluetooth through the speakers, hands free.

"Yo."

"What's good, shawty? What da hell you got going?" Montay's Atlanta slang came out.

"'Bout to bust up the mall real quick. Wassup?"

"Shit, just up here at the club wondering when you gonna show up. You know it's still lots to do before doors open," Montay said. Pimp had him running the club while he owned it and made every final decision.

"Couple hours, say 'bout three," Pimp told him.

"Ok, bet, 'cause I gotta go shopping, too," Montay added, and moments later they ended the call.

It took Pimp another fifteen minutes to get to the mall in the early traffic. He parked the whip, still oblivious to being followed and really not caring, either. He hopped out, leaving the pistol under the seat, and hit the alarm.

Pimp's mind instantly went to his feelings for Icey. This had to be right because it happened so fast and unexpectedly, and it felt so perfect. Sex with her was amazing last night, but being with her was something like heaven-sent. Pimp was loving the feeling he had when they just talked. He was adoring every aspect of their so-fast relationship. Last night he couldn't believe she agreed to move in with him, but he was happy she did. He couldn't wait.

Pimp had promised himself not to ever cheat on this woman. He had promised himself to never hurt her in no form and to protect her in every way possible. He was happy with this one, and that was all that really mattered to him.

The mall wasn't crowded, but people were all over shopping. Pimp had only one store in mind, so he walked into Neiman Marcus and dropped four racks on shoes and an outfit, and then he found Ashley and Cindy something to wear.

\*\*\*

## *Icey*

The club was live. So many people came out tonight to party that it was a shame. Icey saw plenty of ballers tonight while playing the upstairs offices. When Pimp burst through the door, he wore an out-of-this-world smile on his face. He threw open his hands.

"We did it, boo!" He shut the door and came toward Icey. She gave him her best smile as they embraced and shared a deep kiss.

"I see, boo, I see."

"Come downstairs. I want you to meet my folks," he said.

Icey pulled away from him. Her smile stayed painted on her face when she said, "Maybe later, Savarous. I don't feel the crowd right now."

"You okay, boo?" Concern was all over his face. He had love in his eyes.

"I'm fine." Then Icey kissed him with some tongue action.

After he left, she sat back in front of the monitor to see who else was there. She wasn't feeling too good, but didn't say anything to Pimp about it 'cause she didn't want his night to be messed up. She wanted to be as supportive as possible to her man.

The more and more she spent time with Savarous, the more she was falling in love, and she couldn't seem to get enough of him. To be honest, Icey was loving it because he was so caring and loveable. It was like he knew all the right spots for her to reach that point, and he knew just the right words to say to her at times. She loved this man.

Icey was happy and didn't want it to change. She reached into her bag to retrieve her cellphone and called Brad.

"What's going on?" he answered.

"Hey, what you doing?" she asked.

"Having dinner before work. Wassup?"

"I'm telling Savarous about the tracker on his car," Icey said. It was hard to say those words because Brad was gonna feel betrayed. She knew he would not understand, but she was a woman in love with the right man, and she needed to protect him.

"Icey, are you crazy? Do you know the things I saw today?" Brad said.

"I don't even wanna know, Brad. I don't care. I know he's street, but if he's not committed a crime, he's fine by me. And I'm asking for your blessing because I love him." Icey spoke from the heart.

"You don't love him, Icey. You just don't know. He's bad – real, real bad – and I'm not about to let you ruin your life messing with him. I just can't do it," Brad said back.

"I'm sorry, Brad. You know I love you and all, but that's something personal you have going on with him. Like I said, I'm telling him what's up and I'm standing by his side."

Icey meant what she said. She didn't care how Brad felt at that point because, as a friend, she asked for his blessing and got nothing. Icey stayed on the phone with Brad begging her not to say anything to Pimp, but her mind was made up. She was gonna tell him as soon as he came back into the office.

And just as she had that thought, Pimp walked in with two other guys. "Baby, I know you wasn't feelin' the crowd, so I brought two of my main men to meet you. This is Donte, my big li'l homie, and this is Montay. If you ever need anything, these two will be there. These some solid niggas." He put his hands on each of their shoulders and smiled before going on to say, "D and Montay, this wifey Icey Jones. And this is who," he paused, walked toward his girl, took her body into his arms, and gave her a quick peck, "this who y'all gon' forever find me with."

"Baby, we need to talk, like right this second." She gave him a look he'd never seen on her face.

He quickly turned toward the guys. "Say, I'ma catch y'all in the VIP. Lemme have a word with wifey."

Donte looked like he wanted to say something, but for some strange reason he held his tongue. When the door closed behind them, Savarous took a seat behind the desk. A concerned look was painted on his cute baby face.

"Baby, what's wrong?" he asked.

Icey walked over to his desk. She sat on it and they stared into each other's eyes. She was so in love. He was in love. She saw no wrong in this man. He couldn't help being raised in the streets. He was in college at least, and a business man. He wasn't out on no corner slanging rocks or shooting up the streets. So what if he had hood in him? He had more good than bad, or at least that was what Icey thought.

Just when she was about to open her mouth, some knocking came at the office door. Pimp broke their eye contact and got up from his chair. He patted his girl's thigh in passing and walked to the door he opened it up and was face-to-face with two of his bouncers. They held onto a guy who was wiggling, trying to get out of the big dudes' grip, but couldn't.

Pimp wondered what was going on and asked, "What's this?" He pointed.

"This nigga was caught snooping around your whip, boss, and we found this on him." One of the bouncers pulled out a listening device and monitor.

Pimp took and examined it. "Fuck you got going on?" He turned, looking over his shoulder, and saw his girl watching him, so he didn't make a scene. He just faced her. "Baby, I'll be right back. Just hold that thought. Lemme go see what's going on, ok?"

"Baby, I'll just go home," Icey said.

Pimp didn't want her to leave. He turned back to the dude being held. "No, baby this wont take long"

"No, I need to go get packing anyways, and we'll talk when you get done here," said Icey. She walked over and lightly kissed his lips. Pimp agreed and left with the bouncers and a panicking dude whom she hoped like hell wasn't one of Brad's men.

Icey made it out of the club and into her car. She wasn't trying to see what was about to happen and was hoping nothing went down, but kinda knew the situation. So she left, heading home to pack her things.

# Chapter 26

## *Who Can I Trust?*

### *Savarous*

Pimp made his way into the utility room where the bouncers held the guy. He walked in with a mean expression on his face. He closed the door behind him and stood face-to-face with the dude. What was this nigga doing? What was going on? The only people who walked around with things like what he had was the cops.

"Nigga, you can either die or tell me what the fuck you was finna do with this." Pimp held up the device.

"Man, I swear I was just passing through, stealing and sh—"

Pimp punched him in the stomach hard, causing him to double over in pain from the gut blow. "Bitch-ass nigga, don't lie," Pimp stated, then pulled out a knife. He cut the guy's shirt open to check for a wire, then he striped him naked.

"Please, man, I'm telling you the truth," the dude begged, but Pimp wasn't hearing it.

He took the knife and stuck the tip up the guy's nose. "This the night you gon' die."

"Ok! Ok, man. This black dude and white boy paid me $200 to hook this shit up to your truck. I'm just a nigga off the streets, man. I'm just trying to make a living," the dude said, still in pain.

"By doing some police shit?"

"I didn't know, man. I'm fo'real, young blood. I just need me some money, man, that's all."

"What was they driving?" Pimp wanted to know.

"A Dodge Ram SUV, black with chrome wheels. Man, I swear if you let me go—"

"Shut up!" Pimp said while thinking who could be on him. Was it the feds or the local cops? Either way it went, he knew it was somebody of that nature. "Let this nigga go and sweep the entire parking lot. See if you can spot that Ram truck. I'm going to check the video, see what I can see," Pimp told his bouncers and left.

Of all nights this had to happen, why couldn't he just chill and enjoy his new, legit business? Motherfuckers always brought the bullshit out of him, Pimp thought while going back into the office. Coming up the hallway was Montay with a slick smirk on his face.

"Boy, yo' girl sho' 'nough tough, shawty."

They walked into the office. Pimp went straight to the video monitor and said over his shoulder, "Bouncers caught some junkie snooping 'round my whip tonight. The bitch had this." He gave Montay the device.

"What the fuck?" Montay looked at it and instantly knew what it was.

"I know, right?"

"FBI, shawty, is all I can think of," said Montay.

"You right. I thought the same shit. But then, too, the feds don't use junkies and shit. Feel me? They too professional with they shit. This smells like the local cops or some shit," Pimp said, giving Montay his own thoughts.

"True. Damn, I wonder what's up? We clean, though, is all I'm saying. So what's really good is the question," Montay added and took a seat. Pimp kept looking at the TV screens, trying to see whatever was out of place.

"Oh, best believe I'ma find out what's going on. But first things first, I'ma call my lawyer just to see if that stunt they pulled was legal if it is the cops. 'Cause if not, then shid, it's nothing to worry about. But if so, then we gotta move swift from now on, feel me?" asked Pimp.

That's when he thought he saw an SUV pass on screen, but he could only see the bottom part and rims. Pimp rewound it and pressed pause, then zoomed in to get a better look.

"Hell yeah. We need to find out, and fast," replied Montay.

Pimp's mind was at war with his common sense. He knew this act was the cops, but didn't know where they was coming from or how they was coming. He wondered did Murder Black spill the beans about Yummie and her friend? He wanted to find out badly what was going on.

He gave his lawyer a call and told him what had happened, and his lawyer told him it was illegal for a cop to have someone place a listening device on or in his car. After Pimp hung up, he called and had his car towed and swept for bugs. He called Icey, telling her to pick him up when the club closed, and for the rest of the night Pimp sat in his office in deep thought of his next best move.

***

## Icey

Icey didn't know why Savarous was pounding away at her insides. She didn't even bother to ask or to tell him how much he was hurting her. She just let him go until he came with a loud moan, and as he bit down on her neck, she caressed his back. Icey never saw him get as mad as he got tonight, even though he was cute when he was mad.

He rolled from between her legs and said nothing. No *I love you*, no *it was great* or *it was bad*, nothing. He just lay on his back with a hard look upon his face, and she thought she knew why it was there. Tonight, when they were at the club, something happened and went wrong. She quickly jumped in her car and called Brad, who confirmed it was his partner's idea to put the device inside Pimp's truck. He said it was to protect her, and that's when Icey lost it and told Brad off with harsh words of anger.

She was mad at her best friend for going against her and told him to stop or she would report him to his boss. Icey knew she had to let Pimp know what was going on.

She sat up in bed. Icey looked at the man she loved. He turned and looked at her. Pimp reached up, then softly rubbed her face.

"I love you, Pimp." Icey said his new nickname with a smile.

"I love you too, boo," he said back.

Her insides were on fire. She could feel how swollen her pussy lips were because Savarous went crazy inside her, and she was loving every second of it, even though it was painful.

Icey was about to tell him what was going on, but she didn't want to make Pimp dislike Brad because he was her best friend. She wanted both guys to get along with each other. For Pimp it was no problem, but Brad was so caught up on arresting Pimp. It was a shame, and she wanted it to end. Hopefully she'd scared Brad off, and the dude being caught red-handed was a sign to leave well enough alone.

Tonight when she picked Pimp up, he helped her pack all her clothes and small things. They would deal with her big things the next day. Icey's mother went nuts when her daughter said she was moving in with Pimp, and so did Brad, but she didn't care how anyone felt 'cause they didn't care for her feelings. She loved Pimp, and that was that.

Every moment spent with him she realized she was lucky and valued him as a man. Tonight he had a lot on his mind. She noticed and so badly wanted to ease his mind, but she would just let it die under the rug. By now Brad should have had the picture to fall back, and the frame, too. All Icey wanted was to be happy, and she was. She met Savarous and was hooked and loving it to the max.

In the wee hour of the night they both held each other and fell asleep in a spooning position. It felt so right being in his arms. She felt so safe, so cared for, and she thanked God for it.

\*\*\*

*Savarous*

When Pimp awoke the next morning, he found Icey in the kitchen making breakfast. That was something about her he loved: she didn't mind cooking and could cook.

Icey smiled when she saw Pimp take a seat at the table where Icey had pictures scattered everywhere. "Let me clean this table."

She began to get the pictures, but Pimp stopped her by saying, "I got it, baby. Go 'head and finish breakfast."

"Aw, thank you, boo." Icey blushed.

She was so, so sexy to Pimp. He just loved to watch her.

He started gathering all the pictures up when he noticed Brad's pictures. He looked at a few and saw in two of them Brad was standing by a Ram truck on shiny rims. Pimp also saw almost all of the pictures of him had this black guy with him, who had to be his partner. Pimp's mind went back to what the junkie said and looked at the pictures again before putting them in the box on the floor. He was very thoughtful, now more than ever, and only wanted to find out what was up.

Pimp tried to keep his mind positive, but it was hard when the facts stood in his face. He kinda felt in his heart, and almost was certain, that it was Icey's best friend on him, but really Pimp wasn't sure. But he was kinda sorta sure it had to be. Did Icey have anything to do with it? His heart skipped a beat at thoughts of her playing him. Now he was wondering was she a federal agent? Had he been set up like his father? Pimp had to shake those thoughts off.

"Baby, you're amazing," he said. "And I'm happy."

"I am, too," replied Icey and put some plates on the now-clean table. She leaned over and kissed him on the lips. "How did you sleep?"

"I slept like a king."

"Great, 'cause I slept like a queen."

They both sat at the table and ate their food. Icey's mind was on their future, their happiness, and most of all their safety. Life for her was coming together. Savarous was thinking wicked thoughts of her best friend, the FBI white guy. He had thoughts to trick Icey to call him over and he'd kill the white boy and his friend. Pimp's lawyer said it was illegal for them to do what they done, and Pimp ran with that.

His heart dropped when he thought of killing Brad, because he knew he would have to—

Pimp shook his head at the thought. He had to shake it off. He couldn't see himself hurting her. He couldn't see himself doing no harm to this girl, so he had to shake it off as fast as the thought came. He had to do something about it, and do something fast.

"Baby, why you leave last night like that?" Pimp decided to try to get his mind in order, get his thoughts off murder.

"Baby, I was just trying to get out the way and let you handle yo' business. So, what did you figure the guy had going on?" she replied and asked.

"I called my lawyer and asked if that could be done, and he said no," Pimp told her while eating his food.

She, too, ate and pondered what he had just said before saying, "Well, who was it? Do you know?"

"I kinda think I do, baby."

"Who?" Icey wanted to know.

Pimp put his fork down and leaned back in his chair at the table. He looked across to the woman he loved so much so soon and cleared his throat. "Last night that junkie said a white and black dude paid him to put that device in my car. He also said that he drove a Ram truck on chrome wheels. Yo' best friend." Pimp got up and grabbed a picture of Brad. He gave it to her. "Yo' friend drive a Ram truck on chrome wheels, and his partner is black." He sat back down and stared at his girl, waiting for her response.

"You right, baby. Brad, he's so convinced that you this very bad person. He's so bent on proving to me that you have played me, but I don't believe him. I never have, I never will. I was gonna tell you this the other day, baby, but I just asked Brad to leave it alone in hopes he would, but he won't. So, if you can get your lawyer to take that device and turn it in, then Brad would be in deep shit. But it will save you. And at the same time, baby, if you are slanging drugs, then stop, because its haters everywhere." Icey felt so much better when she got that off her chest.

"Damn, baby, how long he been on me like dat?" Pimp was surprised. He was surprised not by Brad, but by her knowing this and not saying nothing. Was she truly his soul mate? Was she really his everything?

"Every since your charges was dismissed."

She told the truth, but it got her no points with him. He was mad. He was hurt by the fact she hadn't told him.

"And you just now saying something, baby?" asked Pimp.

"I'm sorry, Savarous. I just didn't want you and Brad to be at each other's necks. I love him; he's my best friend. I love you; you're the best I've ever had. And I want both of y'all in my life. That's why I didn't say anything, because you would surely not wanna deal with him, and he was only trying to prove to me that you some thug, which I don't even care. I swear, I just wanna be happy how I am," Icey stated, but it was like her words went in one ear and out the other. Pimp was baffled and pissed. He felt betrayed by her for some reason, no matter what she was saying.

But Pimp didn't say anything because he could just be tripping, so he wanted to calm down first. "It's all good, baby. I think I'ma let my lawyer put some fire up under Brad's ass for me. You right, I need to save myself, boo. So, is there anything else I need to know, baby? I mean anything?"

"I promise that's it," Icey replied.

Jerry Jackson

# Chapter 27

## *Different Plan, Same Mission*

### *Savarous*

"Say, Montay? Find the tapes from the grand opening of this club. I need to see something," Pimp said.

"Check!" Montay went to do as told. He walked out of the office and across to the main control room.

Pimp closed his eyes for a second to try to gather his thoughts. It was a pain in the ass trying to figure out who was who and what was what and who to trust. Montay was almost his right-hand man, yet he placed nothing past him, either.

Montay walked in with six tapes in his hands and placed them on Pimp's desk. "These are the tapes from all angles of the club and parking lot."

Pimp pulled out the picture of Brad.

He and Pimp watched every tape very closely, twice just to be sure. He saw the entire truck in two of the six tapes and grabbed some still shots of Brad and his partner, making sure he gave these to his lawyer. He was about to get this boy fired, fuck suspended. He needed to go get out of the picture, point blank.

Since he left Icey that morning his mind was racing trying to figure the best route to take. He calmed down and thought to still trust his girl and his heart, because he saw her intentions were near perfect in his eyes. He liked how she made him feel, and then he also understood where she was coming from, not trying to lose her best friend and her man, so Pimp brushed it off and focused on Brad.

Pimp left the club with the tapes and the device. He called his lawyer to let him know he was on his way over. It only took him 20 minutes to get to the office his lawyer was at.

Icey was moving her big stuff to his house today and putting some in storage. He was happy about that, was gonna love to wake up every day with this woman.

Pimp entered the office to find three lawyers seated at the table with folders and folders of paperwork. Mr. James stood up. He was the man Pimp paid six million dollars to. They shook hands, Pimp gave his lawyer everything, and they spoke only a moment. He had a team of lawyers, but mainly for his father's freedom.

"I'll have him suspended, then demoted, then fired," the lawyer assured Pimp. They shook hands once again, then Pimp left. He had other shit to do. He had a plan set in motion that he had to see through.

He met back up with Icey and the movers at her house to get the last of her things. When Pimp pulled up, she was in the big truck with one of the movers.

Icey rolled the window down as Pimp parked. "Baby, we are headed to the storage. Load the other truck up with them boxes in the basement," Icey told him.

"Ok, I got it, baby," Pimp shot back, heading into the house with other movers. He was glad this was the final trip. The living room was completely empty, along with the kitchen, dining room, and master bedroom. The only things left were one bedroom and the basement.

When Pimp walked into the living room, he couldn't help but notice a black dot in the corner of the wall. It kinda looked like a camera, but it wasn't. He walked up closer on it and noticed it was a small microphone.

Pimp's eyes scanned the entire living room, where he noticed three more. He then checked her entire house; he was heartbroken by what he found as he walked around, looking. He only found four more in her bedroom, which made him feel even worse. Icey was playing a dangerous game. He was almost where he needed to be with his father coming home, and in the midst of it he was being set up by someone he loved.

He couldn't believe Icey had been recording their many conversations, and why? She had just shattered his dreams of their forever. This was her second strike, and she couldn't be trusted.

Her best friend was a fed. He should have known to fall back off her from the jump, damn how pretty she was. There were a million more pretty bitches in this world, but Pimp was swindled by something more than beauty. He was captivated by grace and charm. He was in love. *But love don't feed me*, was his next thought.

Pimp was defeated. He didn't like this feeling. He was hurt on the inside 'cause he had been fooled.

Not anymore. She would not get a third swing at his trust. He'd given it to her twice, and she missed both times.

Inside his truck, Pimp drove to the house, followed by the movers. His mind was in a daze, his heart was in a sling, and his common sense didn't bring any sense. He just was there, down and out, not really caring anymore. Why was he even allowing her to move into his home? She would bug it soon too, probably.

Icey didn't even seem to look the same when he tried to picture her, and he knew then that he had to confront her about what he'd found. He couldn't and wouldn't let a day go by.

Icey and the other movers pulled up an hour after Pimp made it. He took the time to ramble through her personal things and came up with nothing. He found nothing out of place. He was in their bedroom, sitting on the bed when she walked in holding some shirts. She tossed them across her chair and walked over to Pimp.

"Baby, I'm so tired. Lord!" Icey sat across his lap and pecked him on the lips, not knowing that was probably their last kiss. She felt something wasn't right 'cause his kiss was dry, and she saw it in his eyes. She stood to her feet and asked him, "Is everything alright?"

"What's your real name? Where do you really work? Are you the feds?" Pimp also stood up. He took a quick step toward Icey, and she took two steps back. Then Pimp stopped because he had a house full of people, but he was mad and hurt.

"Baby, what is you talking about?" She was confused.

"Don't act stupid. What's this?" Pimp tossed her two of the eight bugs he found at her house.

Icey looked at them, then back up to Pimp and shook her head. "I don't know what it is, baby."

"Baby? You don't know what it is? Fuck you think I am?" Pimp wanted to slap the shit out of her, but he held himself back.

"I swear I'm lost," Icey pleaded. She looked at the bugs again in her hand.

"Yeah the fuck right. What's up with this police shit, you and yo' boy?"

"Savarous, I swear I'm telling you God's honest truth. I don't know what's going on. Where did you find them?" she asked, which made Pimp laugh a little.

"In yo' living room, in yo' bedroom. I guess you forgot to take them down. You was so busy recording us, trying to railroad a nigga, but for what?" Pimp slapped the bugs out of her hands wanting it to be her face. It made her jump in fear, not knowing his next move. He walked off mad, and she knew it.

"It was Brad, baby. It had to be. I forgot when me and you first met, he wanted me to bug the house. But after you beat your case. I never let him finish, and I promise I forgot about it, especially since we got serious. You gotta believe me. I'll never turn on you, Savarous! I love you, for real," Icey proclaimed.

"Bullshit!"

"Please believe me, baby." Icey started crying.

Pimp was hurt and wanted to cry, too, but he was a li'l harder than that. He wanted to believe her. He wanted to give in to his wants and needs, but at the same time one slip could stop everything he'd worked so hard for, and he just couldn't let his heart be the reason.

Or could he? Pimp just walked out of the room, and Icey broke down crying even harder than before.

Pimp needed to clear his mind, so he left her there at the house and hit the streets. He linked up with Montay at the club. Pimp did something he'd never done before when he got to the spot: he fixed himself a stiff drink and downed the entire shot, slamming the glass on the counter, then poured up some more. Montay just watched the employees, really didn't pay the owner no attention, so they didn't notice at all the pain Pimp was going through.

***

## Icey

She was up in bed, waiting on Pimp to come home, and was extremely happy when he walked through the bedroom door. It was 2:00 a.m., and she'd been up crying and in heated arguments with her mom and Brad – especially Brad. Icey gave it to him so bad, and in the end ended their friendship. Brad loved Icey; they'd been best friends since second grade. He could not just continue to hurt her with his own needs, so he promised to fall back.

Icey agreed, and also got the blessing from her mother, seeing that her daughter was madly in love with Pimp and nothing could change that.

Pimp walked in, saying nothing. He just stripped out of his clothes and headed to the bathroom. The door was cracked open and Icey heard the shower going, so she got out of the bed and walked in on her man. The man she was not about to lose, no matter what.

Pimp was brushing his teeth when she walked in and stood to the side of him. She just looked at him while he looked at himself in the mirror, brushing his teeth.

"Can we talk?" She reached out and touched his arm.

"What's up, baby? What?" Pimp said after he spit his toothpaste out.

"It was Brad, and he promised it's over, baby. And I promise it's over, Savarous. I just wanna protect you, baby. And I know it's hard to trust me right now, but I'm telling you the truth. I'll never go against you. I truly got your back. Please, whatever you do, whatever you thinking, please don't give up on us, ok? Please." Icey shed a tear that she wiped away.

Pimp rinsed his mouth and looked at Icey. "Just forget it, baby. I mean, I know I'm clean and all. I just feel betrayed by you, that's all."

"But it's not me, though, baby."

"It's around you, though, Icey, and that shit don't sit well wit' me, you know? I'm just being honest. I love you, and that's why I'm here. That's why I'm home. I just don' know, baby."

"I'm so, so sorry, Savarous."

Icey just broke down crying, and he had to grab her and hold her. Something inside Pimp felt her honesty, plus while he was away he had done a lot of thinking. He weighed his options more than once and gave her the benefit of the doubt. He knew Icey loved him 'cause he could feel it, he could see it. But he was caution now more than anything.

Pimp had made up his mind, and that was why he was home, because love brought him there.

He finally got her to calm down with soft words and back rubs. "I love you so much that if you are against me, I'm willing to spend my life in jail being tricked by you," was all Pimp could say.

"I promise not to let you down. I'll show you," Icey replied, and they kissed.

She sat on the edge of the tub while he showered and talked, then they both retired to bed. Icey nestled under him, never wanting to move, never wanting to let go. She held onto him and talked. She just talked about everything until they both fell asleep around 5:00 a.m.

For the next three weeks Icey and Pimp got situated at his house. She took this time to cater to him hand and foot, to show and prove to him her loyalty. Brad even came around and apologized and explained to Pimp why he was at him. This didn't stop Pimp's lawyers from pushing the issue and getting Brad suspended, as promised, and putting a shield over Pimp. That was something he liked.

Pimp was spending his time at the club or at the house with her, just being around each other. Icey could see a change in him, but she hoped it away everyday in prayer that their relationship would go back to the same, as it deserved to be.

\*\*\*

Icey had happy, confused tears in her eyes. She was overly shocked and surprised to find out she was six weeks pregnant by Pimp. She was happy to share this part of life with him, but disappointed because she knew Pimp didn't want kids at all. He stated that when they first met. But then Pimp had to know what would happen when they had sex and he didn't pull out. He had to know what he was doing, point blank, ain't no way around it.

Six weeks pregnant. She couldn't believe it at all!

As she drove from her doctor's office in downtown Miami, she wanted to call Pimp badly and tell him, but at the same time she wanted to tell him face-to-face. All Icey knew was she would tell him today, not tomorrow, because she promised never to keep nothing from him. She also made the promise to support whatever choice he make on keeping the baby. Though she'd rather have her child, her love for him and his desire was more than what she wanted.

As Icey drove through downtown she wondered what her momma would say. How would she take the news? Would she be happy or be mad?

*Fuck it!* She pulled her cellphone out, pressed one, and let it ring. Icey wanted to cry, yet she wanted to smile. This whole situation was confusing.

"Hi, baby!" Her momma broke Icey's train of thought when she picked up the phone. Her voice alone calmed her a little bit.

She was feeling like a young kid again as she said, "Hey, Ma. What you doing?"

"Oh, honey, nothing. Cleaning up, like always. About to watch my shows." Icey's momma loved her some Charmed with them three girls. Whenever she had issues she would go to her momma's house and they would watch the show and talk.

"Can I come by and watch it with you, Ma?" Icey asked.

"Baby, you know you can. Icey, is—? What's going on?" She knew her daughter all too well, and Icey began to choke up.

"I'm on my way. We'll talk."

"Okay, I'm here."

Icey hung up the phone and mashed on the gas. Twenty minutes later she walked into the house to find her mother right in front of the TV, eating a pickle.

She never even looked up when she spoke. "Go fix you something to eat. I know yo' butt ain't ate, have you?"

"No, I can't eat. My stomach won't take nothing," Icey replied while taking a seat next to her.

"You sick, girl?"

"Som' like that, I guess."

"Icey, girl, don't tell me you're pregnant!"

That remark made the tears fall fast from Icey's eyes. She fell onto her mother's shoulders. Her momma wrapped her strong hands around her baby like when she was a small girl.

"Momma, I'm scared."

"Icey, baby, what was you thinking to let that boy get you pregnant?"

"It just happened, Ma."

"So, you plan to keepin' it?"

"Yes." Icey broke down crying into her mother's embrace.

***

### Savarous

After Pimp switched cars, he called Icey to see what she was doing and when she would be home. He was missing her stupid crazy. She picked up in a very lazy, tired voice. He wondered what was going on with his woman.

"Hey, pretty. Yo, what's good?"

"Hey, baby."

The way she spoke made him know something wasn't right. Any other time she'd damn near jump through the phone at him. "Icey? What's wrong?" he asked.

"Tired, boo. Missing you, also," she replied with a yawn.

"Damn, baby, I wanted you to come out tonight and party with me. Shid, I guess I'll just come home. We'll spend coolin' time then, how 'bout that?" Pimp said.

"That's fine, baby. We need to talk anyways," Icey replied.

"Ah, shit. What now, baby?" He couldn't help but be spooked.

"It's nothing bad, baby. Just come home," Icey said in a humble voice.

"A'ight, I'll be home soon, baby. I love you," Pimp told her.

He disconnected the call after Icey said, "I love you, too."

Pimp drove over to the projects to see what was going on out there. He'd spent most of his time at the club getting it up and running and settling in with Icey. He liked waking up daily with her. It was this good feeling he got when he rolled over and she was there beside him, looking amazing.

It was still hard trying to trust again once that trust was broken, but Pimp put a lot of effort into it and gave trusting Icey another chance. He could never trust Brad. No matter how many *I'm sorry*s he proclaimed, Pimp didn't care. He did tell Icey he didn't hold that against Brad, but he lied, he even told Brad he accepted his apology, but he again lied.

Pimp pulled up to the blue store. It was crowded all of a sudden, and he'd never seen it like that. Just like any hood, Pimp knew what had happened before he got to the door.

There had been a shooting, and Queen got hit twice. He was in critical condition. Police came and went, and all that was left was niggas and hos stressing what they was gonna do.

Pimp saw Ashley posted with her friend, Cindy. He called them both over, rolling down his window. He knew if anybody had facts, then it will be those two. Cindy leaned up in the truck as Ashley stood back.

"Da fuck happened here?" Pimp wanted to know.

"Niggas robbed Queen this morning, all we know. But ChinO and them boys from across the streets said it was them Pine Brooks niggas who be slick hating," Cindy said, and Ashley agreed with a shake of her head.

"Did they get anything? Did them niggas jam?"

"ChinO say they took Queen off for everything. You know, meaning the drugs and money," added Ashley, stepping up on the truck also.

Pimp took everything in they said, then told Ashley, "Aye, go get this dude ChinO."

"Alright."

Ashley went to do as told as Cindy stood right there telling him all she knew of the crew that robbed Queen and shot him. Pimp knew he had to be careful out in the streets 'cause there was a chance he could be watched by the feds. He still didn't trust Brad, or the government for that matter, so Pimp knew to play it safe and not do anything stupid. 'Cause this wasn't Texas. This was Miami, and it was a different time now.

Pimp listened to Cindy ramble on and on about the crew and what they was really about. He had his ears open, but his mind was other places. Diamond had finally agreed to let him visit the doctor with her the last three months. and he was still yet to find her. The situation with the money was going good, and they talked almost every night when Pimp was at the club 'cause he refused to disrespect Icey by having conversations with someone other than her at their home.

He tried his damnedest to ease Diamond's fear of him doing something to her. He wanted to just get to her before she delivered the baby so he could put an end to her bullshit, but Diamond wouldn't budge. Pimp didn't have much time at all to make something happen.

He saw Ashley and two teenage boys come across the street toward him. "Which one ChinO?" Pimp asked Cindy before the three got near.

She turned, looked, then said, "The tall one."

Chino was tall and lanky with short dreads – he was fresh. As he approached the truck, Pimp got out himself and stood there waiting. The boys were around 17 or 18, he noticed.

"What's going on, big bruh?" ChinO asked, stopping in front of Pimp.

"You know them niggas who robbed the hood?"

"Only one. His name Champ. The other two I never seen," ChinO replied.

"What about you?" Pimp asked the dude who was with ChinO.

"I just know Champ," the boy said, agreeing with his friend.

Pimp pondered for a second. If his count was correct, then Queen had just gotten a fresh three kilos and had well over 100 grand in stash. That was a loss Pimp had no plans of taking for free, and the only payment he'd accept was death. Somebody had to die, no ifs, ands, or buts about it.

"'Preciate the info. Y'all fall through tonight at the spot. Its on the house for y'all," Pimp told the teens and got back in the truck. He had to go see about Queen first, make sure he made it out.

Inside the truck he called Montay, telling him what was going on, then he called Icey.

"Baby?" she picked up.

"Baby girl, one of my friends just been shot in a store robbery. I'm headed to the hospital now to see about him, so I'll be a little late on our talk, ok?" he told his woman.

"Is everything ok, baby? You alright?" Concern was in her voice.

"Oh yeah, boo, I'm good. I wasn't there," Pimp assured her 'cause he knew he had to. After ending the call with Icey, he drove to the hospital speeding, hoping Queen made it out alive, and then he wondered how Queen allowed somebody to run up on him like he did. Pimp was always on point 'bout gangsta shit. He was always ready to bust his gun 'cause the first one to pop mainly was the winner of the game, and Pimp had no losses.

When he arrived at the hospital, there was so much going on. Queen's entire family was there. Everyone was crying and falling out when Pimp got off the elevator, which only confirmed what Pimp didn't want to know. Queen had not made it. He died moments before Pimp got there. Pimp was told by Queen's uncle, one of the only people in the family who was calm. Pimp offered his condolences and quickly left before the cops got there.

There was nothing else to do in the streets but go to jail or to die, and how Pimp was feeling at the moment he needed to be at the house. He hated to be tried. He hated when niggas thought they could take what he'd took. Yeah, he had to get home before he did something stupid without thought, and that was something he didn't want.

Jerry Jackson

# Chapter 28

*Surprised by Love*

*Savarous*

He rolled over in the middle of the night to find Icey balled up with a peaceful look on her beautiful face. When he got home she was asleep, so he didn't bother her. He just got a shower and climbed in next to the love of his life and held her small frame in his arms while he thought of the perfect get-back on the niggas who took Queen's life.

He kissed the side of her face, moved hair that was in his way, and kissed her again.

Icey stirred a little, then opened her eyes, focusing on her man. She reached out, grabbed his baby face, and kissed him back on the lips.

Before Pimp could say or do anything, he heard her say, "I'm pregnant. Six weeks." Icey didn't remove her eyes from his own. She didn't want to miss no reaction from him. She wanted to see the real answer, statement, whatever just as long as it was real.

At first all Pimp did was stare at her without words, and he didn't flinch at all. It was hard to read him, and that alone bothered Icey. She started to sit up, but couldn't move due to the firm grip Pimp had on her.

"You said that like you mad, baby. Are you?" Pimp let her go and also sat up. He reached for her shirt, lifted it, and stared at her stomach. He placed his hand over her belly. "I'm not mad."

"Thought you didn't want any kids?" she asked, confused. She couldn't believe he just said those words

"Not until I met you. What about you, though? How do you feel?"

"I feel like how much we did it unprotected, you tried to succeed in knocking me up. But however it go, I am happy if you wanna keep our child, and I'll be supportive, but sad if you didn't."

"Well, be happy, baby, 'cause I am. And that's real. My friend was killed this morning, so it may seem as if I'm not, but to share a life with you is amazing in itself. I love you," Pimp said, then leaned down to kiss her stomach.

He had just made everything perfect with his words. "I love you too, baby."

"Show me, 'cause I don' believe you."

"You better."

Pimp laid her on her back. He got up on the bed on his knees looking down at his lifeline. Icey only wore a t-shirt and cotton shorts that Pimp pulled down her sexy legs and off her cute feet. He pushed her shirt up to her neck and went to sucking on her breasts one at a time, very passionately. And with his one free hand he rubbed her pussy until his entire hand was soaked with her pussy juice.

Icey rotated her hips as Pimp made love to her middle with his fingers and drove her crazy with his tongue. Pimp kissed up and down her chest and stomach softly until he was between her thighs, face-to-face with her fat pussy, which was shaved and wet-wet.

Pimp kissed her there once. He looked at it and kissed her there twice. Then he spread her lips and with the tip of his tongue he made tiny circles over her protruding clit. Pimp clasped his top and bottom lip over her clit and softly sucked, grabbing a moan from her and an arch of the back. Pimp then sucked her clit a little harder and moved his tongue side-to-side. Icey pushed at his head because she couldn't really take it like that, but Pimp didn't stop. He kept going until she came, creaming his entire face.

Her pussy tasted so good that Pimp flipped her over and made her put her ass in the air as he drove his long tongue in and out of her pussy hole. She gripped the sheets from the bliss she felt.

Nobody had ever eaten her, let alone ate her out as Pimp was doing. Icey came again, only this time she screamed her orgasm into her pillow, then lay flat on her stomach.

Pimp was rock hard. He straddled her from behind and slapped her booty with his hardness. Icey turned her head sideways to steal a look at him over her shoulder. Pimp bit down on the bottom of his lip as he grabbed his dick and placed it at her pussy lips. He moved it up, then down, up and down, coating his dick head with her wetness. He eased in just a tease and pulled back out of her, slapping her ass with his dick again.

"Baby, put it in. Make love to me," Icey said in a whisper and moaned as Pimp entered her tightness. He slid in and went to her neck with wet kisses as he began to stroke her, long and sometimes deep. Pimp made slow, slow, hard love to Icey in that position.

He switched it up and they both lay there sideways where he beat the pussy, going balls to pussy lips.

"Shit, baby, yo' pussy good," Pimp moaned in her ear, then said, "Wish I could get you pregnant again."

When pimp said the words, he came hard inside her, holding her tight and grinding into her ,and Icey enjoyed every moment of it. She held onto him, accepting every drop he let out in her tunnel of love.

Pimp let his dick slip out of her. He raised up on the side of her and kissed her beautiful lips.

"Baby, you the man," was all Icey was able to say as she closed her eyes. Pimp cuddled with her. He closed his own eyes, and for the first time ever he thanked God he had her.

Within minutes Icey was asleep, but for Pimp there was no sleep. Even though he was drained, he still couldn't sleep. He had too much on his mind right now.

He heard his phone vibrate a text and grabbed it. It was the wee hours of the night, so it had to be important, he thought.

He looked and saw it was Diamond. Pimp sat up when he saw the message. It was her address. She was in Atlanta, in the Buckhead area.

Pimp jumped up quickly, waking Icey from her ten-minute doze. "My fault, baby. I gotta dip out. Important. I'll text you later. Get some rest, beautiful, ok? Love you," Pimp said.

"You ok? I hate when you start moving faster than your brain thinks the thought. Are you ok, Savarous?" she just wanted to know while sitting up.

"Everything is perfect, baby, I swear."

# Chapter 29

*Either Now or Never*

*Diamond*

Diamond had sent the text and hoped for a reply, but when she didn't get it the fear started to kick in even more. But then she thought about it. It was 3:00 a.m. Pimp must be asleep. He had to be, right?

Well, sleep was the last thing on her mind. For Diamond it was more like worrying about the what-ifs and what-nots. She got up from her plush sofa chair.

She was big as a house, her mother would say. Diamond was almost 6 months now, and all she could hope for was that her son came out healthy and strong and that her dream would come true one day: that she and Pimp could raise him together. Pimp was a good dude, so she knew he would make the best dad any child could get. For the past two months all Pimp had been doing was taking care of her, making sure she had everything she needed. He always texted or called to check up on her, and that meant a lot to her. They shared pictures with each other through the phone, and in every picture Pimp was looking like money.

With every conversation and every picture Diamond became more comfortable with the thought of seeing Pimp face-to-face. It had been so long since she'd seen him, touched him, smelled him. She just wanted to hug him once, kiss him once, just be near. And that's why she was up at 3:00 a.m. texting him while he slept.

Before she made the choice to give Pimp her address, she had a very long, heartfelt talk with her parents, who agreed to let Pimp come over since he was the one paying the bills. They didn't think he would hurt their daughter. He took care of her too well to wanna hurt her like Diamond had thought at one time.

Her mom suggested she place video cameras around the house just in case when he did show up. They would have evidence of anything bad going on. Diamond didn't wait. She called and had nine cameras installed the next day after talking to her mother and father. She was somewhat fearful, but she was also hopeful because, for some strange reason, the past two months Pimp had been acting just as she prayed for him to act. And that was the scary part about it all.

Leaving the living room, her phone in hand, she decided to retire to her bedroom so she could at least try to rest. Her house was large, a three-bedroom out in Buckhead, a nice area in Atlanta, GA. Pimp paid all her bills and car note, too. He made sure she was good, and for that Diamond was grateful to even have anything to do with him. Her bedroom was plush and set in white and lavender. Her bed was soft as she climbed in it, wishing Pimp was there with her so they could hold each other and sleep peacefully.

Everything was going as good as could be expected. Diamond picked up her phone and looked at the screen just to see if any messages popped up, preferably Pimp's. She didn't see anything.

*He asleep*, she thought, and found comfort between two pillows. She let her mind continue to wander, wonder, and pray at the same time until her eyes began to get heavy and sleep took over.

Diamond was just a young girl in love, trying to force her happiness with pure intentions. Pimp was her dream come true, her life crush. If she could only have him as she wanted him, life would be so much better. She was ready to see him, ready to close this distance between them, ready for her son to meet his father, ready for love.

Or at least that's what she thought.

\*\*\*

*Icey*

Icey woke up later that morning and saw Savarous was gone. He didn't really say much last night, but she knew it had to be bad with how fast he got out of bed right after their lovemaking. She was hoping everything was ok, but knew it wasn't.

Six miss calls from Brad and a few voicemails scared her as she sat up in bed.

"Shit," Icey mumbled and called him back. The phone rang five times before Brad picked up.

"Icey!"

"Yes, wassup?"

"I told you! I knew it. I knew it! Your boy, he is big trouble. Government just approved to launch an official investigation on Savarous Jones and his father, who's already serving life in the federal pen. Government has so much evidence that he's a murderer, drug dealer, and mastermind. One of his boys got popped in North Carolina with some diamonds and couldn't take the heat from the home invasion case. He testified that Pimp was the mastermind behind the robbery."

"Brad, that man could just be lying," Icey defended her man.

"I thought about that, too, but it's not me who's been working the case. And from what I was told, that statement was just the groundwork that made us pay him attention. Did you know he's in his last year in college? That he spends $1,000 to fly to Atlanta and $1000 to get back twice a week? Ask yourself, how did he afford the club? Those cars? Icey, baby, listen. Get out while you can. Do not let him destroy your life, 'cause the government got him by the balls, and they will not let go. Trust me on this one, ok?" Brad told his best friend, but Icey wouldn't, couldn't believe him. She had faith in Pimp. He'd shown her nothing of what Brad or any government was saying about him.

"Brad, I'm pregnant by Savarous. I'm happy, and frankly I don't believe what you are saying. I lived with this man a few weeks now. I see every step he makes, so what are you saying?" Icey defended the one she loved.

"Icey, you just dick drunk. This man is a killer, a vicious drug dealer, and you so blind that you can't see it when it's right in your face. Ask yo'self why do he drive a Benz? Why do he own a beachfront? Where do he get his income? Come on, baby girl, you gotta think with sense, not with feelings. The government is coming at him strong, and I just don't want you to be caught up in it, that's all, 'cause I love you for real. He don't love you, Icey," Brad told her, but she had her mind made and heart set.

"Ok, well, thanks for the info. How's your mom?" Icey sarcastically changed the subject.

He didn't answer. "And you're pregnant?" Brad asked.

"Yes, I am," Icey replied proudly, knowing her words would hurt Brad, but he was doing too much. "Anyways, I thought you was suspended."

"Yeah. Not fired, though, and word is out already. It's not a game. It's not me just trying to show you something. This is facts. This is real life, and Savarous Jones' life is about to come crashing down around his feet. He's smart, but not that smart."

"Whatever, Brad. Bye." Icey couldn't hear any more.

She hung up without his reply and called Pimp, but his phone went straight to voicemail. She called two more times to get the same results, then sent him a short text telling him what Brad had just said. All Icey could think about was protecting her man at all costs.

She got out of the bed and just stood there a second. Curiosity had grabbed her, and she did wonder how Pimp lived so high-fashion, from his cars to his crib. But she did remember him telling her he had money when they first met and how he got it.

Icey walked out of their room and into Pimp's office. It was a room he kept locked, but she knew where he kept the key, so she found it and went inside.

His office consisted of a glass desk, table, a laptop and printer, leather seating, and beautiful paintings he purchased from her store. Icey walked inside, closing the door. She needed to just look around. She needed to just find nothing – nothing that would point out any truth in what her best friend was saying.

Pimp's office was neat. Nothing was out of place as she went through his paperwork and bank statements. She saw he only had 90 thousand dollars in his saving and 19 in his account.

Icey looked at the club ownership forms Pimp had sitting on the desk, and it showed where he inherited the club from business with Murder Black and his wife, who were true owners. Icey put the papers back. She searched some more and found the deed to his house. She saw he only put down 10 grand on the property and had a mortgage for $1,900 per month. She also saw Pimp leased his Benz and new truck.

She returned the paperwork and was about to get up when she noticed one of her paintings was leaning a bit to the side. Icey remained seated behind the desk and looked hard for a moment just into space. She got up and thought like a crook. She looked at the walls, touched the walls, but found nothing. She searched every wall and still came up with not even a hidden safe.

Icey searched the floor and window seals and there was nothing – not until she looked over at his coat closet. She walked over and yanked it open. It was small. She pulled coats apart and was faced with a wall that she pushed, but it wouldn't give. She moved the coats from left to right and from right to left, and that's when she noticed the slide handle.

Icey looked, then reached for it. She slid the wall to her right to reveal a hidden door. Instantly she felt hot flashes and wondered what was inside that room. She turned the knob and it didn't open. She would need the key, but where would she find it?

Pulling the wall back in place and placing the coats properly, Icey went to find the key. She looked high and low in his office, coming up empty handed. She left the office, closing the door and going back into their bedroom.

At the thought of seeing Pimp with a tiny key he kept stashed in his jewelry case, she hurried across the room and found the key. Icey hoped like hell the key worked, and it did when she tried it. Icey's heart cracked with the trap door as it creaked open.

The lights were on and inside she saw so much it instantly shocked her, made her stop and stare. She couldn't move. Icey laid eyes on crates of money wrapped in plastic, piled in a corner and stacked from the floor to the ceiling. She also saw large amounts of drugs piled up on an iron table, so many guns and knifes. What really scared the life out of her was when she saw Pimp had pictures of the attorney general, Ms. Greene, and one of the federal judges. He had pictures of federal agents that were dead with an X across each picture, pictures of Brad and his partner, and a few more faces she didn't recognize.

Brad was right, and she was wrong and heartbroken. She had just found out the truth, and it killed her entire dream of them. Icey saw maps, notes, dates, and times. She saw passports, bulletproof vests, and gas masks. Pimp had in that room everything it took to be a killer, a drug dealer, a hit man. What she mostly paid attention to was a picture of an older man who looked like he could be Pimp. There was a circle around him, and underneath the word *Mission* was written. Without touching anything, Icey left the room and put everything back like she found it, then locked his office back, too. Again she called and still got the voicemail. Icey couldn't hold back the tears. She broke down, falling to the bed, balled up with her pillow. She couldn't believe Pimp tricked her.

*** 

*Savarous*

Atlanta had busy streets coming from the College Park Airport, but Pimp weaved in and out of traffic, not caring about speed limits. He just wanted the highway.

He had sent Diamond a text – a beautiful text – telling her he'd be out here tomorrow, but little did she know he was about to make a surprise visit, and make a bloody mess if need be. He could only hope nobody else was around, because they, too, would fall by the wayside.

Pimp sped down Camp Creek, where he was about to hit 285, and all he could think about was murder and how hard-headed Diamond was. All she had to do was get rid of the unwanted child, but like a fool she bucked, and that was even more reason to kill the bitch.

His phone vibrated a few texts as he punched down 285. Most were from Montay saying Shaw and Donte were in Miami, waiting on him to move on them Pine Street niggas. That wasn't the text he was worried about, though.

Pimp had to reread her message two times before it hit him. The feds were coming at him was what she said, and that showed a sign of the loyalty he needed from his woman. He appreciated her for that, especially when she said her best friend was the one who called and told her. Pimp knew he was good. He knew the feds couldn't have nothing solid on him at all. Nobody could take him down but himself, and that was a no-no. Pimp sent an *I love you* text to Icey, then made a call to his lawyer.

"Savarous, glad you called. I was just about to reach you. How are you?" one of his many lawyers said.

"What's good? Talk to me," Pimp stated.

"Ok. Seems the government has placed a freeze on your accounts and has issued a warrant to search your beachfront and club."

"Why they doing all this shit?" Pimp wanted to know, moving in and out of traffic. "Is this shit legal?"

"Yes, I hate to say. But all they are doing is turning over rocks and finding nothing. All your paperwork is good. We've double checked everything. The firm is working to get the government off your back. Let's just hope your home is clear. Is it?" the lawyer asked.

"Yeah, I'm good," replied Pimp.

"As of right now you are safe in standings, so keep a clean look at all times, 'cause the government is watching yo' every move," said the lawyer.

"When are they doing the search?"

"Probably as we speaking, probably preparing, probably been did it. Where are you?"

"Atlanta."

"Ok, you are good. So, let me get back to work with the team so we can have our defense right. Call us if need permits," spoke the lawyer.

"Ok, keep me posted," replied Pimp and they ended the call. He wasn't feeling the news, but wasn't worried either. Pimp felt his phone vibrate with a text; it was from Icey.

*Where are you?*

*Out on business. I'll be home in a few hours. Just got a call from my lawyer, the feds are coming to search the house.* He sent his reply.

*Is there anything here for them to find?* Icey asked.

*No, but leave 'cause I do not want you harassed.*

Pimp waited for a reply, but it never came, so he put the phone down and focused on getting to Buckhead so he could get this over with and get back to Miami so the he could face the feds.

Looking at his GPS, it read that he had 35 minutes before he reached Diamond's address, giving her only 40 more minutes to live.

\*\*\*

## *Diamond*

Diamond was joyous when she received the text from Pimp about showing up tomorrow. She was excited, but she was scared, too, because she didn't know what to expect out of this. And as the saying went, she said it different. Diamond was hoping for the best, looking for the best. All she wanted was the best.

She had, not too long ago, gotten out of the shower prepared to watch a movie, waiting on her mother to get there, relaxed in her bedroom.

She had to give it up to Pimp, for the past two months he'd elevated her status and banked her up. He took great care of her and his unborn son, and for that she respected him. Still not understanding why he left, but sweeping it under the rug was her plan, because for whatever reason he left, he did it for a come-up, and anybody who knew of Savarous Jones knew he was a hustler.

She grabbed the remote from the middle of the bed and clicked her T.V. on, feeling the baby move at the same time. It hurt due to him sitting at the bottom of her stomach. Diamond leaned back on a few throw pillows and started rubbing her big belly.

"I know you ready to come. Just wait on your daddy before you do," Diamond said out loud to her unborn.

Still rubbing her stomach, watching the big screen, she was greeted with so many different thoughts, but was mainly happy she decided to keep her baby and not abort him. All any girl wanted was a picture-perfect life and a protective spouse that they felt safety from. Someone that would lead them, support them, and keep them in line with life's lessons. Females just wanted that faithful, strong-minded man to call their own. Savarous was that and some. He was and always had been an amazing person to her. Even when she was on the outside looking in, Diamond saw perfection when she saw him. Pimp was her world, he just didn't know it. But she would show him, and would do anything and everything to show him he had the world at his feet.

She could never cheat on him, nor disrespect anything about him. All she could do was adore the ground he walked upon, respect his decision-making, and stand by his words. She would be perfect to him only if he gave them a chance. She just wanted badly to follow his lead, live in his moment.

Diamond felt the baby kick in her stomach – a hard, hurtful kick. It made her have to move for comfort. Something was wrong, had to be, and she was getting scared

"Come on, Ma." She got her phone and dialed her mother's number at the same time she felt her legs become wet. She knew her water had just broken, but it was too early, her mother picked up already talking.

"Honey, I'm at the store getti—"

"Ma, my water just broke, and I'm in serious pain," Diamond said, and her mother could tell the difference in her daughter's voice.

"Ok, I'm calling the ambulance. Just sit tight. I'll be there hopefully before they will. Can you move?" her mother said.

"No."

"Ok, unlock the doors with your phone just in case they arrive before me. And try to relax."

"Ok, Ma. Hurry," Diamond said with a grunt of pain that her mother knew all too well.

The pain was growing, making Diamond hold her breath and squeeze the phone in her hand. She didn't expect it to feel like this. Her body began to heat and sweat appeared on her arms, forehead, and legs. She was scared. She needed someone there with her. Not until the pain subsided did she unlock the door through her phone app so the paramedics could get in.

Tossing the phone, she grabbed her stomach with both hands. Her mom told her contractions would happen, but that the pain started off light and grew stronger. If it got any stronger, Diamond didn't think she could make it, and that alone scared her lifeless.

She needed someone there. She needed Pimp to tell her everything was gonna be ok, to hold her hand, to rub her stomach, to keep her safe. Yes, with Pimp there she would feel a lot better. She would feel protected and would be willing to bear the pain it took to have his son.

Just as she thought of him, just as she was about to call his phone or text him, he stood in her door frame.

The contractions started again, making Diamond ball up. Her vision became blurry, her head started hurting, and her mind was playing tricks on her. She thought she saw Pimp standing there, thought she saw him clear as day, but it wasn't. It was her father.

Diamond managed to open her eyes and gain focus to find Pimp walking toward her. The pain was real. She weakly smiled and reach out to her knight in shining armor. He was right on time, as she had hoped .Now she could be strong. Now she could bear their son.

"Baby, it hurts. Ambulance is on its way, and so is my—"

Diamond saw in a blur Pimp pull out a gun and aim at her stomach. She felt the first two shots enter her belly, and her reaction time was slow when she tried to roll over to save her son. Pimp walked over closer, put the gun to the back of her head, and blew her brains on her pillow. He grabbed her shoulder and snatched her over. The Glock he used had a silencer on it that was releasing smoke. He aimed at her stomach and pumped four more slugs into her belly.

\*\*\*

*Icey*

Some people would say a broken heart would heal itself, or that hearts molded with blood would heal more quickly. Most would tell her she would get over it and move on. But to just a few it was hard to let go and get past. Love was not to be taken for granted, to be tampered with, or disrespected. Love was trust, and trust was everything. Words couldn't describe how hurt she was, how played she felt. Nothing could compare to her emotions, regrets.

Brad was right. Brad had it figured out from the beginning, and she didn't believe nothing he said. Savarous Jones was a deadly man, and Icey was swindled into this relationship. If she had known Pimp was anything like he was, she wouldn't have even spoken to his pretty-boy baby face. Now she was sitting there, pregnant and scared for her life.

Pimp had plans to kill the attorney general and a federal judge. He was more than just some street dude from the block. He had already succeeded in killing some investigators and witnesses. Icey wondered what was going on with him. Why was he doing these things?

She thought about what he said when he called, and she got up out of the bed. She went back into his office and made sure she hid the slide flap for the hidden wall, just in case the feds did show up there.

Icey quickly got dressed and headed to her art store. She had two of her students running for her. Gina and Tamia were two young females, like herself, striving to be the best at what they did. The two girls were always determined and always on time for class the three years Icey had been teaching. They were trustworthy and dependable, and that was why she allowed them to run her store, her pride and joy.

When Icey got there, it was quiet as usual, with only one customer being helped by Gina. Tamia was seated behind the counter going through art pictures. She smiled bright when she saw her teacher and her boss.

"Icey, hey. What's up," Tamia spoke, closing the art folder and standing to her feet. Icey smiled at her level of respect.

"Tamia, how are you? How are things at the store?" Icey asked.

She wasn't wearing her true emotions on her face. She hid them pretty well, but it was a hard task at hand. She had to not break down. She willed herself to stay strong, because she didn't want Savarous to see her folding. She wanted to be cool and calm when she told him she found his little room. She wanted to see his face when he was forced to tell the truth. As much as this hurt Icey, she still loved this man, but what was he doing? What was he really into? She betrayed her best friend, cussed him, even was the reason he was suspended, and all Brad was trying to do was help, was look out. And Icey took that for granted.

"Yes, everything is good here. You ok? What brings you down from South Beach?" Tamia tried to make small talk.

"Just passing through. I'll be in the office if either of you need me, ok?" said Icey, then went into her large office.

She needed some thought time. She needed to figure her approach, her words, because she can only step once and only say so much. She wanted it to be perfect. Inside her office space, Icey let the tears that threatened her eyelids finally fall, cascading down her beautiful face in runs. She sobbed, holding herself, hurt and scared, confused and broken by the only man other than her father she loved.

When everything seemed so correct, so right, so in tune, then best believe something was out of place. What had she done? Why was it so impossible for happiness to come as quickly as it had? Icey asked herself if this was something she could get over. Could she forgive him and move on? Could she forget? She wanted to say yes, but that wouldn't be real. She wouldn't forget, couldn't forget. Why did he lie? Why was he aimed at all these big people?

These were questions she wanted answers to because she was a part of it whether she liked it or not.

The crying had her dizzy, and Icey knew that was not healthy for the baby, so she found her leather chair and sat in it. Her entire face was soaked with tears that ran down to her shirt. It seemed she had been crying for hours when it was only for moments.

Who was Savarous Jones and what did he want? She had to confront him. It was only right she did because they were in a relationship, and truth be told, she had his back, so she deserved to know, right? But she wasn't a criminal. She wasn't down for murder and drugs, so how could she truly be down? Was her love so strong it would take over her common sense and morals? Was Savarous that good that she was willing to be blinded by his baby face and major league swag? Icey wasn't raised the way she was acting. She had to come to her senses, had to get it right, because knowing she was wrong and also doing it just didn't sit well with her.

Once she fully calmed down, she grabbed the phone. She called her mother first. "Ma, I'm scared," Icey said when her mother picked up the phone.

"Of what, baby? What's going on? Are you ok?"

The tears started to fall again as Icey trembled and answered. "Of Savarous and what he's capable of doing. I found some shocking things today about him that Brad had been right about all along. Savarous don't know I know," said Icey. She turned in her seat and faced the window behind her. If she told anybody it would be her mother because she could trust her, and Icey just couldn't hold it any longer. She needed to vent, had to get it off her chest.

"Oh my. Icey, where are you?" her mother asked.

"At my store, Ma. I'm safe. The feds are at the house in South Beach, and they'll probably find what I found. I don't know."

"What you find, Icey?"

Pimp's voice almost made her jump out of her skin. She dropped the phone, jumping and turning around to find Pimp standing at her desk, stone look on his face.

Icey didn't hear him come in. How long had he been there? What did he hear? She looked up into his eyes. She couldn't read them. His face showed no emotions. He looked different.

Her eyes traveled down and saw Pimp, the man she loved, the man she cherished and adored, stood there with a gun in hand. Death in his eyes.

*To Be Continued...*
The Heart of a Gangsta 2
Coming Soon

## Coming Soon from Lock Down Publications/Ca$h Presents

TORN BETWEEN TWO

By **Coffee**

LAST OF A DYING BREED

LAY IT DOWN **III**

By **Jamaica**

GANGSTA SHYT **III**

By **CATO**

BLOOD OF A BOSS **IV**

By **Askari**

BRIDE OF A HUSTLA **II**

By **Destiny Skai**

WHEN A GOOD GIRL GOES BAD **II**

By **Adrienne**

LOVE & CHASIN' PAPER

By **Qay Crockett**

I RIDE FOR MY HITTA **II**

By **Misty Holt**

A SAVAGE LOVE **II**

By **Aryanna**

THE HEART OF A GANGSTA **II**

By **Jerry Jackson**

**Available Now**

RESTRAING ORDER **I & II**

By **CA$H & Coffee**

LOVE KNOWS NO BOUNDARIES **I II & III**

By **Coffee**

LAY IT DOWN **I & II**

By **Jamaica**

PUSH IT TO THE LIMIT

By **Bre' Hayes**

BLOOD OF A BOSS **I II & III**

By **Askari**

THE STREETS BLEED MURDER **I, II & III**

By **Jerry Jackson**

CUM FOR ME

An **LDP Erotica Collaboration**

BRIDE OF A HUSTLA

By **Destiny Skai**

WHEN A GOOD GIRL GOES BAD

By **Adrienne**

A GANGSTER'S REVENGE **I II III & IV**

By **Aryanna**

WHAT ABOUT US **I & II**

NEVER LOVE AGAIN

THUG ADDICTION

By **Kim Kaye**

THE KING CARTEL **I, II & III**

By **Frank Gresham**

THESE NIGGAS AIN'T LOYAL **I, II & III**

By **Nikki Tee**

GANGSTA SHYT **I &II**

By **CATO**

THE ULTIMATE BETRAYAL

By **Phoenix**

DON'T FU#K WITH MY HEART **I & II**

By **Linnea**

BOSS'N UP **I & II**

By **Royal Nicole**

I LOVE YOU TO DEATH

**By Destiny J**

I RIDE FOR MY HITTA

By **Misty Holt**

## **BOOKS BY LDP'S CEO, CA$H**

TRUST NO MAN

TRUST NO MAN 2

TRUST NO MAN 3

BONDED BY BLOOD

SHORTY GOT A THUG

A DIRTY SOUTH LOVE

THUGS CRY

THUGS CRY 2

TRUST NO BITCH

TRUST NO BITCH 2

TRUST NO BITCH 3

TIL MY CASKET DROPS

RESTRAINING ORDER

RESTRAINING ORDER 2

## **Coming Soon**

TRUST NO BITCH (KIAM EYEZ' STORY)

THUGS CRY 3

BONDED BY BLOOD 2

IN LOVE WITH HIS GANGSTA

Jerry Jackson